NOW ENTERING SILVER HOLLOW

THIRD EDITION

A Composite Novel by

Lucienne LeBeau

This book is a work of fiction. Names, characters, places, and incidents either are products of the author's imagination or used fictitiously. Any resemblance to actual events or locales or persons, living or dead, is entirely coincidental.

The author isn't sure how locales can be dead, but perhaps that's why they're called ghost towns.

Copyright © 2016, 2020, 2022 by Silver Hollow Stories, LLC
All rights reserved.

All rights reserved, including the right to reproduce this book or portions thereof in any form whatsoever.

Edited by Michael Strong
Cover by Michael Strong
Special thanks to ArtTower at Pixabay.com

For more information, visit the author's page at
silverhollowstories.com

I'd like to thank my spouse and editor for endless patience and for the love I've been given, as well as the encouragement to never give up. I love you.

Foreword

Dear Reader,

There are so many influences in this work, and I think you'll see tributes to some of my favorite authors and stories. Shirley Jackson, H.P. Lovecraft, Stephen King, Edgar Allan Poe… to name a few. I hope that you'll enjoy reading this as much as I enjoyed writing it. This work was born back in 2011-2012, when I first started sketching out an outline, but it really began when I was a kid, and wanted a world of my own, where I set the rules. My world has seen a lot of changes and has shaped into something that isn't 'this' place.

So, if you see something funny, know that you're not losing your mind (maybe), and that you are in a world that's like ours, but not like ours.

You're not home anymore—so take my hand, and I'll lead you to a new world where the rules are unknown, and something is waiting to taste you around every corner.

Don't let go of my hand. I know the way out.

Lucienne LeBeau

October 17, 2016

Atlanta, Georgia

Editor's Note

This third edition has been reworked from the original (formerly published under Anne Hogue-Boucher) and has an additional story not seen before in previously published works. It has also removed a chapter that does not contribute to the overall development of the story. The chapters have been reordered to make a more cohesive composite novel.

Editor, January 22, 2022

MYSTERY MAN

Phil flicked his cigarette to the ground and watched it burn. The smoke danced as it rose higher and higher, to disappear into nothing. Time slipped away as his eyes followed the twists and turns of the pale trails. Closer and closer to the filter it went, the ash leaving a thick, sickly gray trail against the gravel on the driveway. A weak hiss escaped from beneath as he crushed it with one solid work boot.

He no longer cared about Linda. The woman was tired, old news, screwing everyone behind his back. Phil tired of going home to the aroma of incense failing to mask the scent of sex that wasn't his. Hers and another man's.

She said the heavy perfume covered the pot, and she thought the cops would show up, so to be safe, she burned that stale sandalwood.

Phil shrugged to himself and sighed. Not three weeks ago she'd claimed that she hated *smoking* weed, and she made tea instead. He'd given up the green ten years back—it didn't interest him anymore. Sometimes it made his heartbeat zoom too fast the way cold medicine did, so he quit. The cigarettes were something else he wanted to give up, but couldn't. They killed him by inches, every day, and he didn't know how to get rid of them. Like Linda.

He looked up and stretched his neck. A smoky cloud wafted through the clear, blue sky overhead, trying to chase away the sun. The lone cloud failed, leaving a grayish haze that changed a small sliver of it to ash.

Doesn't everything turn to ash?

Time to get back to work.

He put on his safety belt and climbed the side of the building. Working with the harness instead of a ladder made him feel like a superhero. That guy wouldn't use a ladder to scrape paint off the side of a building, and neither would Phil. With his mask secured, he scraped, going somewhere else in his mind. A place where there was no Linda, no cheating, no bills, no Phil's Paint & Plaster. Nothing mundane.

Scrape. Scrape. Scrape. The old white paint lifted and fell in curlicues to the black tarpaulin below.

He was a superhero. 'I'll save you!' Dive-bombing the villains, breaking the necks of the evil-doers, living a double life. There was Phil, the go-to guy for all your painting needs, and then there was his secret identity—Mystery Man.

The villains in Phil's world? True evil. No antiheroes. They murdered for the pleasure of plunging their knives deep into the chests of their targets. Only Mystery Man could stop them.

SCRAPE! Cut. Blood. Pain. A wide gash leaving a drip, drip, drip as it oozed out of him.

"Shit," Phil watched blood pour from his thumb, eyes wide, then narrowing. Red dots of his essence hit the side of the house, scarring the bare wood underneath with a rusty tinge. The flesh on his thumb opened like a hungry bird's mouth. His stomach attempted to leave via his chest for a moment, and he growled.

He lowered himself to the ground and got into the back of his truck. The first-aid kit was somewhere inside with the road flares and the flat-tire fixer. After using his good hand to sort through the pile—success—soothing salvation was moments away. Phil slammed it onto the van bed and grinned as the damn thing popped open from the force. He liked being that strong. Whenever he used too much strength on something, he felt like a superhero. But Phil's grin soon turned to a grimace. His thumb was throbbing now from the effort.

Alcohol pads, gauze, and tape in one hand, he set them on top of the box and cleaned the gash, letting it bleed. Grabbing the Quikstopper (stops bleeding fast!) out of the kit, he poured it on the wound, and waited. A few moments of pressure and adhesive, and the bleeding stopped. He added his liquid bandage and skipped the gauze and tape, hoping that would be enough.

Satisfied that he wouldn't bleed to death, he headed back to the house, and climbed back up to the spot where he'd been working. He needed to clean up that spot of blood, so he got his turpentine out of his utility belt (Mystery Man had one of those, too), and a clean brush.

The spots weren't there.

Phil did a double-take. He looked at his thumb. The ugly wound looked back at him, resembling a screaming mouth. No, he hadn't dreamed it up.

He looked back at where the spots should have been. Nothing but bare wood, the paint chips scraped off as he'd left it. Except those damn spots. What, did the house eat it?

Phil shook his head. Ridiculous. Guess he hadn't bled as much as he thought.

Back to work and back into his head.

Mystery Man rescues The Girl just in time before Baron Badass strangles her. Punch, kick, roundhouse! POW! Baron Badass goes down in only one round. Yet he gets one last, rueful laugh. "Oh Mystery Man, you fool. You'll never disarm the Doomsday Clock!"

With one deft move, Mystery Man takes his Shuriken and throws them at the ticking bomb at the edge of The Clock Tower. The sharp blades cut the wires, stopping the timer and saving the city from Plague Most Foul: PMF. Yes—the worst plague to attack a human. Once again, Mystery Man saves the city, and no one will ever know it.

For he is Mystery Man, and he must stay in the shadows of rumor and whispers in the dark.

The sound of humming pulled Phil from his reverie. It made the hair on the back of his neck raise, just like it did when Linda placed soft kisses on his neck. He couldn't remember the last time he'd received such an intimate gesture. The humming was bit sing-song. Breathy. A gentle breeze at the beach.

He swung his harness around to get closer to the window, following the sound like a Siren's song. The house had been empty for years—heck, the Silver Hollow Historical Society was paying for the job. The house sat, rotting away, and the Society had tried raising the money to restore it to its former glory.

They had enough in the budget to restore the building itself. A city doctor had given them a generous donation. Phil consulted with seven different historians to help him use the right methods of restoration—he wasn't an expert, but he was what SHHS could afford. So he tried to do everything just so. Donating bits of his funds to the experts for their time. Made him warm inside to do something like that.

The frame of the house was in excellent condition (a shock to everyone involved in the project) and supported his harness. He was a slim man though. Not much to hold up.

The humming continued.

He peered in the window. No one was there.

Phil shook his head. Maybe it was from the woods out back, and the voice just carried funny. There was a trail leading throughout the entire forest, branching off to a house a mile away. It cut deep into the woods to the other side—about twenty-five miles of thick, overgrown trail. On day hikes, it was a way to escape Linda and her incessant yammering. Phil knew the forest well—the thickets, river, and the cavern network that sprawled out for miles, soothed by the sounds of running water, birdsongs, and little crunches of animal footsteps on the underbrush. It led to an enormous chasm with moss-covered rocks and rushing waterfalls.

Back to work. Phil abandoned his Mystery Man story in favor of pondering the house and its awkward history, and the tour with Dr. Francis Langelier, head of the SHHS. Phil had no head for history, but because there was money involved, he paid attention to everything Dr. Langelier and his overgrown, butternut squash-head had said.

"The original owners built the house before the Strife of East Versus West, in April of 1861 by a Union officer who married a Secession Nurse. An unusual pairing, to be sure. She had tended his wounds and saved his life. This young nurse, a credit to her profession, once said, 'I help

the sick and the wounded, I don't ask them what side they're on.' But far more interesting is that they built this place on top of a ruined crematorium. Digs performed on the grounds by the Historical Society unearthed dozens of people who had been cremated incompletely—the workers never pulverized their bones. The majority of the remains, anthropologists have found, are of women, aged eighteen to twenty-five—they came from a nearby asylum."

Phil's mouth hung open, eyes wide. He wanted to tell Langelier that he never knew that, but no sound came out of that perfect 'o' of lips. He'd lived in Silver Hollow his entire life, and the only thing he ever knew about Dubbs House was that the other kids called it haunted. They had for generations. But even when he was a little boy he didn't believe in that haunted house stuff. He believed what he could see, and that was it. Once he found his words again, he spoke. "What kind of asylum was it, Doctor?"

Dr. Langelier smiled. It wasn't genuine—it never reached his eyes.

"Well, Mister Hausmann, we haven't found out yet. There's quite a debate on the subject. Some say it was for the mentally disturbed while others claim there is evidence to support a TB asylum. However, we may never know as the fire wiped out the town records. The fire in 1894 burned so hot, it leveled the former church, half of the constabulary, and the nearby farmhouse, but Dubbs House still stood. Only a handful of townsfolk survived. They were a superstitious lot. In fact, they recorded only that they would never speak of the 'atrocities' committed before the fire. They feared 'bringing back the Timeworn Order's displeasure.' Not a bright lot, would you say?"

"Oh yeah, not at all." Always agree with the guy who signs the checks. "I never believed in that hocus-pocus, anyway."

The doctor laughed and clapped Phil on the back, knocking Phil's teeth together with the impact. Phil forced a smile of his own.

"Good man, Mister Hausmann. Now, as you can see..."

The doctor had gone on about the house, even including the second fire at Dubbs House in 1955. Phil squinted at the side of the house as he worked, the vast haze of words gathering like fog on the horizon of his brain. Words telling him the asylum was filled with women, and that some of those bones were not just found in what was the crematorium area. No—they found remains all over the dig site.

He wasn't stupid. He could imagine enough to piece together what happened. In his mind's eye, they burned alive. They burned, they screamed, they choked and gagged on the smoke. All of them vomiting last night's dinner of undercooked chicken and bland potatoes as the flames overtook their bodies. Bladders voided, bowels emptied—shitting themselves as the fire consumed them in a fitful embrace.

"They found rusted chains and parts of iron bed frames..."

Burned alive in the second fire of 1955, chained to their beds. But how did the wood not burn? Why just the people? If it leveled the buildings nearby, why didn't it level Dubbs House? How was that possible? Just stone and asbestos, or something else?

Phil shivered.

The paint. Back to the paint. Scrape off the old skin, bit by bit. Scrape it off and keep moving. In front of Phil was the paint and the task at hand. His heart was beating too fast and his stomach filled with a sick heaviness that came before he puked up its contents.

Doubtless, Linda would make fun of him if he told her. Stupid, insensitive Linda. The way she looked at him was the same way she looked at roaches crawling on the floor—the nasty little sneer that made her face scrunch up till she resembled an anteater. "You need to stop thinking about that shit and start thinking about making more money," she'd say to whatever he tried to confide in her.

One time he got a big bid under his belt and brought home flowers and a promise to dinner up in Terrace Lake. She scoffed, stubbed out her cigarette, and shrugged. "That's still not enough to put the down payment on that car I told you about last week," she said, snatching the flowers from his hands and tossing them on the counter.

Maybe tonight would be the night he screwed up the courage to tell her enough and pack his things and leave. He'd stay at a hotel in Terrace Lake. There had to be one there he could afford. Just to get away. For now, he settled with getting away in his head, remembering.

Dr. Langelier had talked about how the place went from a hospital, to a home, then to a bed-and-breakfast, then a temporary asylum, and then fell into disrepair. The damn gas bag never shut up when it came to history—or any other subject.

"We purchased it thirty years ago, in 1982. I was just out of university—impressive that I've kept most of my hair, isn't it?" Langelier chuckled at his own joke and touched the thinning grays at the top. "Such a difficult thing to put the history of the house together, yes? Research isn't exciting the way it is in adventure films. What's amazing is that the fire did little damage to the structure thanks to the stone masons. It only damaged the people."

Langelier seemed to realize that Phil was tuning him out with a glazed-over look in his eyes. Phil's ears were ringing, boredom bringing too much attention to his tinnitus. The aging bag of wind changed his tack. "Do you remember Saul Boggs?"

Phil nodded. "Old Haul Saul. All the kids used to call him that."

"Indeed. Well, some fifteen years ago Boggs was helping do the first major cleanup of this place. He was the only one whipcord thin enough to go up to the attic and not do any damage to the floorboards." *Langelier gave a smile at this, and Phil forced a small laugh.*

But it was true. Old Haul was average height, but slight and wiry. Phil waited for what was coming next.

"Up in the attic, he was hauling out junk. Belongings of the dead patients or residents, and the occasional gem from the Sellers-Kellogg-Watson fortune. I came in one day by a hunch just to check on him and see if he'd made any important discoveries."

Phil fought the urge to roll his eyes and managed not to grunt by clearing his throat. "I take it he found something good."

"Something great—he'd uncovered documents about the history of the house. Naturally I recognized them for what they were and took them back to the Society."

Phil coughed again. Yeah, naturally. Self-important longhair. "I'm sure you did. I mean, you went to school for it, right?"

Langelier looked at Phil as if he'd found a pot of gold. "Oh yes. I worked hard to recognize and authenticate such things. As I was saying, I rushed back to the Society and examined the papers. Alas, it left me with more questions than ever before. Water damage smudged the dates to illegibility, and some were so waterlogged only a few sentences with names remained."

It seemed to Phil that Langelier was just talking to hear his own voice. He didn't bother to reply—it wasn't as if what he said mattered. Langelier just kept talking.

"I tried investigating around town—I was the maverick back then, you know. Even after my time here they see me as a newcomer. You know how it is." Langelier gave a belly laugh so big that Phil thought the man might burst something.

"Yeah, I do." Phil forced a smile and tried to laugh along with the older man. "People keep their mouths shut if it might become gossip about them."

"Yes, indeed. Indeed." Langelier said. "No matter who I interviewed it was like getting apples from an orange tree."

In Silver Hollow, there were things that people wouldn't say as if they were afraid of calling attention to themselves or whatever had happened would somehow happen again. He was one of the silent ones, himself. Not out of superstition—but upbringing.

What mattered now, though, was that they were restoring the place back to an old war hospital, at least half the house. Other parts would be preserved as the Dubbs House where they lived. "Preserve the Old Ways" and that stuff.

As he worked, he tried humming to himself the way he always did when stress took over, but his mind wouldn't let him rest. Flashes of dead bodies and charred remains kept staring back at him in his head, their mouths agape in eternal screams.

Linda yelling at him about leaving the coffee pot on too long with a voice as shrill as a tea kettle overheating, waking him from his morning rest on the couch.

Another mental volley to people being chained to their beds while the parts of the building not protected by asbestos burned. While the *people* burned. While they screamed and cried for help. His face grew heated. He was burning, too. Burning with them. Beads of sweat burst over his forehead and raced, stinging his eyes as he went up in flames with the house—with the women.

He took a deep breath, chest tightening. Phil forced himself to take another deep breath, and then another, focusing on nothing else for the moment but how his heart moved in his chest from a hammering, jack rabbit pace to a slow, calm, steady beat. "Fuck," he slammed his scraper on the ledge, cursing at his endless monkey chattering mind and dented the wood underneath the chipping paint. *Damn.* He picked up the scraper and put it back in his tool belt.

Phil cursed at himself under his breath for slacking off, the ringing in his ears growing. He sighed from the pit of his stomach and climbed down from his harness, feet making a solid *thump* as they hit the ground. It was time to move to the other side of the window. He had to hurry. The light wouldn't be good on this side of the building for long, and he didn't want to risk another cut.

Stop daydreaming and being stupid, Linda said in his head.

"Shut your fucking mouth," he muttered. When it wasn't Linda in his head, it was one of his teachers. He often heard the put-downs of the past echo in his head—a frequent reminder he was nothing, and that his life didn't matter.

As he moved the harness to its new location, Phil climbed to the other side of the window. He made sure his mask was secure (just like Mystery Man would) and peeled off the old paint with more care this time. He'd have to go back and fix that dent he made, and he'd have to do it for free. Phil bit his lip and tried to ignore the lump in his stomach that was punishing him for his rash behavior.

More humming. A throaty, distant sound that gave him warm sensations down the back of his head and neck, making his prick do a half-stand at attention.

This time, there was no mistaking it as a noise from the woods. The sound was resonating from inside the house.

The interior was cleaned and empty of items, except for the essentials. The Society sent out most of the furniture for restoration and the asbestos removal team had left behind bits of caution tape, but otherwise it was ready for the historical restoration people to come in and take care of the walls and floors, bringing the place back to its former glory. "*Vagrants pass through here often. Watch out, they can be dangerous,*" Langelier said.

Phil scowled, denying his body a shiver.

It was the right time of year for a drifter to come through. It wasn't uncommon fifty years ago whenever the house wasn't being used (like all abandoned buildings in the town), and it happened still. No matter what, there would always be transients.

He swung around on his harness, looking around the grounds. Trees shed their leaves and dried out brown-green grass stared back at him in silent judgment. The breeze picked up and brought the perfume of wood smoke with it.

Vagrants. The town was typical of any rural area. The Haverty family knew the Hausmann family, the Pipers knew the Knotts, ad nauseam. Speckled with summer people and people who blew through on their way to the city, there was always someone new or something new to talk about among the townsfolk. Maybe the town got up to fifty to seventy people in the summer (looking for cheap accommodation and peace and quiet). At the end of October, though, there were only residents remaining for the harsh winter to come. There were fifteen permanent residents now, counting Phil and Linda. They lived on the far edge of Silver Hollow's boundaries, encased in its embryonic sac—with no one to cut them out to make their escape.

The bright autumn sky was a whisper through the first turning leaves; blood red. Phil inhaled deep into his lungs and sighed. The humming had stopped.

He turned back around toward the window and saw her. He dropped his scraper and yelped.

The woman stood there, bare, full breasts pert and round, slim waist exposing a flat, peach-colored stomach, and down further to a natural but groomed bush. Her legs were long and thick with strong muscle, the way Linda used to look before she stopped exercising because of her knee. (Now she was chicken-legged and shriveled). She resumed humming a tune that danced into Phil's ears with the grace of a prima ballerina.

The woman just stood there, staring right at him from inside one of the former patient rooms. Her long, dark hair pulled back behind her neck, hanging loose down her back. His eyes roamed over her body and he kept staring, unable to tear himself away.

Phil felt a wave of greediness wash over him, and he battled the urge to slide down the ladder, run inside, and slide into her. He hesitated, looking away from that hourglass figure and at her face, into her eyes—this girl could be mental—*who in Perdition stands naked in the middle of a run-down asylum? A nut job that's who.*

She smiled at him.

"I need you to come in here. Can you help me?"

Phil balked a moment. He shook his head that no, he couldn't come inside—angled walls and drop cloths obscured his view. There could be others waiting to mug him or something. His imagination saved him in this case, playing out potential scenarios where his stupid mistakes based on his lust got him killed.

"What do you need?"

The girl turned away and said something. What, Phil didn't know. He leaned forward and strained, but no luck.

"I can't hear you. Can you come closer?"

He swung his harness over to get a better look inside. The girl moved to the middle of the room. Closer, but still far from the window.

"I need help. I don't know where I am."

Phil nodded to himself—this girl was likely a junkie blowing through town (although she was healthy looking for a junkie). This wouldn't have been the first time it happened. Silver Hollow was an attractor for the desperate ones. Though he'd never encountered any himself, his friend Paul told him about three guys who wound up in Dubbs House. Paul said that they were sleeping inside when he got there, smelling of old piss and fresh cheap alcohol. One of them still had the needle in his arm.

First time for everything. Phil decided he could get his coat from the van, call nine-one-one, then go inside, and put the coat on her while they waited for an ambulance.

"Okay," he said, and though he tried to keep his voice low, it broke like a teenage boy's. Not because she was beautiful enough to bring tears to his eyes, and not because she was naked (she was both), but because there was something familiar in her features, and the setting. A former patient?

He shook off that idea in a hurry. *Phil, you ass,* he heard Linda's voice chastising him, *your imagination is ridiculous.* "I'll tell you what. I'll go to my van and get you a coat, and get you some help. What's your name, sweetie?"

"Name?"

"Yeah. My name is Phil."

"Phil."

"Yeah, that's my name. What's your name?" *High as fuck,* he thought.

"Norma."

"Okay, Norma. Nice to meet you. I'll be back as soon as I can get down from here."

"Hurry. I need you." She sat in the middle of the floor, hugging her knees, and sobbed.

Phil rushed off the harness and hit the ground, running to the van and grabbing his coat. His phone was on his tool belt so he called nine-one-one from there.

"All circuits are currently busy. Please hang up and dial again immediately. All circuits are currently busy--"

Phil stared at his phone. He'd never gotten that message before. This place wasn't so populous as to keep emergency dispatch in Dover busy. He shook his head. Help wasn't coming for now.

He grabbed the coat and turned to go into the house while his phone kept redialing for him. As he made it to the front steps, an operator came through the speaker.

"Nine-one-one. What is the address or location of the emergency?"

"The old Dubbs House in Silver Hollow. One King Street."

"And the nature of the emergency?" the voice on the other line asked. It sounded distant, like she was talking through a tin box.

"There's a squatter here, looks like a junkie. She's naked and keeps telling me she needs help. Says her name is Norma." Phil said.

"Is she bleeding or incoherent?"

"I don't know if she's bleeding. I haven't gone in the house."

"Remain where you are, sir. Sending police and ambulance now."

Phil sighed. "Thanks."

"Are you going inside now?" She asked.

"Yeah, I'll go put my coat on her and treat her for shock if she needs it," Phil said with another sigh. It felt like an hour had passed.

"Is this Phil Hausmann?"

"Yeah, who is this?" He asked, brow furrowing. That voice wasn't familiar.

"It's Debbie. Debbie Carnassy."

Phil shook his head. Who the fuck was Debbie Carnassy?

"I'm sorry, I don't recognize the name," Phil said, pursing his lips into a frown.

Debbie laughed, but when she spoke, her voice sounded far away and strained. "I'm the girl in the house, with Norma. We're dying, Phil. Help us."

Phil's eyes widened as his heart skipped a beat, and his mouth went dry. He couldn't find the words to reply as the phone went pure static, cutting in and out from silence to noise.

No. That didn't just happen. The sun is going down, and my mind is playing tricks on me because I'm spooked. It's almost Halloween, anyway, and I'm overtired, Phil's mind echoed back at him. He stood on the porch, determined to stay out of that house until the police or an ambulance arrived.

Disappointment washed over him as he chastised himself for being stupid. That's not something Mystery Man would do. He wouldn't let his imagination run wild.

Don't be an idiot, Linda's voice chided him once more. *You're no hero.*

"Hello?" The voice said, now loud and clear over his phone.

"I'm still here." Phil's voice was creaky and small again.

"Sir, I asked you what your name was," said the voice. It didn't sound like Carnassy anymore. This voice was lower, smoother, and pitched with concern.

"This is Phil. Phil Hausmann."

"Okay. Are you all right, Mister Hausmann?"

He wasn't sure how to answer, now. There was no way he'd tell her what he'd imagined had just happened. He wasn't that far gone. Instead, he swallowed hard and started, "Oh, uh, call me Phil. Yeah. I guess I'm in shock myself." He gathered his courage and opened the large front door with a now still hand. "I'm going in the house."

"I can stay on the line with you, Phil, until service arrives," the operator said.

"No, that's okay. I'll be fine now," Phil said, his voice strong and deep again. The house seemed less ominous as a hint of Mystery Man came over him. It was just a house. There was an odor inside—fresh flowers and summer rain. It didn't smell like the musty, old, charred underneath remodel that it had when he first visited.

He hung up the phone with a dulcet beep.

He heard the girl whisper. "Help."

"I'm on my way," Phil craned his neck up to the second floor and raised his voice. "I'll be right there."

He hustled his way up the stairs two at a time. The paint was peeling when he was at the bottom, but by the time he got to the top, the paint looked fresh.

Something felt wrong, at least at first. The hallway seemed to stretch on for ages and tilted in ways he couldn't walk. He slid on something slippery. A hiss, a strangled cry. Did it come from him? Something else? Pain shot up through his knee into his groin, setting fire trails up his spine. He looked down, jaw hanging open as he saw his knee was leaking scarlet onto the wood floor below—and then disappearing.

"Wha—what's going on?" Phil said, his voice a hoarse whisper. His vision blurred and his face felt like it was running off onto the floor. The wood seemed to absorb the water runoff, too.

A voice at the end of the hall, soft and breathy. He strained to hear what the whispers were saying.

"Phil, we need you. This is all for you."

A long time ago, when Phil was little, he had to have his appendix removed. When he was on the operating table, the anesthesiologist put him under with ether. He felt like he was falling into a comfortable, warm bath. That was how he felt now. Something in him was slipping.

Phil just accepted it. There was something special going on here. Something just for him. He didn't know how he knew it, but he knew it. It was like being part of an intangible thing, greater than he, and he wanted to be there.

This was where he belonged.

He forgot about Linda, and Dave, and Paul-Not-Good-Paul, and Wally, and whoever else she was screwing behind his back. This was where he needed to be, and he needed to help that girl know she belonged here, too.

She deserved to know.

It was all okay. Everything fit. The time was right.

He approached the girl and put his coat over her. She shivered and writhed. Phil didn't move away. He reached out to touch her and hold her close.

She changed. Phil still didn't move. His face was slack, eyes wide. The fine hairs on the back of his neck stood erect, his spine ramrod straight. His vision clouding, he could do nothing but drool and feel his whole body stiffen as it did during feverish masturbation fantasies.

Mystery Man would have broken the spell and wrapped the monster up in some magical device. Phil didn't.

A trickle of red flowed from Phil's nose and spattered on his shoes, then the floor, making blooming red roses as they dropped. Drip, splat. Drip, splat.

The girl was no longer a girl, but a twisted, gooey, abyss-shaded slick of a being. It engulfed him, its tendrils long, supple, and slick as it took him into her—into *it*.

Phil saw stars burst before him and inside its body. Such brilliance! Aligned with perfection, he heard the singing of the heavens, the smell of blooming spring, and his skin growing warm as the blanket of bliss overcame him.

The stars grew fatter, large as saucers—growing and bursting forward until they encompassed his vision in a brilliant white light.

Then nothing.

DUBBS HOUSE

"Son of a bitch, Chet. You don't mean to tell me there's a junkie squatter where Phil's workin'?"

Chet gave a half-smile. "Yep. Only Phil would have this kinda shit happen to him, eh?"

"That poor son of a bitch." Postman said, a scowl crossing his boyish face.

George Postman was a young deputy, but he was competent, in the constable's estimation. Chet (*short for Chester, thank you very much*), was the old constable, and the days of waking up and hopping out of bed were long gone for him. The joints creaked and cracked even when he sat down.

Chet was too old for this crap. Phil was a hardworking, nice guy, and he had to fall for that crazy bitch, Linda. Linda was mean, demanding, and what the intellectuals would call an ignoramus. Bigoted, rude, and conniving.

Everything Phil wasn't. Unlucky bastard making bad choices, Chet had said on more than one occasion to Postman, whether the kid was listening or not.

"Yep. Let's go see what we can do." George said.

The prowler rumbled and roared to the scene before the paramedics got there. Chet checked his time. They were there in less than one minute from the when the Phil made the call. Record time. The ambulance would take another eighteen to twenty minutes.

Chet got out of the police car first and pointed George toward the van—where the end was open—and it looked a right mess. A first-aid kit was ripped open and the contents strewn on the ground and over the back of the vehicle.

"Be careful not to disturb anything, George. Remember your contamination rules."

Contamination rules was a reminder to the eager deputy not to crap all over the crime scene. If there was a crime scene.

The little voices belonging to whatever lived in the pit of his gut were screaming at him that this was a crime scene, and to not believe what his eyes were telling him. His face stood out in stony, grim relief as he approached the property.

With each step he took, a scream settled into his throat, and he kept swallowing it. It settled in the pit of his stomach where the voices came from though his heart was strong and steady.

He hated this place—Dubbs House—with a passion. When he was a boy, it was a house again, and the ladies who lived in it were bat-shit crazy. Mary Sellers-Watson-Kellogg was one of them. The socialite was from Beanton (where rich people had to have multiple last names—he didn't understand that and he never would—nonsense pedigrees) but moved to Silver Hollow with her *friend* when she was in her late forties.

She hadn't started out insane. No, sir. This was a respectable woman who ran a bed-and-breakfast when she'd first purchased it, and she and her *friend* ran the place which drew a crowd because of its strange history. When people suggested to her she should play the place up as haunted, Miss Sellers-Watson-Kellogg refused with a "tut-tut. The history of the place is what's fascinating, not the *fairy tales*."

Elizabeth Maxwell-Hunter (another one of those pedigreed women), however, was much more into the fairy tales of the place.

The lover, Elizabeth, held a séance there one Halloween, and his parents attended. They went, because not only were this couple of so-called spinsters two of the most interesting people in the town, and both rich, gorgeous, and different—they were charming.

He remembered that he'd gone trick or treating in Silver Hollow, which, back then, was an active but small community. Chet was only five years old, climbing up onto porches in his big-boy bandit costume, holding his pillowcase open and greeting neighbors with a voice so small they had to strain to hear him. The people he greeted laughed and gave him everything from sweets from Haverty's to caramel apples. He remembered the apples wrapped in cellophane and tied with orange or red satin bows. With each visit, his mouth watered but he remembered his manners, gave a whisper of thanks, and hopped away from each house.

Then, he had to stay in with his big sister (who was nineteen and had just gotten a job as a secretary down at Hudson's law offices in the next town over). She helped him bathe, count his candies and treats, have a handful of his loot, and then put him in his jammies. Chet could still see the Sunny Train pattern hand-embroidered on the faux pocket of the red flannel.

Gretchen told him a Halloween bedtime story where a brave constable saved a young boy from werewolves with his silver bullets. He closed his eyes, the bed turning into a fishing boat, rocking among the stars, circling the pregnant, glowing moon—where a werewolf howled in the far off distance, then sang of mares and does eating oats.

When he woke up with the sun shining through his window and forcing little Chet's eyes to open, a brick had settled into his stomach—maybe the candy was no good. Beads of sweat covered his brow, and his mouth was dry. He swallowed sand and thought that the sandman must have missed his eyes or used too much of his sleeping dust.

The little boy in the Sunny Train jammies climbed down the stairs to a silent house, rubbing the grit out of his eyes. Every morning the house was full of activity, even after his parents had returned from a party. There was the clattering of dishes, the smells of bacon and eggs for breakfast and fresh coffee brewing in the percolator on the all-gas stove.

But not that morning. That morning, his parents were not at the table, and his sister, pale and drawn, was sitting there, wringing her hands and staring into space.

"What's wrong, Gretchen?" he asked, his voice smaller than even last night, when shyness had taken over his throat. This time, it was dread's icy cold hand clinched to his neck, squeezing the air out of him.

Gretchen looked up and pushed her long blonde bangs away from her eyes—an automatic movement, as if she was in a trance. She turned to him, sniffed, and said in a stuffy, full voice, "Mom is in the hospital. Something happened last night."

Chet didn't understand. If she was in the hospital, then wasn't she going to be okay? That's where sick people got better, they'd always told him. Why was Gretchen crying?

Mommy hadn't gotten better, and his father never talked about what happened. Chet never asked. His father had been an open man with his children, but that was one subject he refused to discuss—except to forbid Chet and Gretchen to go near that house or have anything to do with the people who lived and boarded there.

So they didn't.

Chet learned why later on, when his father passed away.

On his deathbed, he'd called for Chet, who was a young deputy at the constable's office back then. Ever the obedient son, he did as his father said, even if it didn't settle with him.

Chet shied away from death and hospitals, and the house his father was in (which was right down the street from the damned Asylum-House) was a mix of everything that made Chet want to scream and run away. But he went just the same. Max Callfield was his father, and he would show respect—the man continued to take care of him, even after Lisette Callfield was long in the ground. Though Max was never the same, he didn't become a monster or wind up beating on them. He was just a shadow of a person afterward, eating tomato sandwiches for fun.

"You have your mother's eyes," Max said to Chet. Chet smiled.

"Yes, sir, she willed them to me."

Max coughed and shook his head. "Got an answer for everything, boy. But I have little time left, and I need to tell you some things."

Chet turned serious and pulled his chair closer, cursing himself for wanting to pull away from the acrid odor of shit and vomit, the stench of death looming over his father like a cloud of Perdition. But he stayed in one place, so his father didn't have to struggle to speak above a whisper.

His father sat up as best as he could, and leaned toward his son, closing the gap between the two of them with the stench of rot mixed with antiseptics clinging to the air.

Max put his hand up and touched Chet's shoulder. Chet was a child again. Helpless to stop the Grim Reaper from claiming his prize, helpless to lose yet another loved one. First, his mother, when he was five, under strange circumstances, then Gretchen, who'd died when she was twenty-eight, due to sudden cardiac arrest. Not that it made a lick of sense to Chet—it never would. It had something to do with this damn house he was standing in front of now. His instincts told him that then, when he was only fourteen-years-old—that's when Gretchen died, and he trusted that.

Max had not taken his daughter's death well, and things got worse. That was when the drinking started. He'd drown himself in booze every night just to get himself to sleep, a cigarette dangling from his mouth, hopeful he'd set himself on fire. This kept up for six months, until one night, in a fitful frenzy, the man tried to burn down Dubbs House—a can of gas in one hand and a book of matches in the other. The plan failed when he got to the driveway and broke his ankle.

That seemed to sober him up (in the figurative sense), but it seemed to Chet that he still blamed the house, too. It was there, in his eyes, whenever someone mentioned the place, and whenever he had to go near it to leave town.

Whether he would admit that to his son was another thing, but Chet was an observant man, and he knew his father's signals, if not the thoughts behind them.

The son patted his father's side, waiting for the old man to speak between the wheezes and rattles.

"Listen, son, I have to tell you about your Mother, and what happened that night," his father said at length.

"Dad, you don't have to do this—you—" Chet said, feeling his ears warm and cheeks turn red as that icy grip tightened around his throat, silencing him.

"Don't interrupt me, Chester Emmett Callfield. Listen close. I owe this to you. You were a little tyke then, and you deserve to know the truth of what happened that night."

Max told Chet the events of that evening, from the séance held by the enigmatic Elizabeth Maxwell-Hunter, to the events leading up to his mother's death. He let his father talk as Max described events he said he couldn't bring himself to believe, and Chet had wanted to tell him not to hold back, but said nothing.

That was when Chet found out that his mother never made it to the hospital alive. His father said she disappeared into the Asylum-House. There was no body buried in her plot because they never recovered one.

Chet shook his head, unable to speak. Unable to believe what his father had told him. That morphine drip must have been something else, he started to say, but held back, unwilling to hurt his father's feelings. The old man was hallucinating a memory for him, and it was coming out as a haunted house deathbed confession.

But now that Chet, seventy-five-years-old, was standing at the front porch, his father's strange tale and his sister's death came back to him.

Phil was in that house, nowhere in sight, his van messed up and things thrown askew, work boot tracks in the dust that accumulated thick on the old graying paint. Everything seemed to conspire to make the constable sick, his stomach rolling as if to tell him that danger was near, and he should vomit to make it go away.

Even though Chet was over ten years past retirement, he was young in body and in good health. He'd outlived two doctors (his pediatrician didn't count) and his third young internist told him he had the health of a forty-five-year-old man. He inherited that from his mother's side of the family—both his mother's parents lived into their early hundreds.

Chet realized now that had been rough for them. They outlived their only daughter. Now, Chet wondered, if he would outlive his own son, a frown creasing his features as he tried to push the thoughts away and consider the matter at hand.

Perhaps his mother would still be alive today if that—*no*—he clenched his fists and grunted to himself as he forced his attention back to the house and what he might find inside.

Chet took a deep breath and climbed the beaten wood of the front porch and used his flashlight to push the door the rest of the way open. He stepped across the threshold, treading as if on ice during a spring thaw, as if the house might sense him and swallow him whole, as it did his mother.

"Hausmann, you in here?" Chet asked, his shout hoarse as it reverberated off the walls, making an echo that sounded like it was mocking him.

He waited.

Silence.

Chet had never been in the house before and always sent his deputy to chase out the squatters and drifters, or chase away the kids who shouldn't be anywhere near this place. Not that kids were a problem these days. The town was dying again, and the children were the first to go.

This house killed my mother and my sister and now it wants more, he thought, then pushed it away.

Now he had to find Phil, but this place was enormous. The foyer was bigger than his bedroom, and the stairs that led to the bedrooms/patient rooms (*what a morbid place*) loomed over him. A nagging sensation tugged between his shoulder blades, like when someone watched him during practice on the gun range. But who was watching him here? The unseen observer sent a chill washing over him, gooseflesh erupting over his arms and shoulders.

He had his service pistol, and his pepper spray. An old house wouldn't intimidate him from finding this young man and the woman that Phil was trying to help. *Fuck's sake, Chet, it's only a house*, he admonished himself.

Sweeping through the main room, the kitchen, and down to the sunken dining area, he saw nothing, at first. All he could smell was dust, ozone, and the odor of almost-dried paint hanging in the air, a heavy blanket of chemical stench. His head throbbed.

Out of the corner of his eye, a shadow passed. Chet turned, saw nothing, and shook his head.

Fuck this place.

The wind kicked up outside, scattering leaves everywhere, crying through the trees.

"Hausmann?"

Still no answer. Just the creaking and groaning of a settling house.

With a grunt he saved for when he was forced to do chores, Chet made his way up the stairs. CRACK! The noise made him jump, and he fell backwards down the steps, catching the railing to prevent him from falling down more than one.

It was his radio. Postman was calling him.

"Constable, come back," the young man's voice sounded static-filled and staccato.

"Callfield here," Chet said. His voice was as mild and steady as ever, despite his racing heart and the urge to shit his guts out.

"No sign of Phil or the woman. There appears to be some blood in the back of the van," the deputy's voice cracked at the word *blood*. It was climbing in pitch as if he were holding back a scream.

Chet sighed. "Copy that. Get an investigator's team out here from Centerville and tape off the area."

"Ten-four, sir," George said. Silence fell once more.

Chet's legs grew heavy as he neared the landing, and he slowed his pace, that pull of dread stronger than ever. It wasn't anything but his instincts talking to him, the way they'd done for as long as he could remember. There was a quick whoop of a siren in the distance

At the top of the stairs, he found Hausmann, battered and bloody, but his chest was rising and falling. Chet leaned over to listen to his breath and to feel for a pulse. It was faint, but there.

But where was the girl?

"Paramedics!" Distant voices, footfalls faint and the metallic crash of a gurney rolling over the threshold came from below.

"Upstairs," the old man said, raising his voice. "One male, forty-six years old; female nowhere to be found."

The medics hurried up the stairs and worked on Phil right away, busy chattering at each other to start a line and get a backboard as Chet searched the maze of other rooms for the girl who vanished.

Maybe the place ate her.

The layout of Dubbs House, regardless of the fact it was a bed-and-breakfast as its last incarnation, was far more like a hospital than anything else. The rows of rooms stretched out forever in front of him. It made him dizzy to look at it. Even larger than it looked from the outside.

Chet walked from room to room, hand on the butt of his gun, which felt slippery. But the gun wasn't covered in oil, no—it was the sweat from his palm.

It took the girl like it took my mother and Gretchen, he thought, beads of perspiration gathering on his face. He kept going in spite of his ever-increasing heart rate. There was no sign of the girl in any of the rooms.

He turned away, leaving the other rooms unchecked. Chet was coming back with George in a minute to come help him do a sweep of the rooms. The junkie or whatever she was didn't leave a trace that the constable could see.

A noise.

Quiet sobs from the room at the end of the hall.

"You've got to be shitting me," he said under his breath.

He headed for the room faster, lungs expanding to their limits to calm his heart. Inhale, exhale. Again and again as his heart thrummed, then slowed, obeying the flow of his breath.

Pushing the door open with a timid hand, he expected to see what the dispatcher's call had described—a naked, confused girl, maybe a junkie, needing help.

What he saw almost pushed him into the arms of the Maniae. His mind reeled as he recoiled at the sight.

The woman he saw was dressed as if she was going to a high-society soiree or dinner. But it wasn't the fact she was dressed, or weeping—it was that she looked like Lisette

Callfield—a clone of his mother. The woman was staring off, toward a point to his right and behind him, and he shuddered. It was as if he wasn't even standing there.

Chet remembered the way she was dressed before she went to the séance, and this woman was wearing the outfit she wore that night. His jaw dropped. That burgundy dress, pure silk. Nylons. Kitten heels. The constable admired her with his five-year-old eyes once more, the way he once admired Yuletide presents under the tree.

But it *couldn't* be his mother. His mother was dead, right?

Now he stood there, expression twisted in bewilderment. No one ever recovered a body. He had checked into his father's story a while after his father had passed. The death records read *presumed dead*, and there had been no corpse at the memorial service. No funeral procession, no interment. Chet never gave it much thought, unwilling to question the circumstances surrounding his mother's death. It had been too painful, too strange, for him.

He got himself together with a deep breath and kept his hand on his gun, taking a step toward the weeping woman who was now looking straight at him. There was a flash of recognition in her eyes.

"Ma'am?" Chet said.

"Chester? Is that you?" Her voice was familiar.

Chet stepped back, unable to believe what he was seeing. He listened to his instincts, and his instincts told him to beware. Now they were screaming for him to get out.

He drew his gun.

"Chet? It's Mommy," she said, extending her arms, "please, you have to help us. We're trapped here."

With a firm grip on his gun he kept it lowered, finger outside the trigger guard. He continued to stare at her, lips pulled into a tight line. His heart hammered in his ears.

"What do you mean, and who are you?" the constable asked.

The woman, or thing pretending to be his mother cringed, scarlet mouth round.

"Chet, it's me, your mother." Though she sounded the same, this was not the woman who read to him every night.

"Not possible. My mother would be dead by now. She would be geriatric, so unless you're 110 years old, and the best looking 110-year-old I've ever seen, you're not her." Callfield set his jaw.

"Chet, please. I don't know why I look young and why you look so old. I know you're my Chet, though. Gretchen is here, too. We need your help. There are so many of us here, Chet. We need you!"

"Enough!" Callfield said, raising his gun. Sweat broke out on his forehead in fat drops. "You stay where you are."

A loud set of footsteps behind him caused Chet to reel with his gun, coming face-to-face with George Postman.

"What's the matter, sir?" Postman asked, raising his hands in synch with his eyebrows.

He turned back around to make sure the woman wasn't moving against him or trying to get away.

There was no one there.

The surreal washed over him—walls seeming to bend and bow, the floor coming in closer and then further away—and for a moment, he reeled forward, legs buckling underneath him before he could right himself again.

"Nothing. I—I thought I heard something," he said to Postman. His voice sounded small to his own ears, and he cleared his throat.

George nodded, face drawn and pale. Callfield holstered his piece and huffed a long sigh.

"Something's not right with this place, is it, Constable?" George asked.

Chet turned on his heel and pushed past Postman.

"You're got-damned right, Deputy," Callfield said under his breath. "God damn this place."

George took a quick glance around the room. Seeing nothing, he turned and followed the constable.

Chet kept walking. His head hurt, his stomach turned, and everything had a twin. His vision blurred, but he kept walking. Down the stairs, and out the front door. He felt something push him. *Push* him out the door.

(*Mother?*)

He went behind the bushes and vomited.

"Constable, you all right?" It was Postman, on his heels again, face pinched with worry.

The fresh air helped Chet return to normal. He turned to Postman. "I'm fine. Must've been the smell of the house."

"Yes, sir." George said with a huff.

"Get that worried look off your face. What's going on with Hausmann?" Chet asked, using a handkerchief to wipe his mouth.

"They said he's in shock and his spine might be broken," Postman said, keeping his face neutral. "They've rushed him off to the hospital. No one can get in touch with his kin. I tried Linda's cell phone. It's off or she can't hear it. Left a voice mail to call the hospital."

"What about parents?" Chet asked.

"They're dead, Constable." Postman said with a shake of his head.

"I hate to think of him wakin' up to that Linda—if he wakes up, that is."

"Same here, sir."

Chet put his handkerchief back in his pocket and headed toward the prowler. "Well, let's get there. If Phil survives—and I hope he does, we can ask him questions when he wakes up."

The crime scene crew arrived and Callfield told the detective what little info they had. The crew combed over the yard, starting at Phil's van. Chet knew damn well they didn't know what they were doing. What in Perdition was there to look for in this little pissant town? Some drifter that was long gone into the woods by now.

They got into the car and headed for the hospital. The only noise was the roar of the engine as they sped down the highway.

George broke the silence. "That house. It doesn't seem to be anything but trouble."

Chet nodded.

"When we were kids, there were all sorts of haunted stories about it. We used to dare each other to get in close," the deputy said.

Chet nodded again.

"There's real creepy stuff there," George said, trying again. "I don't know why the Silver Hollow history people don't just have it demolished."

"Yep."

George seemed pleased with himself for getting a word out of the constable.

"I heard people go to the house and never come out again." George said.

"Uh-huh." Chet's lips drew into a thin line.

"And I heard that the house is cursed, you know. Some people say that's just hocus-pocus but I think there might be something to it; something's weird in that house. I think—"

"George?"

"Yes, sir?"

"Shut your fuckin' mouth." Chet's tone cut through the air between them.

"Yes, sir." An audible swallow clicked in George's throat.

The corners of the deputy's mouth turned into a frown, and he looked at his trousers, picking the lint off them. He looked up and out the window, nodding to himself.

Chet glanced over at him, a look of semi-satisfaction crossing his face as he looked back at the road once more. The deputy continued chewing on his lip, looking out the window and begging to be anywhere but in the prowler at that moment.

The rest of the ride to the hospital was quiet.

THE DIARY

Silver Hollow Historical Society Archives

Archive Number: 000312

Date: circa 1942-1944

Historian's note: Found in the Sellers-Watson-Kellogg / Maxwell-Hunter House, formerly The Walker J. Dubbs House, during a cleaning of the property in preparation for asbestos removal crews. Dates not included or illegible due to water damage. Records show Maxwell-Hunter and Sellers-Watson-Kellogg owned the building from 1935-1945. -Francis Langelier, PhD

Diary,

It is with great dismay I write such words this evening. These forays of mine into the realm of the unseen have, as dear Mary had predicted, have come back to chew me apart like a feral dog.

Since the incident, I haven't written, because I've been under a sedative for the past three nights. Ever since the Halloween séance has resulted in a disappearance.

It is this god-forsaken house.

Here I, in my infinite hubris, believed that the fortunes would be in my favor. How wrong I was. But, as usual, I pushed. I always get my way. This time, I wish I hadn't. Now I wish I'd listened to Mary.

"Elizabeth, I don't think it's a good idea to hold a séance in this place," she said, "not ever since Mister Parker met with his accident."

Ah, I should start at the beginning. When we first moved into the renovated house, with the full intention of making it a popular bed-and-breakfast stop, we had never stayed at the house for more than a few hours at a time. But we both felt it was special.

We set the workers to their tasks and received reports of accidents on occasion. A few times, a worker went mad and did something unfortunate—for either himself or others, or both. Once, one man set about another with a hammer to "kill the bugs."

Kill the bugs, he had not. Killed his fellow worker, well, he succeeded. One would suppose repeated hammer blows to the face would do such a thing. They told me the victim was no longer recognizable.

Dear Mary found these reports horrid, a testament to the historical violence and memory surrounding the place. I, however, took it to mean something different—a spiritual energy in it that was too much for mere men to take. It was like a giant spiritual dustbin, collecting terrible energy in the center. Cleanings with incense and a spiritualist would make it right again.

Once we moved into the house, though, it was blissful. As if it had been waiting for us. With fresh paint on the walls, flooring restored to its former mahogany glory, and custom furniture we brought in from Nottingham's in Grace City, we had created our own paradise.

Mary was familiar with most of the history of the place. The first fire claimed many, but they rebuilt and carried on. It was a hospital during a wave of illness—which reduced the town's population by two-thirds. Walker J. Dubbs, a retired officer from the East Territory, and his lovely Western Territory defector of a wife who was also a nurse, took care to ensure people survived. Her dedication to saving lives during the war meant that she had aided Eastern soldiers against orders, and she'd paid for it by being called a traitor to her people.

Ridiculous once one thinks we were all in the same country. That might be my modern, Northeast sensibilities talking.

At any rate, the home, a symbol for the two of them uniting, and far from the Hansom-Warner Divide, had become their care center. They didn't renovate it much for the transition.

The nurse (her name escapes me at the moment) Dubbs had married could not have children, or perhaps Dubbs could not, instead. The couple adopted three children orphaned by the war. All of the children passed young, so the townspeople say, and the records of their deaths are lost or wherever they were, I couldn't access them. The two of us never gave it much thought. Well, Mary didn't.

It's of no consequence, I guess. Jewel Grove Hospital purchased the house, and renovated into an asylum to take their overflow. They had little work to do because of the many rooms to house boarders—and it was ready with little changes to keep patients. The records are missing on most of these things. What kind of patients lived here? No one knows. Some speculate consumption, others speculate mental illnesses.

Ah, I remember her name now. Constance Hayes Dubbs.

Constance Hayes Dubbs. Yes. What an interesting couple. One can only speculate what their relationship was like, what with so many records missing after the Great Fire. The Great Arson was what they should've called it—records burned when a man from Silver Hollow went mad and tried to erase humanity by setting town and city halls on fire. This resulted in many towns burning to ash, and the death toll reached the hundreds before the marshals stopped him.

But I have seen her. Seen the Dubbs woman, and others, now, in this place.

I was bathing in the claw tub of my private bath, just off the master suite of what one would call the keep's room. Surrounded by the hot water and stillness of the room, the scents of lavender and roses filling my nose, sleep washed over me in little waves. Forcing my eyes open, I went under a moment to wet my hair, and when I came up, I gasped in shock. There was a woman who wasn't Mary, and she was looking at me. Her eyes were wide and jaw dropped in surprise.

This was no transparent ghost, either. No, she was solid. She had her hair up, and wore a white dressing gown, unbuttoned with black lace trim, as though she was on her way to bed or on her way to get dressed. The lithe figure outlined through the sheer garment underneath showed me a woman who kept herself well.

She had stopped to look right at me. As if I was interrupting her from her routine, rather than she from mine.

I was not seeing a memory, but was seeing an actual being, whom I should not have been able to see—she was dead. Constance was just as surprised of me as I was of her.

"Nurse Hayes?" I recognized her from the history books, but part of my mind had closed to rational thought. The room felt cold—colder even than it felt after a hot bath—and gooseflesh erupted over my body.

She opened her mouth to speak. No sound emitted. Just a whisper of air. That made it worse.

I sat forward, too shocked to be modest, and not thinking I was hallucinating or dreaming.

She reached out toward me and I shrank back.

"What are you doing?" my tone was shrill and echoed off the tiles.

The woman stepped back, then looked as if she would say something again. She looked sad as if she had realized that something was wrong. I shivered—cold air hitting my exposed skin from the bathwater.

Then she—well, she disappeared. Not as if she popped away, out of existence. She faded.

I scrambled out of the tub, put on my gown, and found Mary.

Yes, I was hysterical from what I had experienced, but I hadn't been hysterical when it happened. Hysterics don't come at the mere entering of a bath or during washing, or even when a person has an experience like that—for me, it comes afterward when I try to speak of what I'd seen. I suppose I was in shock, at first, and then so overwrought by her sudden appearance and *disappearance. When I found Mary, it came out of me in sluices of gibberish.*

Mary, known for being calm in any situation, brought me a cup of tea and listened, bright eyes intent as I told her the ghost-who-wasn't-a-ghost story. As I told her what I'd seen, and that it was no apparition. She kept me from flying into hysterics once more by placing her hand on my back. Her cool hands kept me grounded.

Once I had calmed, she was silent for a time. I sipped my tea and waited.

"Perhaps you imagined it," she said. "It's a soothing, quiet bath, meant for relaxation. You may have fallen asleep in the tub and had a vivid dream."

Mary is practical. Practicality is her greatest virtue and is likely the reason I love her so.

I am not so practical. I am very much a woman of my passions, and I give in to flights of fancy. But Mary's reassurance brought me comfort; so much so I went upstairs to bed.

"I suppose you could be right," I said, finishing the dregs of my tea. The bitter leaves give a scratch to my throat on their way down. I sighed. "This was just more real than any dream I've ever had."

"You're a creative soul." Mary gave my knee a gentle squeeze. "It doesn't surprise me that the history of this house has sparked your imagination."

The corners of my mouth turned up, and I kissed her lips.

"Thank you, love."

Mary didn't convince me this was my imagination, and it showed in my faint smile and furrowed brow. Still, I went upstairs and fell into an uneasy sleep, waking a few times in the first hour. I started as if she would be there by *my bedside, reaching out to me again. After the third or fourth time I woke, I fell into a hard slumber.*

Sleep has such a delightful way of repairing damage. Rest can conquer everything from parrot pox to hangovers. I didn't dream that I could recall, and when Mary woke me up with breakfast, I was as calm as I had been when I first got into the bath and settled.

With a few scrambled eggs, crispy bacon, toast, and freshly squeezed orange juice, I forgot about the previous night's upset. There was far too much to occupy my time with preparations for guests, who would pass through soon for the summer and staying for the leaf changing season. Silver Hollow in autumn is a feast for my senses. The weather is crisp and cool, and the leaves are brilliant in shades of gold, red, bright yellow, and rusty brown. The air is perfumed with wood smoke, fresh apples and pickling spices. People gravitate to the area.

Three maids, two cooks, a groundskeeper, and a porter—that was enough to keep the place running.

Mary managed the books, and I managed hostess duties and receiving of our guests. When I checked the reservations in the mail and placed them in our registry, we were booked solid for the entire season.

This meant we were far too busy to pay attention to the strange goings on in the house, like the claims that belongings around the place were missing. A thorough search of everyone's belongings showed that there was no thief among us. Pots and pans, linens, personal items such as watches and rings just disappeared. I lost a hair pin with an emerald scarab on it. It was on my dresser, and the next time I looked, it was gone. No one was with me.

Another search proved fruitless, and some staff complained of other things happening in the house while they were working. One maid claimed to have been locked in the pantry for an hour (but there's no lock on the pantry door). She fainted away and Mary sent her to the doctor.

We assumed it was the employees raising a fuss so we would pay them more. But they stayed. Why wouldn't they? The bed-and-breakfast brought in the work, and we pay well enough compared to other places in the area.

Even though Mary had a logical explanation for everything, and I took comfort in that, there is nothing normal about this place, even with logical explanations. The groundskeeper couldn't get the hedges to grow in spots. He insisted it was the ground—the ground was sour, he would say. I wrote it off to his poor gardening skills and a lack of knowledge with those species, and Mary wrote it off to a lack of education in general.

Now I am not so sure.

I should get to Mister Parker now.

Mister Parker was the owner of a lumber company that met with success during the building boom. He was to stay with us for an extended time over last summer, and to enjoy the seasons changing before returning to his winter home in Covet Stream in the Southeast Territory. Compared to that palatial home, our bucolic bed-and-breakfast was quaint and rustic to him.

The first week he was with us was non-eventful. He mentioned that his bed was uncomfortable, and we offered to change rooms or change mattresses, but he refused, saying he believed it was just a matter of getting accustomed to sleeping in a new place. What's funny is that he also refused a partial refund. Mister Parker said he didn't need it and apologized for mentioning it.

"Surely it's my imagination. Have you ever slept on these mattresses?" He asked, tone mild as he cracked into his poached egg.

"Yes, but I'm well-accustomed to the newer innersprings," I said, refilling his coffee cup for him. "There should be a way to make it up to you, Mister Parker. Perhaps a twenty percent refund would help?"

He waved his hand. "No need, dear Miss Kellogg. I'm hearty enough. I wanted to let you know, in case others complained."

No one refuses a partial refund. Not anyone I've ever met, anyway. The man was honorable, and a gentleman. Why he complained? That could be to make conversation—not everyone is capable of proper social behavior. The rest of the time, he was agreeable and pleasant. Even complimenting the staff on their orderliness and the chef on his cooking skills. Most people of Parker's ilk don't bother with recognizing the staff as people, let alone paying compliments.

After the first week, however, he changed. He became irrational, making strange demands of the staff, complaining that there were rats in the walls, and telling Mary to stop wandering into his room at night with an ax.

At that accusation, Mary balked.

"Mister Parker, if I were to enter your room with an ax, you'd not be around to discuss it over breakfast," she made a huffing noise.

I held up a hand before Mister Parker could respond. Mary turned away. "If you'll excuse me."

She left the room, skirt sweeping out behind her.

"Mister Parker, I assure you Mary sleeps sound during the night, and only the gardener uses an ax to chop firewood. If you'd like, we could add a deadbolt lock to your door for added security—no charge, of course."

Parker frowned and looked as if he were having some kind of internal debate. "Yes, I suppose that would be acceptable."

We added the deadbolt to his door. For two or three weeks, we had few complaints from him, but his eccentricities increased. Singing was his favorite pastime, but his songs were becoming stranger, and he spoke in a foreign language that neither of us could identify. Mary asked him, but he wouldn't identify the language. He said it was an ancient, dead language, and that few knew it.

Mister Parker spent more and more time in solitude. Sometimes, the maid would hear him singing, or chanting, in that ancient language. He wouldn't let her in to clean his room.

Mary and I were at a loss. We couldn't evict him from the premises as he had paid in full, and we had no policy on making it mandatory to let staff into the room to clean it. As long as he wasn't burning the place down or being a nuisance to the other guests, there was little we could do. In the Northeast Territory, a person has to be a 'pervasive nuisance' to be evicted from a place of boarding. Since none of our guests complained (they stayed away from him), we had to tolerate his change in demeanor.

One night, just after the solstice, he came to dinner with the other guests. Mary and I often took dinner with our guests to hear stories of their adventures in the woods or exploring the landmarks in the small township. Sometimes the occasional tale of local color proved amusing. But when Mister Parker joined us, my entrée formed a pit in my stomach, and I had difficulty finishing my meal. Instead, I wound up drinking more of the wine.

At first there was no need to feel ill at ease. Mister Parker was back to his jovial self. That's when I saw it.

The smile that didn't reach his eyes. The way he looked at everyone as if he were trying to figure out a rousing whodunit. Forced chatter and laughter, strained to the point of breaking.

It broke.

Mister Parker got into a heated debate with a gentleman over a trivial matter, and the knot in my stomach grew tighter.

"Gentlemen, please—civility at the table—we can discuss this later," I said, using my motherly tone.

That was when he drew a pistol.

Several people scattered, trying to duck under the table and scurry away, while others sat, gape-mouthed and clutching pearls. I gripped the table, my hand inches away from my steak knife.

The gentleman with the pistol in his face, a fine guest by the name of Eustace Kirchner, spoke in mellow tones to him and agreed with Mister Parker's points. Kirchner was a psychiatrist, and skilled at his job. When he spoke it transfixed us, and my hand slid away from the steak knife.

With his hypnotic tone, Kirchner persuaded Nicholas Parker to put the gun away, and Kirchner helped him back to his room with a sedative.

We finished dinner then and left the table in silence. Slipping out of the room, I went to the office and called the constable, clicking the lock and ensuring there were no eavesdroppers.

The constable was unwavering in his insistence that since Dr. Kirchner got the situation under control, there was nothing they could do about it. The noise of spitting chaw made me glad he couldn't see my face twist with disgust. Filthy habit.

"What do you expect from me, ma'am—I don't know," he said, voice tinny and distant over the telephone. "Fact is, he didn't use his weapon, and there are no laws in the Northeast Territory that state a person can't carry a weapon with them. Sounds like people should be sure not to rile this man up."

I held back a sigh, and a growl of irritation. "Well, I suppose then we'll call you when he shoots someone."

He chuckled. "Ma'am, in my experience, men like that are made of talk, you see. Those types carry guns and wave them around, but when it comes to it, they don't act on their threats. I'm sure you're safe, no need to get hysteric—"

The receiver hit the cradle so hard when I hung up on him that the bell rang.

Either he didn't believe me because I'm an outsider to his little town, or because I'm a woman. Had I been a *man, or had a husband to verify the information, I'm sure he would have listened. But no, not being a hysterical woman—even though I was calm and lucid over the phone—he didn't trust me. Or he thought I was doing it for attention. He started to call me hysterical, so I'm inclined to believe my womanhood stood in my way of being believed.*

For the record, that wasn't Constable Max Callfield. It was one of his idiot lackeys. Max would have believed me, but I'm sure no one told him.

With my head in my hands, I sat there, trembling from fear and anger. If we were lucky, Mister Parker would take his leave from us in the morning. That he might commit suicide with that gun gripped my heart, but not out of pity for the man. For self-interest, I admit. I didn't want this man ruining the dream that Mary and I had spent so much time and effort building.

Yet it was not a gunshot that took Nicholas Parker from this world.

We don't know what happened to him—we couldn't be sure. Mary called it "his accident," or "the accident."

He vanished and took no belongings if he left, and he must have gone through the window, because we had to cut our way into his room after he didn't come downstairs for two days. He even left his pistol behind.

The staff, Mary, and I expected a gory scene as we opened the door.

Instead, we had a scene of a closed window, clothes folded and waiting for after a bath, with everything in place as it would be common for someone staying in a hotel or bed-and-breakfast. The room was spotless though there'd been no maid service in the room for cleaning. He changed his bedding and left them and his used food trays outside his door every other day, but there wasn't even a hint of dust in the room.

The suitcase in the closet was empty and the drawers were full with two seasons worth of garments. Cologne, shaving items, everything in place. Reflecting on it now still makes the fine hairs on the back of my neck stand on end.

It was as if the house ate him. That sounds humorous. Yet I'm not laughing at the notion.

Mary called his family, business colleagues, and others that might know his whereabouts, but to no avail. We turned the matter over to the constable, and they took his things. As far as local gossip, there wasn't any—we attempted to be discreet about it. I'm certain Mary ensured that money kept lips shut tight.

With careful inventions, we could even hide it from the other guests, telling them that Mister Parker was called *away on urgent business and we would send him his belongings. Since the guests who'd encountered him that night with the gun were eager to see him go, they didn't query further.*

I suppose they suspected things on occasion, but they said nothing, and it didn't get out as a splash story, because more guests came and went after that. We had several frequenters and long-stay guests. The visitors forgot Mister Parker.

After Mister Parker's strange disappearance, Mary was not too keen on having me hold a séance, despite her skepticism. I insisted.

Looking back, she had been right. Mary was often right, damn it. But I am a stubborn woman who wants to follow my own path, and I often learn lessons the hard way.

This time, Mary's instincts were correct, though she was not one to go on instincts, preferring logical arguments over emotional ones. But I thought a séance would be a good idea, and felt it needed to happen—and I was curious.

We needed to communicate with the spirits to get things to settle down in the house—not just for us, but for them. That's what I believed. Mary thought it was nonsense and would invite trouble. After a fortnight of chasing after Mary, I cornered her while she was doing the laundry.

I sat in the clothing basket, bottom getting soaked by wet clothing, and I wouldn't let her finish her chore until she acquiesced.

"Do I ask for too much?" I looked up from my station in the basket.

Mary frowned at me, sighing with exasperation.

"No, you don't. But why is this so important to you?"

I squished around in the basket for a moment before answering. "If it's all nonsense, like you say, Mary, then what trouble could it cause?"

"Séances don't attract a desirable element, Elizabeth."

"Don't be such a snob," *I said, wagging my finger at her.* "What are you afraid of?"

"I'm afraid you won't let me get these chores done." *Mary said, one hand on her hip, and the other waving me off. I didn't move.*

"No, I won't until you let me do this," *I said, crossing my arms across my chest.*

"Fine, you can have your séance." *She gave in with a laugh, then pushed me from the basket to get back to work.*

The night of the séance brought high winds, a cloudless sky, and a glittering, fat full moon. Storm clouds, far away, rumbled in the distance. An ideal All Hallows Eve night. It would be perfect for communicating with the beyond, and whatever forces were alive within the house.

Only a couple remained as guests at our bed-and-breakfast once I'd told them about the séance. The rest had gone elsewhere for the upcoming winter. We didn't tell everyone about it—I wasn't that careless, but Thomas Lind and his wife, Diana Schuster-Lind, expressed interest in spiritualism. After several dinners together filled with discussions of the supernatural, I couldn't resist.

The only other couple I invited were locals, the lovely Mister And Missus Callfield. They were a dear pair of people with two beautiful children and had been the only people who were kind enough to welcome Mary and me to the town. With those four, and the medium, there were only seven of us—a lucky number for me.

Pragmatic Mary didn't believe in lucky or unlucky numbers unless they were plus or minus in the ledger.

My love still held to the notion that Mister Parker went mad and disappeared into the forest. But a body was never recovered, and there was no evidence that wild animals carried him off, and she had no answer for that. Plus, the windows were closed in that room. The dogs called in by a hunter in town, found no scent of him out of doors. Parker went into his room that night and never returned, as if he'd evaporated like mist in the mid-morning sun. Mary refused to see it, saying he must have gotten out another way.

But I knew, deep inside, that the house had claimed Mister Parker. I was determined to get him back, and any others the house may have claimed. There had to be others, and this séance would reveal them—I was certain.

The Traveler woman I hired for the evening had not wanted to step over the threshold.

"The grounds are cursed," she said in her deep voice. I nodded, trying not to bubble up with giddy enthusiasm.

"An ancient evil lives under the soil. Its poison has seeped into the walls," Madam Palmer said, still standing on the porch. "The house has a mind—a hateful, vile, and wretched mind."

I love Traveler theatrics. Fascinating people of all walks of life who took up the nomadic style.

"Perhaps you can help us get rid of the evil then," I said with my best party smile.

"You don't understand. This isn't something that one chases out—it's something that gets inside of you, and changes you."

"Would an additional payment change your mind?" I asked. "Fifty dollars extra."

She shook her head. "No, you still don't understand."

"One hundred more," I said, hearing my voice straining with desperation. This wasn't the best position to be in with the woman. I took a deep breath and tried to wash away the strain of unease in my stomach.

"No."

"Two hundred. Please. We need your help. I promised an authentic medium to my guests."

The authentic medium bit her lower lip and looked up at the house. She grew pale, but I could see in her eyes she wanted that money. The old woman looked like she was having a tennis match in her head. I started to sweat in my evening dress.

"Fine. I'll do it," she said.

Palmer was from a poor family—all Travelers struggled for their living and she was no different. Her children and grandchildren moved about looking for work and they needed that money. Theatrics or no, it seemed a brave attempt to get as much money from me as possible. It worked well.

"I'll pay you once we're finished," I said. Mary, who had heard the end of the exchange, gave me a look that told me I would get a stern lecture about money matters later. I looked back at her and shrugged, caving to the Traveler's wishes. I couldn't back out of the agreement now.

I never got a lecture from Mary, and the psychic woman told me she would not collect her two hundred dollars after that night. "It is tainted money," she said.

Instead, she took food: a roast, vegetables, and bread to ensure her family received a decent meal for the night.

"Please, take the money, I insist," I said. Palmer held up her hand and shook her head so hard I thought she might snap her neck.

"I won't take it." Her charm bracelet littered with Traditionalist god heads rattled as she shook her hand to keep the money out of it. "If you're worried about word getting out, I assure you I'll be silent."

I wasn't worried so much about that, though I likely should have been. Palmer was a Traveler and in general, the Travelers were true to their word.

She left after that, and I went back inside. I didn't understand what she meant by 'tainted money,' but I thought she was all about getting as much from me as possible. She disproved me into shame.

Mary tells me I shouldn't tell a story out of order. Let me start at the beginning of that evening.

The séance started as expected, after the party gathered and ate from the spread provided by our chefs—who left after service, as did the staff. I didn't invite them to stay and they were eager to leave. They weren't all residents of Silver Hollow—some lived in the next town over. No doubt they were eager to get home (half of them acted disgruntled at a séance going on where they worked).

The séance began at midnight. The lot of us gathered in the intimate sitting room where I had a round table set up and the Psychic was waiting.

I need not expound upon how a séance goes—what's important was how much it differed from those I attended in the past.

We joined hands, and some closed their eyes while others watched for signs of tricks or a setup. Though the *knocking method had proved to be a hoax (Mary gloated for several weeks over that), some tricks weren't so simple.*

This evening was different. No tricks. No hoax. The Traveler woman channeled something. A wretched thing took over and refused to depart. Her eyes opened wide, and she made a sound that no human had any right making—a guttural growl that sounded like there was more than one voice coming out of her. None of the voices sounded human.

The noise was in a language that none of us recognized and sounded similar to the gibberish that Parker had chanted once. I tried to break contact from Mary on my left and the Psychic on my right, but I couldn't loosen my grip from theirs.

When I was young, we were among the first people in our neighborhood to get electricity, and I saw a man working on the wiring get electrocuted. He couldn't let go of the live wire, and when he collapsed, the wire was still stuck to his hands. I don't know how awful it must have felt, but the jolt that was causing me to cling to both Mary and the Psychic burned through my body.

A crash from the basement resonated through the house, and that broke the spell that was holding us together. I rose to my feet to get away from the circle. To break it so that whatever was taking over her body.

That's when the electricity went out, and I heard a woman scream. I wasn't sure if it was Diana or Lisette. I knew it wasn't Mary (being familiar with her voice).

The candle was the last light left in the room, and that blew out, plunging us into near darkness. The only savior was the full moon overhead, casting a silvery shine on the room and on the six figures frozen in place.

"Who blew out that candle?" It was a man's voice who asked, but I couldn't tell which one.

An awful groan emanated from the Traveler gain, and then she collapsed onto the table, arms flailing outward, making her look like an Egyptian painting on the pyramid walls. "Is she dead?" Lisette asked.

"No, she's just—stunned." Thomas stepped forward and helped the psychic onto the settee. She was unconscious.

I looked around again at the group, my eyes better adjusted to the darkness. There were only four figures in front of me. "Someone's missing," I said.

Ice gripped at my entire body and I did a mental roll-call. Diana and Thomas were standing together at that point, his arms around his wife. Mary was in my peripheral vision. I couldn't see her but I could smell her perfume. That left—

"Where's Lisette?" Max's voice sounded strained. "Lisette, where are you?"

A scream for help came from the basement. Mary took off for one door that led to the cellar.

I followed on her heels and Max Callfield followed me. "What happened?" he asked.

"Mary, check the fuses," I said, trying to open the basement door. The heavy oak slab wouldn't budge. I pulled harder, and nothing.

Max pushed me out of the way and I didn't protest. That was his wife screaming down there.

He banged on the door as Mary opened the faux curio cabinet which hid the fuse box. I ran out to the kitchen, through the back door, grabbed a hatchet used for splitting wood, and ran back inside.

"Out of the way," I said. Max moved.

If anyone would break down that door, it would be me. But as I raised the ax over my head to crack it into it, the door popped open.

At the bottom of the stairs were two shapes in the shaft of moonlight beyond our shadows. The first looked like the figure of a woman, and next to that figure sat an enormous dog or wolf. Only their outlines were visible.

"Don't come down," Lisette's voice carried up the stairs, just above a whisper. "If you do, we'll all be cursed."

Max shook his head. "Come up here, Lissie," he said.

"No, I can't. They're holding me back."

Mary got the lights back on, but the basement was still dark, and only their silhouettes were still visible, casting elongated shadows off the dim chandelier's golden light.

Max grabbed the ax from my hand and ran down the stairs to hack up the wolf-dog-shape thing. I turned away to beckon the rest of them to follow, but they didn't.

They were further away, and Mary was standing by the fuse box.

"Lissie? Where'd you go?"

I turned to the sound of Max's voice and saw that both the wolf-thing and Lisette's shadow were gone. Max turned back to look at me. "She disappeared right in front of me," he said. Now his voice sounded small and shaky.

"There's a secret passage for the servants that leads to the upstairs rooms," I said. "Lisette might have gone through it."

The doubt in my voice sickened me. Everything about this evening sickened me.

The group searched everywhere for her, well into the night. Mary and Max explored both ends of the passageway until they met in the middle, and Thomas and Diana went down to the basement with me once the lights were on to search there.

Poor, dear Lisette. Her husband was beside himself, so much so that at first I wondered if he was just acting. Perhaps he had done away with her and was playing up a scene for the rest of us.

I was about to open my mouth when the group met again in the sitting room and accused him of it. He became pale, then fainted. A real faint where a person falls forward, rather than a theatrical one. Max hit his head on the round, solid oak table, hard enough to make it shake.

Mary called for a doctor, and for the constable. Thomas and Diana left for home. We didn't argue. No one gave thought to making them stay or worrying if they paid their incidentals.

The constable (the same one who called me hysterical) let them go after brief questioning. They questioned Max, Lisa (the Traveler woman's name had escaped me until now), Mary, and me, and they cleared the four of us. They trusted Max. He was their boss. If he had harmed Lisette they wouldn't have pursued it. That's how it works in small towns—they protect each other.

That's because no one was involved in Missus Callfield's disappearance. The house would be the only suspect, and the constable insisted it was just a prank by Lisette. Max didn't argue with his deputy—the bereavement swallowed him whole. The man took one punch after another, even when the deputy implied that we were doing it for publicity.

I would not dignify that with a response.

Neither Mary nor I knew what to say to Max. Neither of us have spoken to him since, and I think none of us will ever be the same.

This happened only a few nights ago but it feels longer. The constable didn't question us again, and there will be a service for Lisette next week up in Terrace Lake. If Max will allow it, we'll go to pay our respects.

No one has mentioned the house, and it's as if the people in town, even the constable, know it was the house, but what could they do about it? What could any of us do about it?

I don't understand this town, and the people in it. No one got arrested that night, and no one has been since. The lot of them act as if nothing happened, as far as we can tell. Though they play dumb, they seem to be the ones hiding something. Such a strange place.

The night when Missus Callfield disappeared, I sent the Traveler woman away with a hamper full of food, refusal of money, and her promise not to so much as mention this place. I know she won't mention it, not for our sake, but because she believes in those curses.

As do I.

Not that I know nomadic culture that well, but I've never known poor people to refuse money. She said the money was tainted because it was tied to the house, but there was something else she said when I asked why the food wasn't tainted, then.

"The food belongs to the cooks and the cooks are clean. That money has touched cursed hands."

I shook my head. "I don't understand."

"You will."

She left into the darkness, and her group moved on, I suppose.

Now, looking back on the past few days as I sit here in a now quiet Dubbs House, I understand. I allowed the evil of the house to work through me and let it harm Lisette. The psychic woman is right—my hands are tainted.

I wish I could take it back. I wish I had listened to Mary.

Lisette Callfield's disappearance is my fault, because I insisted. I pushed and got my way because that's what I do. Max will never forgive me, and I don't deserve forgiveness.

If there is an abyss—Perdition, as the old religious cult says, then I'll be cast there upon my death and face eternal torments, but they can't be as bad as the ones I'm facing right now. With what I've seen and endured in this place, maybe death will spare me by bringing me peace.

But I doubt it.

— Elizabeth Maxwell-Hunter

MERCY HOSPITAL

Paul slipped in and out of consciousness as the ambulance wailed and whined its way through the narrowing streets of Terrace Lake. "You're doing great, Paul. Stay with us," they said as they hooked him up to tubes through his nose, mouth, and arms. "We're going to Mercy Hospital. We'll be there in ten minutes."

The young man didn't answer and slipped into the dark water that kept surrounding him.

With a sticky little noise, Paul opened his eyes when the ambulance slowed down. Out the back window, he could see the enormous stone building looming on a steep hill. The place looked like a giant bat, with multiple floors and a spread out configuration, with the ER entrance making up the body of the bat.

Nurses in classic white uniforms and hats greeting him on the gurney, the noise they made sounded like squawking and trumpeting. Paul moaned.

They were talking underwater—he could almost understand them, but couldn't answer them. Paul opened his mouth, heard the buzzing of bees, and looked away, wishing his body would stop hurting through every pore. Or he could at least lift a hand to say yes or no.

Nurse whites turned red as they leaned over him to stop the bleeding. A man in white scrubs asked him questions about allergies, about medical history and other things. Through the commotion, Paul nodded and shook his head. Sometimes he answered with nods and shakes when they were talking to each other.

The voices became clearer, sharper. They asked what happened, and Paul struggled to give a small shrug that made his shoulders burn like they were full of glass shards. The last thing he remembered was working the back patio of that house, refinishing the wood, and seeing something that surprised him. Could have been that a board snapped. If that was it, he thought, he would sue the Silver Hollow Historical Society for a fortune. Injury on the job had to be worth a claim against them. If he made it.

The team asked him to hold still. Paul did. Every joint seared with pain as if he'd stayed out in the sun for too long. When he was eighteen, he'd fallen asleep at the beach when he was visiting the Southeast territory, and didn't wake until five hours later—and the reward for that was burnt skin that pulsed tight over his body. Paul put boiled lobsters to shame with his reddened self, and the blisters that erupted all over him were the size of half-dollars. Had to go to the hospital then, too.

This was worse.

Paul slipped back into the darkness just as a nurse spoke to him, another one talking underwater.

A woman's voice—a different woman—spoke to him.

"Can you wake up? Sir?" the voice was deeper, more authoritative, and tinged with an overseas accent. Proper sounding.

His sticky eyelids peeled open once more, and he focused on narrowed blue eyes, looking at him with concern, but distance.

"What's your name?" she asked.

"Paul Ingersoll." His voice sounded rough and faint.

"Good. And do you know where you are?"

Paul didn't move his head, but his eyes examined the room he was in, and he cleared his throat. "Mercy Hospital."

"Yes. Do you know what day it is?"

"Wednesday."

The woman nodded. He tried to sit up, but the doctor put her hands out on his shoulders and pushed downward.

"Don't move, Mister Ingersoll. I'm Doctor Kathryn Cross, and I'm going to be treating you today."

She asked him more questions, who was the leader of the country, did he recall what had happened, and stuff like that.

"Don't remember," Paul said when she asked about what had happened. "I was just doing some sanding and restoration on house—the back porch that leads to the kitchen. There was…" he squinted as if he could see what he'd seen then and shook his head. "I saw something, but I don't know what, and then I don't remember anything after that."

The doctor nodded. "That's okay. Just try to relax for right now. We'll give you something for your pain and more fluids and blood. Don't try to sit up until I tell you to, okay?"

She excused herself for a moment and a nurse came in and injected something into his IV line. A warmth spread over his body and he sighed in relief, then a more pleasant darkness washed over him

The angry bees that were stinging his body went away, and the sounds of beeps and boops faded into the background, like the rhythm of a heartbeat.

The rhythms called his name. "Mister Ingersoll, Mister Ingersoll, Mister Ingersoll."

There was a badge staring him in the face when he stirred: KATHRYN CROSS, MD. He looked over the badge and at the person behind it. A tall woman with fine bones, prominent cheekbones, full lips and blue eyes that made him think of cloudless summer days at Terrace Lake. Those eyes were deep-set but had a hardness to them—the way a person looks when their environment has toughened them.

"How are you?" she asked. When she opened her mouth, he heard the Albion accent. That explained the hardened appearance. *Oh yeah, she was the same doc from earlier.*

"Better already, but I thought I'd died."

"Oh?" Doctor Cross said.

"Yeah, I'm surrounded by beautiful angels," he said with a grin. He felt his face get a little warm, and he looked away, shame-faced for the cheesy line.

"That's just your morphine talking. Enjoy it while it lasts. We're going to run a few tests and make sure you won't surprise us with anything." Cross's voice was clipped and professional, but her lips twitched in a slight smile.

"Okay. So I'm not gonna die, though, am I, Doc?"

Doctor Cross shook her head. "Someday you will, but not today. Although you came close, your numbers are remarkable now. I believe you'll be fine."

"Okay," he said. That accent of hers was silky smooth. The woman sounded like a queen to him.

Doctor Cross looked over at the screen displays that were monitoring his condition. Paul looked at them for a moment, unable to interpret them, and watched her instead. Her swan-like neck curved as she jotted something down on a tablet using a stylus. He giggled to himself then quieted, biting his bottom lip and his head swam a little.

She turned those blue eyes on him again and he tried to make his face return to its neutral state.

"Well, your vitals are stabilizing, and you seem to be improving," Doctor Cross said. "But we're going to keep you, run a series of tests, and if everything looks okay, we'll let you go home either tomorrow or the day after. How does that sound?"

Paul gave her a goofy, drug-addled grin. "That sounds nice."

Doctor Cross smiled. "Okay. Glad you think so." She took his hand and squeezed it. Paul believed he'd fallen in love. "I'll be back to check on you later. If you need anything, Lauren Gilley is your nurse."

Paul didn't speak, but just kept smiling up at her.

Doctor Cross left the room. Paul slept.

He woke up to the noises and interruptions of blood tests and scans, then fell into a smooth, drug-induced sleep.

Paul was in Dubbs House. The aroma of wood oil and old must was familiar to him although where he was inside the house was foreign. The room was dim, and the moisture in the air settled into his skin, giving him a shiver. Lit in a blue-gray light, he could see nothing but walls swollen with water damage.

There were sounds in the distance—cries from the dark of fear, pain, and despair. Disembodied whispers called out to him, too. Pleas for help and nonsensical raving.

Madness whispered in the darkness. Some in complete gibberish.

Paul scratched his head in wonderment and tried to bring the room into focus. He had been lying in bed at Mercy Hospital, and now he was somewhere in Dubbs House. Swallowing a lump in his throat, his heart raced, and he had to sit for a moment on the cold concrete floor to get it to slow down.

Once his heart calmed, Paul rose from the floor, exploring this empty, yet claustrophobic room. How it could be so huge and seem so close to him made his stomach churn and his breath come in quick gasps.

It's a basement—it must be a basement. So where was that light coming from? There were no doors nor windows he could see. He approached the walls.

They were thick with some kind of slime. Paul examined the floor. This wasn't concrete. In fact, it was slimy. He touched it. The walls were pulsing. *Cold and pulsing.*

Face twisted with disgust, he wiped his hand on his pants and fought the urge to vomit.

Something was wrong, and Paul looked for the exits. A door, window—anything to get out of this room.

That's when he saw the man.

The guy who had lured him into the house in the first place—tall, sinewy, and blond. It clicked—that's what he'd seen out of the corner of his eye while he was working. But this time, he didn't go near him. Paul backed away, back toward the walls as the beautiful man smiled at him and unzipped his pants.

That's when a rope of flesh snaked its way around Paul's arm. It burned him like acid, and he felt like his skin would tear off his bones. He screamed. Another rope grabbed him, snaking around his trunk, then his legs, and his arms.

When he looked up, he saw the lights of the hospital's ceiling. *This is just a memory.*

The man, godlike beauty with chiseled features walked over to him, moving first like smoke, then speeding up as he got closer, faster—becoming a blur in front of Paul's eyes.

"You're stuck here, bastard," he said, now in complete focus, sticking an accusatory finger in Paul's face, heavy jaw jutting out in defiance. "You should have helped those women. Now you're stuck here with the rest of us."

Paul opened his mouth, but all he could do was cry out in pain. Another rope grabbed him, then lashed out at the other man, wrapping a tentacle around the man's neck. Paul watched, unable to move, as the tentacle squeezed tighter and tighter, then pulled back in another blur. The force and the acid, or whatever combination it was separated his head nearly all the way off.

Blood gushed over Paul, and he threw up, mixing yellow bile into the dark red spattering all over the coveralls. His bowels and bladder let go, and the smell of his excrement made him retch again.

As he grew weaker, he felt something like teeth breaking through his skin. Something in the house would devour him, and he couldn't do anything to resist. He screamed for help, his voice hoarse, and then growing with strength as he willed himself to not give up and let whatever this thing was take him. He screamed for his mother, for his father, and for any god that might be listening.

A siren screamed in the distance.

Everything went black.

The hospital ceiling greeted him, and his body responded by pouring out sweat—his heart hammered so fast and so hard he thought it might rupture. Tears mixed with the sweat and he sobbed. He tried to put it away—to blame it on hallucinations from the medicine they'd given him. The images wouldn't fade.

Doctor Cross entered the room with Nurse Gilley, making him forget about his problems for the moment. The two came up to him on either side of the bed.

"How are you doing, Mister Ingersoll?" she asked, face pinched with concern.

"I—don't know. A little weirded out. I don't remember much, just a nightmare."

Doctor Cross nodded and examined him, then looked at his vital signs. "Must have been a bad one, but you're normal again."

Nurse Gilley put a cool compress on his forehead and Doctor Cross pulled up a rolling chair to sit by his gurney.

"You have a concussion, Mister Ingersoll, and I'd like to keep you here until you're doing better—just a couple of days to make sure you're strong again. What do you think of that?"

"I guess that would be okay," he nodded. "Better to be on the safe side."

"Good. Practical man. Now, there is another matter we need to address."

"Yeah?" He tried to sit up, but the dizziness hit him hard. Paul laid back again and let it pass. Doctor Cross waited before speaking again.

"Your emergency contact, Gary Platt. What is his relation to you?"

"That's the soon-to-be ex-boyfriend. I was going to get that changed. But, uh, my brother, Jeff—he's a good guy—he can make decisions on my behalf."

Doctor Cross sighed and smiled the way she might smile at a kitten rolling around with a ball of yarn—*isn't that sweet*. "Good, I'm glad you have more than one person to look after you. I'll make sure that's put in your file, too. About Jeff. I doubt it will come to that though."

"Why? I mean, why are you glad?" Paul asked, shifting in bed, still flat on his back.

Now it looked like she'd tasted something rancid. "Because your ex, or soon-to-be ex refused to show. He said he 'didn't want to hear about it,' and hung up on me." Cross's eyebrow twitched, and she shook her head. "Now, you said your brother's name was Jeff, and I assume his last name is also Ingersoll. Am I correct?"

"Yeah. And I'm not surprised Gary said that. In fact, I'm kind of glad. Not the best way to break up, but at least it's over."

Doctor Cross nodded. "This is true. Although getting in such a bad situation is *not* a great way to end a relationship. So don't do it again, okay?"

Paul wanted to say something, flirt with her, but kept quiet. Cross was way out of his league, and he knew it. It had been a while since he'd been with a woman, and she wasn't likely interested in a bisexual woodworker who was a patient, too.

"Get some rest, and I will check on you a couple more times before you're admitted. Making room for you in Critical Care will take time. The police want to question you about the emergency call, but I told them it would have to wait until later, when you're feeling up to it. As long as you're my patient, you're under my protection." She jotted something down on her tablet again. Paul focused on the jet black stylus, and it changed into a jet black tentacle, roping its way up the doctor's hand. Cross didn't react, and Paul closed his eyes. *It's just the medicine.* He shuddered to himself and opened his eyes. It was a stylus again.

"Thanks, Doc." Paul said.

"Of course," she tapped the stylus against the side of her tablet. "You don't strike me as the type."

"Type?" Paul shook his head.

"Violent type. The constable will ask you about the missing man. In fact, I'm curious myself."

Paul sighed. "Me too. I mean, curious. I remember him now. But when I got downstairs to the basement, something happened. An attack, I think. I don't know." He didn't want to recount his dream. Not yet. She might put him in the loony bin if he did.

Doctor Cross nodded. "Don't think on it too much. Just rest. If it's any consolation, I believe you. I'm told by some of the nurses that strange things go on in that place. Since I'm not a local, they don't tell me everything, though." She got up and crossed the room, her slender legs carrying her to the next emergency—she moved like rushing water.

"Doc?" He said, urgency in his voice.

She turned back. "Yes, Mister Ingersoll?"

"Please call me Paul." He said.

"Okay, Paul. What can I do for you?" She said, taking a step toward him.

"Something bad happened to me in that house." He said, feeling like he was a ten-year-old all over again, telling his mother about the tree outside his window that was alive and hungry for him.

"Yes it did, and it was a surprise you didn't die en route to the hospital." She said, putting her hand on his arm for a moment before withdrawing it.

"Why?" He asked, wanting to sit up, but the jelly that took over for his muscles made it impossible.

Doctor Cross sighed and sat down again. "Well, I didn't want to tell you and scare you, but since you're tough, I think you can handle this. Your body was covered in lacerations and you lost blood volume. You were in shock, and your vitals were everywhere. When you first got here, you were in and out of consciousness. We treated you, and you stabilized better than expected because you're in excellent general health. But you were in bad shape."

She paused and closed the jacket to her tablet, putting the stylus away.

"It was far worse than you realize. Though no bones are broken, you have a mild traumatic brain injury—a concussion I told you about before—and we need to make sure your blood pressure stays stable. That's why I want to keep you, to ensure you're one hundred percent better in the morning. If so, you should be able to leave."

Paul took a minute to digest everything Doctor Cross said. After a moment he realized he'd been holding his breath and exhaled. If his dream had been any sign of what happened, well, it wouldn't be a surprise if he had checked out for good.

"Thanks for being honest, Doc."

"You're welcome, Mister Inger—Paul."

She patted his arm again and left.

What seemed like only a few minutes later, the staff moved Paul to a room. Then after that, Doctor Cross returned to check on him. One of the nurses got him a Braxbury Cola with extra ice and offered him a sandwich. She also offered him extra blankets and kept coming back to check his temperature and read his vitals. With this much attention, Paul wondered if he was doing worse than he thought, or even than the doc let on earlier.

"This is it for at least a few hours," she announced after listening to his chest and stomach through her stethoscope. "I'm lending a hand in CC for the next few days, so I'll be your intensivist as well. They'll send me reports on you and I'll be back in the morning."

"Thanks, Doc." He said, reaching out for her hand. "That's a lot of work. I, uh—I appreciate it."

"You're welcome." Cross took his hand and gave it a friendly squeeze. Her hands were chilly, but the smile wasn't. "And it is unusual, but not so much for an understaffed hospital." She wrote on her tablet again as she left the room.

Paul could hear her speaking to someone in the hall about him—a nurse. She was giving medicine orders and checking on other patients, using big words he didn't understand. Paul drifted on the sound of her husky voice. Two men's voices joined it. One, he recognized as Chief Chet—that's what the locals called him, and the other had to be his deputy—Postman. He opened his eyes.

He wanted to call Jeff and ask if he'd arrive tonight, or be there in the morning to drive him home. Would he be allowed to go home that soon? Home to an empty house, missing valuable items, like the collection of first editions he'd inherited from his great uncle.

Gary would be gone with them though. That was a plus.

But what if he wasn't? What if he had to see the bastard?

He pushed that thought aside, stomach turning.

Something terrible had happened to him at the SHHS site, and the last thing he wanted was to come home and have to deal with that bullshit on top of everything else. The more he remembered, the less he liked it, but forced himself to stay calm.

The man was real. Paul had tried to tell him. They'd gone into the basement—he followed where handsome man went. It was the lure of the Venus fly trap. Paul shivered and pulled up his blanket.

He couldn't recall how he'd escaped—how they knew where to find him, but he'd lost consciousness so often, it was like trying to see something down a long tunnel. No matter how hard he squinted, it wasn't coming into focus.

With a sigh, Paul looked at his arms. They were covered in cuts and scrapes. It looked like something chewed on him.

I've been eaten by a house. That is some freaky bullshit. I must be out of my fucking mind. I'll be damned if I'm gonna tell anyone about this.

He wasn't sure how he'd answer the police. He didn't want to lie, but he knew the truth sounded bonkers. Silver Hollow had always been strange, so they'd understand. They might know something he didn't.

The guy had been there, and he could've told them what happened. He'd been trapped in the basement (or wherever in Perdition that was), too.

Maybe he'd claim it was an animal attack. Since it looked like a huge animal mauled him, he could say one got into the basement and attacked him. Did that make any sense? Not more than what he believed happened. What he could recall. The choice was between honesty and insanity, or lying and incredulity.

Resolving to be honest, no matter how much he sounded like a nut ball, Paul closed his eyes again, hoping to keep away the nightmares.

A RED CAT

Silver Hollow Historical Society Archives

Archive Number: 000366

Date: 13 December, 1936

Historian's notes: Found among several books and sherds of pottery. This is a partial diary found in the Sellers-Watson-Kellogg/Maxwell-Hunter House, formerly The Walker J. Dubbs House. Found during a cleaning of the house to prepare for asbestos removal crews and signed by Mary Sellers-Watson-Kellogg. This is the only portion (two entries) that survived. -FL

Diary: 13 December, 1936

Weather: Freezing and blustery. Snow in the afternoon.

It has been months since Elizabeth and I settled in and received our first guests, and a shorter while since Miss Emily, our chambermaid, hanged herself in the

pantry. But we have a business to run, and we must take care of our guests. Life must go on as the cliché demands—and things must return to some semblance of normal.

At least Elizabeth has stopped bursting into tears and has stopped hiding in our room. These past weeks have been a dizzying cycle of me bringing meals to her room, asking if she would come out today, and her silent refusal to budge from the bed. I would sit with her during those meals, just to make sure she ate.

No bid for conversation drew Elizabeth out of her shell. Sometimes, she stared out the window, a tear slipping down the apple of her cheek.

I would collect the tray and leave her be. There was little else I could do.

Then, a fortnight ago, Elizabeth came out of our room and spoke for the first time in so many days.

"I think the outdoors will do me good."

"Why not," I said. *Hope created tension in my voice and I winced, wishing I sounded casual. A fuss could send her back into hiding.*

Earlier, I found out what had attracted her to the outdoors. Elizabeth has taken to sitting outside with the most unusual animal. Well, it's a cat. If it weren't for its strange color, it would be an ordinary feline.

It is a red cat.

Red as the maple leaves changing in late October, with long, fluffy fur. We have never seen a cat this color, and we're feline aficionados.

The cat is enamored with Elizabeth and likes me well enough. But one would think he is her son, he follows her so. She says he is a familiar as the witches of Salem must have had. I try not to scoff at her whimsy—instead, I smile and remember that's what attracted me to her in the beginning.

I would be foolish if I said that cat didn't have a kind of extra sensory perception. The feline seems to know when Elizabeth is frightened, upset, or otherwise unhinged and comforts her with his deep, rich purr. But I'm not convinced it's supernatural. Because he is a cat, his keen senses can pick up smells, sights, and sounds we humans cannot.

Elizabeth said she is never afraid to be in any of the rooms with him because he chases the evil out of them (so dramatic!). At night, he sleeps with us, pressed against Elizabeth's back, and sometimes, I wake to see him alert and sitting as a sentinel at his post.

One morning after a long night of The Sentinel and his watchful eye, I told my love of this.

Elizabeth cut into her sausage link and smiled. "He does. The night watchman, my guardian angel."

"Yes, of course," I said, doubtless she could hear my skepticism. "But what's wrong with this house? I mean, Emily was likely just an unhappy woman—she was probably trying to get away from her husband."

Elizabeth made a face as though the sausage had turned sour and then stared at me with stony eyes. "Right. Because sometimes couples aren't as happy with one another as they pretend to be."

My eyes widened and I shot her a look, eyebrow raised. "Is that a commentary?"

Elizabeth sighed. "No, Mary. It's not. I just—I think they were a happy couple until this—this goddamn house."

Silent, I turned back to my breakfast. The woman didn't use such coarse language often, and when she did, it was sheer frustration. This was not an argument to be had at the moment, so I changed the subject to business.

At first I thought that the cat being her guardian angel was an odd, childish flight of fancy. I also believed none of our guests or Elizabeth when they described the supernatural activity that seems to be so prevalent in this house.

That is, of course, before the incident, but I refused to admit it to Elizabeth, even though it was upsetting to her and something she needed to discuss.

I am not so full of hubris that I lie to myself—and my silence to Elizabeth was a victory for her. The two of us have been together for so long she puffed up with pride when I deferred to her opinion—meaning I don't defer often. But in this instance, how could I not? My silence and subsequent changing of the subject was my admission of her being right. That's just the way I communicate, but I am old and stuck in my ways.

The strange occurrences in this house have humbled me, as I cannot explain them away. I have been devastated by the suicide and violence—the disappearances. This house has been nothing but a curse and burden, filled with weirdness. Nothing bizarre has happened to me, but all around me, which is enough. That, and sometimes I feel I'm being watched, or I see a shadow out of the corner of my eye.

Then, this cat arrived.

Elizabeth named him Oscar. After Oscar Wilde. Apropos. Not because of his looks, but there was something about him that was playful yet dark—much like the man himself.

The animal's appearance was sudden, and his demeanor remarkable. I am fond of cats, but I've never been so enamored with one until I met Oscar. He would follow Elizabeth from the gardener's shed to the house, and would sit with her on the porch while she updated the guest registry, waiting for her to feed him.

When mealtime arrived, he sat outside the kitchen. Elizabeth would take whatever meats and bones (and the occasional vegetable) were on the menu to him on little plates and let him "select" his meals from there. Then she would go about her business, and, when he finished eating and cleaning himself up, he would go find her, and sit, purring, in her lap. That's his payment for services rendered.

Now he gets to go inside the kitchen to eat—and he doesn't jump on the counters in there, as if he can sense that Elizabeth doesn't want him up there.

So far, not one guest has complained about him. Which is fortunate as he makes Elizabeth so jubilant. Not that it's of any consequence. Should anyone complain, I would tell them they could try to find another place to stay.

Good luck with that. The nearest lodging is up in Terrace Lake.

What is most interesting is that when Oscar is around—well—this is strange for me to admit as I am not much of a believer in the supernatural. However, with everything that has happened, I will place my ego on the shelf and write what I think instead of fearing what others will think of me when they find this after I'm dead.

When Oscar is around, the supernatural activity stops.

If something is happening in a room—like the sensation one is being watched, and Oscar enters, the feeling stops. Elizabeth had commented on it once while we were in my office and I was going over the books, getting ready to place my orders for the coming months.

I looked up from the books and raised an eyebrow at her. "Oh, really?"

"Yes. When Oscar enters, it goes away. I'm not imagining it."

"Hm."

"'Hm' yourself all you like, Mary, but it's true. Whatever it is, it's frightened of Oscar."

Sighing, I set my jaw. This would not turn into another sleepless night of me putting my hands on her and being turned away, leaving me to service myself.

"Yes, well. He's a special cat," I said, hiding the disbelief from my voice and smiling at him in her lap.

Oscar raised his head and stared at me as if to say, *I know you're lying.* He put his head back down and turned away.

I went back to my books, still unbelieving. Still skeptical—refusing to accept it as truth despite past evidence that there was supernatural activity in the house.

Until it happened to me.

The night it happened I was in the library, organizing my books, separating fiction from non-fiction, as I had a case of new titles in and I wanted to ensure that the guests could find them.

So while moving the older books to the higher shelves, I was standing on a tall ladder. That's when the eerie sense of being watched began.

I ignored it and continued to shelve the books. The room got chillier. Blaming the draft, I shivered inside my sweater, pulling it closer to my body.

That's when the ladder shook. I gasped, gripping the sides hard and trying to regain my equilibrium. My feet slipped and I gripped the ladder till my knuckles turned white, determined not to die from falling to the oak floor and bursting open my skull.

Oscar came in and ran up to the wall. The cat hissed, and batted at nothing. Such strange cat behavior but not uncommon, I've observed.

But then the sensations went away—of being watched, of being dizzy—and, the ladder stopped shaking.

The cat saved my life.

Once I climbed down from the ladder, I went over to him. He stopped his wild behavior and wound around my legs, butting his head into my ankles and starting that stentorian purr. Offering him my hand, he let me pet him.

"Thank you, Oscar," I whispered so no one would hear me, as they would confirm my fear I was mental for talking to a cat.

For that moment my skepticism about the house faded away, and I understood that this feline was a protector. I picked him up, carried him to the kitchen, found a tin of sardines, and we split the booty.

That was when Oscar won me over—and he has been so good for Elizabeth, who is prone to deep, dark moods. How could I not adore him? He is such an unusual cat, both in color, and in personality—and, he loves my Elizabeth.

Another peculiarity of this cat is that, when a room is "active," as Elizabeth calls it, he will rush ahead to enter before anyone else, and the "activity" will vanish.

I hope that whatever it is in this house will continue to be afraid of Oscar, and that it will even go away if Oscar stays.

We're not sure how old the cat is, but he is playful and active, so I imagine that he is but a young cat. Elizabeth, who had an uncle who was a veterinarian, states that by his teeth, he is only one or two years old. This is welcoming news. Perhaps that means he will be around for many years to come, and, whatever is plaguing this place will grow tired of its games, and will leave for good.

That would be most desirable.

As the sun sets, I must leave my office and join our straggler guests for our dinner. I hope Elizabeth will mingle tonight. That is one of the things she does so much better than I.

— Mary.

Diary,

Oscar is not to be an indoor cat. Though he enjoys following Elizabeth wherever she goes, he needs to be let outside with frequency. Though he always returns after these brief jaunts, Elizabeth frets while he's away from home.

The two of us are attached to the boy, and hope he stays out of the road. There aren't many automobiles in this town during the winter, but when there are, they drive too fast, slipping and sliding over the icy streets. I hope Oscar is wise enough not to give them chase.

It's difficult to determine whether Elizabeth frets more for Oscar, or for how boisterous the house gets when he is away. A boisterous house seems like a silly notion, but there's no other word for it. Precious items disappearing and then reappearing in places they have no business being, and food purchased from the market not two hours earlier rotting in the pantry. There are other things I've not seen with my own eyes, but the staff has reported them.

Before, I didn't believe in the supernatural, and, even when presented with things I could not explain, I dismissed them as strange, but colored by the vivid imagination of the human mind. Even still, I can't just go about believing everything I hear.

Belief is a funny thing, and I will always question things.

A recent incident happened where I could not find Elizabeth. Oscar was on one of his outings, and I tired from working on the plans for next year's events. I plan at least one year ahead to ensure that we have enough business from the surrounding communities and those passing through to keep us sustained.

Elizabeth had come up with several ideas for summer festivals and themes, and I was going through each one, matching it to our budget, and choosing the best and most cost-effective. After a few hours, my stomach started rumbling and whenever I read the themes, the Taste of Esperia or A Night of Bharatham Foods, my mouth watered.

As we have limited staff during the winter (just a few maids to keep things tidy and a chef who comes in a few times a week), the cooking this evening was up to Elizabeth. She is an excellent cook, and can bake with the skill of a five-star confectioner. But cooking for many is an all-day undertaking, so she preferred the staff to do it.

Though we scheduled the chef to come in and cook for us this week, the man we retained for the winter had met with a most unfortunate burning accident. The poor fellow was at Mercy Hospital's burn ward for six weeks. We had a difficult time coaxing him to return, but he promised to do so once he healed. The doctors still haven't given him permission to go back to work, so I'm uncertain when he'll be back.

"The house burned him," Elizabeth said. "This place made it happen."

What could I say to that? Deep inside, I agreed, though I wouldn't admit it.

Elizabeth told me she would make a hot soup to fight off the cold weather, and fresh, hot bread. As time passed, I stopped being able to focus so much on my work, and more on the fresh bread, dipped in a hot tomato soup. When I wrote a brochure and used descriptors such as delicious *and* scrumptious, *I headed to the kitchen to see how dinner was coming.*

I closed the door to my office and locked it behind me (the safe and other valuables are in there), then entered the kitchen through the swinging side door.

"I'm half-starved," I said, then stopped when I realized that the soup was off the stove, and everything was served on trays, but Elizabeth was not in the room.

"Liz? Hello?"

No answer.

At first, I didn't think on it, imagining she had gone into the deep pantry, looking for garnishes, or the linen closet, looking for napkins. Only the two of us were there that night. A storm was due, and the staff had gone home before the weather became impassable.

I laughed. Dear Elizabeth didn't need to go all out with an elaborate meal—there was no special occasion, but that's Elizabeth—she enjoys doing something special when there's no cause for it. The woman is the Merry Unbirthday queen, I'd say.

I picked up the trays and brought them into the small breakfast alcove where Elizabeth and I dined in the off-season and there were no guests to entertain.

That's when I noticed the soups and bread were cold, meaning that supper had been ready for some time. That also meant that Elizabeth went a fair distance for finding garnishes or linen napkins.

I didn't fret, not just yet, thinking she'd gone into the pantry and gotten distracted, finding a trivial thing to organize and forgetting her stomach. Or locked herself in and spent time dwelling on Emily's death. Not unusual for the dear woman.

"Elizabeth?" I called, louder this time so if she were in the pantry she would hear me. "Our soups have gone cold."

My stomach growled, and I sighed, then turned to the pantry, walking in and getting ready to give Elizabeth a lecture on letting our food sit for so long. The light was off. I turned the switch, and the light came on with a crackle. The dim light cast shadows, but not one of those shadows belonged to Elizabeth.

The silence was palpable—a heavy blanket over the long, narrow room. That's when I felt something strange.

Eyes on me, even though no one was there. The heavy stares of a crowd just waiting for someone to lynch. Lynch, like poor Emily did to herself.

Setting my jaw, I headed out of the pantry, switching the light off and closing the door with a slam. My hands shook, fingers icicles.

I then headed for the linen closet, reassuring myself that she would be there; again, organizing things or distracted by something she had found. I threw open the door to another long, narrow room that shelved the linens and opened my mouth to call her name, but fell silent once more.

She was not at or anywhere near the linen closet, either.

"Elizabeth? Where are you, dear?" I felt the muscles in my face tighten in a frown, and my heart picked up its pace.

There was no answer. I swallowed hard, trying to get the image of Lisette out of my mind. The house made a gentle creaking noise, foundation settling. The low hum coming from the basement told me our new radiator system (central heating) was working, yet I felt colder than ever as goosebumps erupted on my arms.

Then I went back toward the kitchen, thinking she would reappear there, since she hadn't finished with her kitchen preparations.

That's when I heard a scratching at the kitchen door—the door to the outside where the chef would toss away leftovers into a special bin for the gardener to use as compost during the growing season. It's in the far back of the kitchen next to the breakfast alcove.

I peeked outside.

Oscar returned from an outdoor excursion, red hair puffy as a cotton ball. He came in and looked around, but instead of his fur going down from the warmth of the house, his hackles raised.

It was then I could no longer be skeptical. Something was wrong.

"Elizabeth?" I called, even louder this time. Oscar took off. On an unusual whim (I seldom follow whims—it

was desperation), I followed him. He was running through the house, toward the library, his paws skittering on the floor.

Hissing and growling, he pawed at the door. I caught up to him and opened it.

There was no sign of Elizabeth, but Oscar was detecting something. His senses were even keener than other cats' perceptions, I think. He pawed at a bookshelf.

So many old houses have secret passageways (the home I grew up in had several), and Dubbs House was no different. Even though I didn't know about this one, I knew what it had to be.

I pushed on the side of the bookcase, and the disguised door sprang open. Elizabeth, bloodied and bruised, tumbled forward with a shriek.

I gasped and grabbed her to keep her from hitting the floor.

"Are you all right?"

Elizabeth nodded and pulled away a moment. I let go and looked at her. Reddish marks covered her neck and had a bloodied lip.

"I'm okay. What happened? One minute I was in the kitchen, finishing up our dinner trays, and I went to the linen closet for napkins. We were fresh out of them in the cupboard. When I opened the linen closet, something grabbed me. I know you won't believe me, but something grabbed me!"

"No, I believe you, Elizabeth. Something hurt you, it's plain."

The sleeves of her top were rolled up, and there were huge, finger-like bruises on her forearms just under the elbows. Her blouse was torn. There were bruises, which I assumed to be grab marks, near her throat.

Not wishing to alarm her, I made no mention of them. I wanted her to know I believed her. After all, she could not have made those marks herself (they were too big for her dainty hands), and there was no sign of a human intruder.

Had her attacker been a person, I would have expected to see someone in there with her, as her wounds were so fresh—and Elizabeth would have said there was someone there with her. There was no room for anyone to run in that small, hidden space. It looked like one of those protection areas built for when and if an enemy came to the door; or a prayer closet.

But there were no prayers to be had in there—or far too many that went unanswered.

I helped Elizabeth to the couch near the fireplace, poured her a brandy, and poured a rye for myself. Then I sat down next to her. We drank, and it eased our nerves.

Oscar paced in and out of the open passage way, a deep growl emanating from his chest. He circled, and, satisfied that he drove off with whatever force hidden in there, he came out and jumped up on Elizabeth's lap. The cat stared at her with sharp green eyes.

"I'm all right," she said, stroking the cat's head. Then she turned to me. "I promise I am. Just a bit banged up. Let's finish our drinks and I'll warm up dinner again."

"Are you certain?" I asked, giving her the once-over. She looked better now, more stable, but I had to be sure.

Elizabeth gave me a weak smile. "Yes, dear. I have to be sure to keep Oscar around."

Upon hearing his name, Oscar purred in his thunderous voice. It had a calming effect on us. Color returned to Elizabeth's face, and my heart slowed from its racing. The house became safe again.

There is something special about this cat.

— Mary.

Historian's note: No further records exist. -FL

PERMANENT VACATION

Linda hung up the phone from the hospital and sighed. She had been in the middle of packing her things and writing Phil a note about why she was leaving. That wasn't his fault. He was a nice guy.

Too nice for her.

Linda ached and yearned to get out of this little town and live. Nothing ever came out of her plans despite her desire to make them work. Like her plans to take up skydiving, or her idea to gamble herself into a fortune in Succubus City. Grand schemes to get rich or famous always fell apart, and to Linda, it was nice guys like Phil who were to blame. Nice guys held her back.

People called her ignorant, some people called her a bigot. Truth was, she was none of those things. She sometimes behaved that way because that's what she thought they'd expect. "Might as well give them what they want, right?"

The suitcase didn't answer.

"All I want is to be free," she said to her pants as she folded them and packed them away. She grabbed her vibrator and took out the batteries, then tossed them in the interior side pocket. "Oh, and to fuck my friend Colleen—she might like you, little hummer."

Colleen made her plans work. Linda met her through Phil's best friend, Paul Walker. Colleen was Paul's sister, and she and Linda hit it off right away. They'd bonded. Colleen was smart, sophisticated, and bisexual. One night of drunken play, Linda discovered fingers, toys, and girl-on-girl action was a fuck of a lot better than any dick she'd ever had. At least in this case.

There was no way she'd go back. Sex with Phil was like eating vanilla ice cream when she wanted chocolate.

Now her chocolate ice cream was going back to the city. Metro living. Grace City was a huge, cosmopolitan area, and Colleen was a marketing executive there. She was tall, glamorous, and salon blond with tawny, smooth skin and eyes so dark brown they were almost black.

Colleen was glamorous in the way Linda wanted to be, but couldn't. Every time Linda looked in the mirror, she saw the copper hair and sliding, caked eyeliner—the too-pink rouge on pasty cheeks dotted with freckles, and the split ends frizzing her hair out like a scrub brush. A scrub. All her hair lightening and attempts to dress up just made her look like a little kid imitating her big sister. A crude attempt at what a bumpkin thought was sophisticated, with dresses that didn't fit right or pants that hung off her where they were supposed to hug, or worse—hug where they were supposed to hang.

Linda didn't just want to be with Colleen, she wanted to *be* Colleen. Oh, no, not in that weird psycho way, maybe being near the woman would help her not look like such a rube in sophisticate's clothing.

When they were lying in bed afterwards—Phil's bed—Colleen invited her.

"No, I couldn't," Linda said, voice a husky whisper. She realized she'd been holding her breath and exhaled.

"Sure you could. What's keeping you here?" Colleen sat up on one elbow, the sheet pulling away to reveal a rounded breast with light pink nipples.

Linda didn't answer. Colleen didn't push.

So she took it out on Phil. She nagged him to make more money. Nagged him to take her on vacations. Bitched the moment he walked through the door and carried on until she exhausted herself, turning every comment he made into a fight. It was wrong.

But whenever he was around, the guilt stopped—bitch now, repent later. She resented him for keeping her in Silver Hollow, and it wasn't even his fault—not all of it. But she couldn't stop herself. That made it even worse. When Linda got mad at herself for it, she took it out on Phil, and Phil would just take it. He would sit, and listen, and apologize in the right places. On rare occasions he'd lose his patience. The last time they argued like that, Linda realized it was over—Phil had enough.

"Real sick of your shit, Linda," he said.

Linda's hands shook as a surge of rage spilled from her stomach outward.

"Oh, and what 'shit' would that be?" She asked in a high-pitched, near-screech. "That I want something more? That I'd like to do something other than just make ends meet?"

Phil shrugged and sighed, getting up from the recliner. He pulled out a pack of cigarettes and set them on the table.

"I quit."

He started for the door.

"Where in Perdition are you going?" Even her ears were getting hot with rage.

"Out."

The door slammed in time with Linda slamming her fist into his pack of cigarettes, which only hurt her knuckles. She stomped into the bathroom, raided the medicine cabinet, and found a baggie of white powder. After she sniffed up her sorrows, the numbness came.

Hours passed of nods and cigarette burns on the dining table, then Linda woke up and went upstairs to bed. Phil slept on the couch.

She called Colleen the next morning and asked if the offer still stood.

It did. Colleen said that if she went to Grace City, she would be there for a long time. Colleen hated visiting and only came to see Paul when she had to—she preferred for Paul (Walker not Ingersoll) to come see her.

Walker and Phil were good guys. As Linda stood there by herself, bright coral lipstick in one hand and a half-eaten chocolate bar in the other, she felt pangs of guilt for a moment.

Sweet anticipation replaced the guilt lining her stomach, and then the rest of that chocolate bar made her forget the rest. She wanted the excitement that Colleen's world offered. Linda wanted the parties, the wild night life. Grace City gleamed with promises.

Closing her suitcase and setting it on the floor with an audible thump, Linda crossed the bedroom to Phil's desk, scrounged around for a piece of paper and pen, and sat down.

Phil —

I'm leaving to go to Grace City with Colleen. She invited me, and I accepted. I hope you'll be able to deal, and that Paul won't be too mad at her for it. See, she's the one I've been with—I knew you suspected I was fucking someone. I don't want you to blame Paul or Dave, because they're your friends, and they wouldn't. Paul Ing. or Gary, either—they're not into that, I don't think. I think they're just straight up gay.

Colleen and I are bisexual—guess you knew that about Colleen, but not me. Fuck, I didn't even know. But, now I do, and you do, too.

Anyway, sorry that you're in the hospital. I couldn't deal with that. Not after the whole Ingers and Gary thing. It's been too much for me, and I'm no good with stress.

Hope you're all right, anyway. Like Gary said, I'm just not ready for that kind of commitment, and I can't deal with all that heavy shit. I suppose that means I don't love you, because if I did, well, I'd probably be with you no matter what. But I can't. I think I love Coleen, but who in Perdition knows. I didn't love Paul W., but his sister's another story, you know?

We won't be friends after this, but I'm sure that's fine with you. I hope you find someone who will make you happy. You're a nice guy, Phil, and you deserve better than this. Sorry I couldn't live up to your expectations—or anyone else's.

I'm sure George will be around to take care of you, like any good friend should be. I wouldn't know. Everyone in my life's been a piece of shit, except you most of the time.

Have a good life.

—Linda

It'd be good enough, she didn't have to be a wordsmith or whatever. She left the bedroom with her suitcase and stuck the note on the fridge with a fat tomato-shaped magnet.

Now it was time to leave and get better. Linda was a high school graduate, and with Colleen's money, she could afford to go to school—Colleen said she'd pay for school if she wanted.

Her feet froze with trepidation. Would she pay for school for Linda to become a celebrity stylist like she promised? It was no joke the woman had connections and knew famous people—Linda saw the pictures, but what if it was just another lie? Just getting used and tossed aside like so much garbage.

With a look around the entryway cluttered with dirt and stains on the wall, Linda stepped out of the house and slammed the door behind her.

Once she read a story about a man who went on vacation to Merribelle Island down in the Southeast Territory and then decided he'd never go back to his nine-to-five job. The guy opened a tourist shop and lived in the upstairs part. For him, that was like heaven. Made a great living off selling souvenirs and lived his dream. That's how this felt to Linda—all of it. She was going on a grand holiday and she was never coming back.

Climbing into her car, she set the avocado green suitcase in the backseat and started up the engine, taking a deep breath. This was it—soon she'd be at Colleen's in Grace City, partying in the penthouse with celebs, doing blow and getting her brains fucked out by the talented fingers and tongue of that tall blonde bitch. The part that wondered how long it would last silenced by gold chains and a gag made of silk.

She turned onto King Street and saw Phil's van.

On a whim, she pulled up to the house. Police were around the van, but nowhere near the house. The cops didn't take notice of her pulling up, either, which was weird.

She felt a pull in her belly overwhelm her. *Have a look around.*

Not the type to disobey her whims, Linda marched right up to the house and opened the door. No one stopped her, or even acknowledged her presence.

Phil's now-ex wanted to see where he'd been attacked. That was all she knew. Phil had gone into the house and someone attacked him, according to the doctor who sounded like a snotty bitch. Doctor Kathryn Cross, whose accent and tone of voice that just dripped with condescension.

"You're saying that you don't want to come to the hospital, or that you can't?" she sounded like she'd heard this before—and she probably did, with Paul and Gary.

Linda sighed. "It's not really your business, Doc. How about you just go back to taking care of him and doing whatever it is you do? Why don't you let the social worker take care of it?"

There was silence for a moment. "Are there any *family* members we could contact?"

"George Postman's his third cousin." Linda snapped her gum into the phone and popped a bubble in the doctor's ear.

"Fine, we'll work on our own. You've been an enormous help." The doctor's voice got far away as she hung up the phone. "No wonder he doesn't want to go home." Click.

Doctors. They all thought they could say and do whatever they wanted, especially the foreigners from Albion. Their uptown accents and the way they looked down on everyone, even if Linda complained about her nothing would happen.

As she stepped over the threshold and looked around at the crystal chandeliers and gold etchings against wood columns, Linda could tell the house had once been a palatial getaway for socialites and sophisticates. She could picture them drinking champagne from crystal flutes and eating foie gras, snorting coke off of tiny silver spoons they kept in elegant hand-blown vials that hung around their necks.

Now it was just a rundown shadow of itself. Complete with peeling paint and a musty odor, splintered wood, and tarnished brass. Thick dust hung in the air, illuminated by the weakening light streaming through the windows.

She walked up the stairs, looking around at what the place once was. The wood groaned under her sneakers.

A noise—a giggle from what sounded like a little girl, echoed in the hallway at the landing.

Linda stopped and looked around, curious. Why would a young girl be running around where a person just got attacked? Was she with the cops or something? Maybe it was take your daughter to work day or some shit. She laughed at the thought.

Even though the coke from the morning had worn off, it wasn't a big downer this time. Because she would move on to better things soon—and that was an upper on its own.

Grace City was the epitome of better things. Just 250 miles away, the fashion hub of the world, glitz and glamor, waiting for her to arrive. But first, she was going to investigate. That'd make an interesting story to tell Colleen and her famous friends as they knocked back flutes of champagne and snorted blow laid out on the service table.

Giggles.

"Who's there?" Linda asked.

"Me," came a voice, sounding closer this time. Linda laughed and turned a corner.

There was a little white girl in a pink dress, white tights, and pink Mary Jane shoes to match. Her little red hair was done up in neat side braids with pink bows tying them off.

"And who is 'me?'"

The girl giggled again and ran away.

"Wait!" She ran after her. What was a little girl doing here? Something wasn't right, and Linda would make sure this little kid met with the police. "You shouldn't be in here, it's not safe." The protest sounded lame to her own ears.

She ran down the hall to the room at the end, where the little girl had entered.

"What are you doing?" Linda asked the girl who was standing there with a large dog, a kind of German Shepherd mix. Mixed with what? A bear? The dog was taller than the girl and looked at Linda with intelligent eyes—the brightest blue eyes she'd ever seen on a canine. Not like the huskies with the faded blues, but the aqua of the shallow South Pacific. She swallowed hard and did her best not to make eye contact with it. Her heart rammed in her chest as the animal bared its large teeth at her.

The animal made no sound, not yet. All it did was snarl. That was enough.

"My doggie ranned away so I was trying to find him," the girl said.

She knew that face, those braids. Linda's face fell. "I've seen you before."

A picture popped up in her head: a black and white of that face and those pigtail braids. Where had she seen it? The caterpillar tickles in her stomach, which had been from anticipating her trip to the city were now angry bees in her gut. She was alarmed, but why it was bothering her so much still eluded her.

"You have?" The little girl asked, her hazel-green eyes shining hard. "No one's seen me in ages."

Linda frowned.

A memory of a headline flashed before her eyes. A headline from the Grace City Examiner from when she was a teenager over twenty years ago. She remembered it because the paper mentioned everything but the name of the township.

PROMINENT BUROUGH FAMILY HOLIDAY ENDS IN TRAGEDY

GIRL, EIGHT, AND FAMILY DOG FOUND DEAD AT HISTORIC HOUSE

FOUL PLAY SUSPECTED

This place. This house. The little girl had her name—Linda Sue. For a while, her friends here had told her it was an omen, that she would die in this house. They'd been messing with her head. That's what friends did best—but a creeping feeling settled over her after that happened—a feeling that took a few months to escape her teenage mind. Now, it was back in full force. She yelped.

The dog growled, and the sound made Linda's ears ring. The girl smiled and giggled again. This time, her laugh was cold—her smile a snarl.

"Oh, fuck." Linda said, backing away. "What the fuck is going on?"

The dog lunged. Linda screamed.

Outside, the crime scene investigators carried on, hearing nothing.

Linda's car sat across the street, empty—not even a suitcase left behind. A tow truck rumbled in as the sun set, taking the vehicle to the impound yard over in the next town.

Inside Dubbs House, silence.

NOBODY SLEPT HERE

"We're lost," she said, for what seemed like the fortieth time.

"We're not lost. I know where we're headed," he said.

Afternoon silver clouds hung in the sky, unmoving as the car slowed to a crawl. The woman sighed. A typical springtime in the Northeast Territory. With a little more sun, she would have suggested pulling over for a picnic and not letting the sandwiches she made go to waste.

The blonde grimaced. Once around the circle and back to the General Store. Twice. Three times. A fourth. If there was a hotel, it wasn't nearby. There was nothing that resembled a bed-and-breakfast there.

"The hotel is supposed to be near the General Store, off Main Street." he said, slowing down. "This is Main Street, so where's the damn place?" The man looked around as if the hotel would appear by magic before his eyes. "There's the roundabout, and that town hall thing, but no bed-and-breakfast. The lady said 'left off Main Street.' Well I don't see it, do you? *Women*."

"Why don't we ask?" Jill's lips pursed so hard the cherry lipstick seemed to disappear.

Ted growled under his sigh. "Fine. Go ask. Or we can keep driving through Silver Hollow and head right for Nashton Lake. But that means we'll be on the road for another few hours, which means *you* will have to drive."

His wife gave him a scathing look as he pulled up in front of the General Store, dust kicking up and settling on the yellow walls. She opened the car door, glaring at him again, and set her jaw. The slam behind her punctuated an unspoken opinion, and her heels clicked a staccato rhythm on the old sun-bleached and splintered hardwood porch.

As she entered the store, the first thing to greet her was a pleasant aroma—a mixture of baked goods, soaps, cosmetics, and spices wafted to her nose. She took a deep breath and smiled at the scent as she approached the counter. The store was quiet, transporting the woman away for a moment to that old town cult in the Southern Territory, where the only noises were the whispers of prayers from the parishioners.

There was no one in the room, but she spotted a bell with a hand-lettered sign in perfect block print: 'Please Ring Me for Service.'

Jill tapped the bell once, a pleasant ding echoing.

"Hold on, I'll be right there, Mabel." Came a man's voice from the back. "The apple pies are ready, just wanted to keep 'em warm for ya while I baked for tomarrah."

The young girl smiled. Mabel—what an old-fashioned name. How quaint. She heard footsteps and waited, not turning toward the source of the sound.

An old man, in his sixties or seventies, wearing a well-floured apron that read 'Haverty's General Store' on it in hand-painted stencil, came to the front. His eyes widened and jaw dropped upon seeing the stranger, and for a moment, she thought the man might turn around and hide in the back of the store again.

"Oh, well, you're not Mabel," he said, appearing to recover from his surprise. "What can I do for you, Miss?"

The tanned woman in the red dress smiled. "My husband and I are passing through, and we're looking for The Hunter-Kellogg House—the bed-and-breakfast."

"Ah, I see," he said, his voice growing more confident. "Well, you're looking for King Street. Go all the way to the town hall—follow the circle and take a left out of it. That's King Street. If you see Maple Street, you know you went the wrong way. The place you're looking for is the first house on the left, 'bout a tenth of a mile off the circle. There aren't any other houses near it, so you can't miss it."

"Okay," the young woman said, "follow the circle after reaching Town Hall, take a left, and I'm on King Street. Tenth of a mile on the left, can't miss it. Got it." She smiled as the elder man nodded. "Thank you, sir."

"Name's Hal Haverty," he said. His voice was soft and kind. "And you are?"

"Oh, how rude of me," she said, a light blush rising to her cheeks. "Missus Jill Braxbury. We—my husband Ted and I—are heading through to Terrace Lake on holiday."

"Ah, I see," Hal said. "That wasn't gentleman-like, making you get out for directions."

Jill laughed. "Oh, he was too embarrassed to come in to ask. I don't mind at all." She looked around. "In fact, it gives me the chance to purchase that wonderful-smelling bread you have baked."

Hal looked at her as if he didn't understand what she had said. Then he nodded. "I'll wrap a loaf up for you."

Jill fumbled with her purse while he wrapped a hot loaf of bread in tin foil, then popped it in a paper sack.

"That'll keep it warm and moist, the way my Hannah used to bake 'em." Hal said, a hint of nostalgia in his voice. Jill's smile faltered.

"I'm sorry for your loss, Mister Haverty."

"For what? Hannah isn't dead. Poor girl's crippled, though. Can't get around so much with the arthritis."

Jill looked into her purse again, face heated. "How much do I owe you?"

"Most times I charge twenty-five cents, but for you, because you're visiting, I'll charge you twenty cents." He said. Though he didn't smile, his tone was kind.

She pulled out two Coolidge dimes and paid the man. *Things were cheaper in the country,* she thought—and she didn't believe Ted when he told her that. Guess she owed him at least one apology.

Jill took the loaf from Hal with thanks. It was like a warm newborn in her arms.

"Be careful, Missus Braxbury. Have a good day."

Her expression twisted for a moment. Be careful? Did he think she'd drop the bread? "I will, Mister Haverty. Thank you. You too."

Ted scowled as Jill got into the car.

"What on earth took you so long?" He was either talking to her, or grumbling because he was being grouchy about having to ask for help.

"The shopkeeper gave me directions, and you know me—I took a while to get them right. But we didn't go far enough. You had it right. Take the circle at town hall, make a left, and that's King Street."

Ted gave her a small smile. At least now the bruises to his ego faded. He was so handsome when he grinned.

She might want to stroke more than his ego later that night. The thought made her neck tense up, and she found it hard to swallow.

"What's in the bag? Smells good," he said.

"Fresh bread. Can you believe they charge a quarter for it?"

"Everything's less expensive in these more rural areas, honey—except what they have to bring in from outside. I told you that." Ted's sounded like her father, and Jill fought the urge to roll her eyes.

"But I only paid him twenty cents," pride leaked into her voice.

"Oh?"

"Yes, he gave us a discount."

"I see. Well, it's because he can't refuse a pretty dame." Ted's face broke into a lopsided smile.

Jill snorted laughter. "You sound like Sam Shade."

"*Spade*."

"Right." She fell silent and let him drive.

They followed the street to Town Hall, which sat at the end of the circle. In the center of the circle, a kind of ugly fountain that looked worn and cracked stood. The copper was green and moss grew from it. Jill shook her head. A lion's head on a man's body was an odd choice of art.

Traffic was dead, like a ghost town. There was a gnawing inside her belly that became a pressure, dread expanding. Were they the only tourists there? Even though it was only March, heading into April, it seemed like there should be more people outside on such a warm day.

"Where is everybody?" Ted asked.

Jill shrugged. "You read my mind. I guess we were so caught up in finding the place we didn't notice how dead it was." *Dead.* As soon as the word came out of her mouth, Jill shivered.

They went onto King Street, and the bed-and-breakfast was unmistakable as it loomed in the distance. How did they not notice it before?

There were three cars parked in the long drive—status vehicles—and one that screamed millionaire with chrome and fine leather seats. They pulled up in their convertible—a testament to Ted making his way up the corporate ladder. Earlier, she wanted to let the top down when they were driving, but Ted said it would rain. It hadn't.

Jill glanced around the property. Some of the bushes were struggling to grow buds from a harsh winter. Large trees were getting a head start on spring, growing fat, hanging leaves, though she didn't know what kind of trees they were. A groundskeeper was busy tending to a row of rosebushes, buds forming in blood red dots against the green. Birds sang greetings from every direction. Without the traffic of the city, they had no competition for noise, and the volume of their songs rang in her ears. She smiled.

Ted grabbed one suitcase out of the trunk and looked over at Jill, eyebrows raised with a question. She shook her head.

"I'll need my makeup case, too." Jill said. He nodded and took it out for her.

Ted allowed Jill to step ahead of him until he got to the door, then held the suitcases under one arm and got the door for her with the other.

"You didn't have to do that, dear." She said. "But thank you."

"Yes I did. I have to make up for being a chump on the way here."

Jill gave him a small smile, shook her head, and entered the massive foyer. Oak wood floors and furniture polished to a mirror shine. Fresh flowers on a center table brought spring indoors, and the tick-tock heartbeat of a grandfather clock greeted them with a half-past chime. It seemed almost alive to her, and she was standing there, open-mouthed, enchanted by the crown moldings and the decorated ceiling of white fleur-de-lis.

Smelling tobacco and clove smoke made her look to the front desk. An older, pale-skinned woman, with gray eyes and dark hair, sat smoking and reviewing her ledger. The strangest looking fluffy red cat lay sleeping on the corner of it, near the woman's arm.

The cat stared at the both of them, and Jill would swear it was intelligent looking. Intelligent in the way an alligator looks—crafty, as if it were plotting something. Jill backed up near Ted, her heart skipping a beat.

The woman at the counter didn't look up, enamored by her ledger. "The cat won't bite," she said. Her voice was husky, the way smokers' voices got after years of the habit.

Ted walked up to the desk. The cat sniffed him, and sat up, stretching. Ted offered his hand. A few sniffs, and a head-butt later, the cat purred. The woman looked up at the couple.

"He likes you. You can stay," she said.

Jill tittered. The woman looked at her, unsmiling.

"Something amusing, young lady?" she asked, raising one well-groomed eyebrow.

Jill's face fell. The cat looked at her, his eyes making fun of her as he gazed. Jill tried to shake it off. "No, ma'am," she said. "I'd just never visited a place where we had to be screened by cats before being allowed to visit."

The woman smiled. "That's all right. Oscar is special. He knows whether people are good and whether they're trouble."

Jill approached him, afraid that 'Oscar' wouldn't like her. Then what would they do? Would the lady ask them to leave?

Oscar sniffed Jill's hand and licked it.

The woman at the desk laughed. "He likes you, so don't worry."

Jill breathed a sigh of relief.

"I'm only teasing," the lady said. "I would let you stay, even if Oscar didn't approve, you know," she stubbed out her cigarette in a crystal ashtray and blew out the smoke. Oscar backed away from the trail of blue-gray and settled back down at the end of the desk. "But I'd just make him watch you."

Ted chuckled and Jill tried to relax, although Oscar kept watching them with intent, and she squirmed under his firm gaze. *It's just a cat*, Jill thought, *let it alone*.

"Fill out the form, if you please," the woman handed a registry sheet to Ted. He took it and scribbled their information on it. "And you two are?"

"I'm Theodore Braxbury, and this is my wife, Jill," Ted said without looking up.

The woman checked the register, put a check mark next to their names, recorded the time and date, then handed him another piece of paper. "Ah, yes, Mister

Braxbury. The deposit charge is on the slip. Calls outside the territory cost extra, and there is a telephone in each room for your privacy. We expect the standard deposit now, and you can settle up calls at check out. Meals are part of the total price, and dinner is served at eight o'clock this evening. There are four others—two couples—who will dine with us tonight, and we dress for dinner."

The woman handed Ted their key and continued her well-rehearsed speech. "You're in room five, which is upstairs on your right. For the record, I am Elizabeth Maxwell-Hunter. The co-owner, whom you shall meet tonight, is Mary Sellers-Watson-Kellogg." She rang the bell and looked over at Jill, giving her a wink. "Tough to fit that on the sign, you know."

Jill smiled. She had just been thinking those were long names. *Names like that meant they were important people,* she thought. Jill wasn't important until she met

Ted—then she had money, a standout surname, and a chance to educate herself to act like a proper lady. Her meager beginnings were all but forgotten now she was *Missus J. Braxbury*, of the Braxbury Soda Company.

A young man who still had acne spots on his face and baby fat on his pale cheeks came and took their suitcase. He looked at the key. "Room 213, if you'll just follow me, sir. Ma'am."

Elizabeth looked at them once again, and said, "Your bellhop, who seems to have forgotten his own name, is Edward Postman. If you want any room service, just let him know."

Edward blushed. "So sorry, sir. Ma'am." He bowed his head toward Elizabeth, who shook her head and looked away.

"It's all right, Edward. Just because the girl is pretty doesn't mean you forget yourself."

Jill blushed as Edward looked like he wanted to melt into the floor. Ted laughed and clapped the young boy on the shoulder.

"It's all right," Ted said, "she's a catch, I know it."

Jill's stomach turned, and not in a pleasant 'butterflies in the stomach' way. *I'm not a damn fish.*

She pushed the thought aside with another—a voice that sounded much more like her mother's. *Be grateful he considers you worth his time, otherwise you'd be a spinster slinging hash in a city shit-house.*

When they were upstairs, the bellhop apologized for not introducing himself. "The owners aren't local, and they're real formal. I'm supposed to introduce myself before I take your bags. That's how they do it in the big city, I guess." He glanced at Jill and back to Ted, then blushed again.

Once shown to their room, Ted tipped Edward a dollar, and the young man's jaw dropped for a moment before he recovered. "If there's anything you need, sir, please dial four. That's my line."

"After dinner, if you would, bring a bottle of champagne to our room, well-chilled," Ted said.

"Yes, sir," Edward said. His voice had the eager edge that Jill sometimes heard in herself when Ted praised her for something.

"Thank you," Ted said as the bellhop made his departure.

Jill grinned up at him, looking at his expensive suit, high-shined shoes, and wad of cash. Her heart swelled with a mixture of pride, lust, and love. All the times he spoke to her as if she were a slow child: forgotten. All the times he turned over and fell asleep while she wound up lying in the wet spot with a red face and a snarl etched on her lips: forgiven.

She turned away from Ted, taking in her surroundings. The room was sumptuous with velvet, satin, and silk adorning the room, plush carpeting underfoot and velvet drapes open to let the light in once the sun came out from behind the clouds. A rich perfume hit her nose. There were fresh cut spring flowers on the dresser, in a vase. Jill tingled all over and sighed with contentment.

Jill kicked off her shoes and sank into the rug, toes grabbing each fiber as an ecstatic smile spread over her face. Ted moved over to her, picked her up, and threw her on the bed. Jill descended into it, soft and warm.

"Ted, this place is wonderful," she said.

He kicked off his own shoes and joined her on the bed, kissing her. "It is. You've got to trust me, Jill. I know what's best."

She exhaled to mask a sigh. Ted kissed her neck, unable to see her roll her eyes.

The afternoon breeze wafted in through the windows as the bed shook underneath Jill's back—they had married seven years ago and had produced no children. This was met with their parents' constant expressions of disappointment coupled with occasional hostility. They needed this second honeymoon. This was it. Tired of snapping at each other, tired of waiting for babies that would never come, Ted said that he wanted to try again. If they had the honeymoon they wanted this time, rather than what they could afford back then (before Big Mister Braxbury released the purse strings and let Ted get promoted), it would be the catalyst that would produce a son or daughter.

Jill was delighted with that idea. Not only did Ted have that promotion and they could afford to go to Nashton

Lake for a week (even that buxom blonde starlet Scarlett Rose enjoyed Nashton Lake, the society pages said), she wanted children. Even when she was a little girl, she always favored baby dolls—dressing them, changing diapers, singing them to sleep, and feeding them their bottles before burping them and putting them in their cribs with little kisses to their powder-scented foreheads.

A mother and a teacher. Those were the two things she wanted. Though she had gone to college, Ted said he would prefer she didn't have to work. After five years of teaching while Ted worked at his father's soda company, she could quit because he was making plenty of money with his steady promotions. Big Mister Braxbury didn't just hand out work, even to his son.

Now, he was a VP in the company, and she had no way to justify working to Ted. So she quit. Her life consisted of bridge clubs, social gatherings, getting her hair done, cleaning house, making breakfast, lunch, dinner, opening her legs before bed, using her hand when Ted rolled over and fell asleep, getting up the next morning, and doing it over again. The constant loop of being a housewife. Tick-tock, tick-tock.

Bridge clubs and socials were nice, but shaping little minds was what she did best. The kids—high school kids, paid rapt attention to her and understood the lessons she gave in calculus, algebra, trigonometry, and geometry, and *not* just because she could have been that bombshell's body double. No. She captivated them by making it fun—telling stupid jokes and admitting how stupid they were, throwing chalk at kids who fell asleep in class or getting the other students to prank them. Listening to them and their problems and being a mentor to the ones who were struggling. Housewifery wasn't *her*. There was nothing wrong with it, but it didn't excite her the way teaching did.

But Ted grew sullen and acted embarrassed that dinner wasn't ready when he got home. He nit-picked the dust accumulating in his study. He got cross with her often.

"The guys at work ride me hard about you still working."

"So?" Jill said, slicing white mushrooms for a casserole.

"So it's ridiculous that you're still working and our home life is Perdition. I mean, this place is a pig sty." Ted said with a clenched fist. Jill looked around the kitchen. She'd just cleaned it yesterday after dinner. She said nothing. He kept complaining.

By the time she got to the onions, tears were streaming down her face, but at least she could blame the fumes.

So she wrote her letter of resignation.

The promise of two or three children kept her going. She purchased school supplies and chalkboards and put them in the two spare bedrooms hoping she could teach them once they got old enough. It would be her job to help them learn, grow, and be whatever they wanted to be when they were on their own.

They tried to have babies. After two years with no luck, and with the two of them snapping and at each other's throats all the time, Ted came up with this gem of an idea. Well, Jill came up with it, but Ted would refuse it if he couldn't get credit. Instead, the brochures and mailers wound up in conspicuous places in the den, mixed in with bills and accounts.

As soon as she packed, she had a tickle of hope in her heart it would work.

With some good fortune, she'd even catch this same afternoon. The air heady with perfume, the afternoon sun coming out from the clouds and streaming in through the windows, and the soft, plush bed underneath them, she felt it was possible.

This place was like paradise, the stars clouding her vision, the smell of Ted above her, and then nothing. Bliss took over her body until she couldn't sense anything else but the pleasure.

It was possible this place *was* paradise. She hadn't had that happen in months.

Jill dreamed of babies and stars, and a red cat running through the house, chasing shadows.

***

Ted ran about the bed-and-breakfast, chased by a *thing* he couldn't see, but could at the same time. A shadow with long arms reaching out to him, yet the shadow was *solid*. He felt the wind from it as it reached out to grab him. His heart beat faster as he moved, closed in by wet, dripping walls. They formed closer, melting, collapsing, and Ted pushed against them, hands sinking into what was once firm wooden paneling. Punches against them stuck as if putting his hands in molasses. The gooey substance swallowed him as the walls expanded—it crunched him up and stretched him all at once. His lungs tried to expand as they crushed his ribcage. A pocket opened around his mouth, allowing thin strips of air for him to breathe.

Love cannot live here, came voices speaking as one from all directions. Enveloped by the void, he felt his whole body drain of energy.

The world began in darkness and will end in darkness, chanted the voices in the blackness.

Then it disappeared and Ted's eyes snapped open. His limbs were heavy, immovable. He lay on the bed, gasping for air, a lump in his throat. Jill stared at him, her eyebrows knit, little wrinkles around her eyes.

"Are you all right?"

For a moment, Ted had no answer. Where was he? After a moment, he oriented—the bedsheet stuck to his skin, the cool air assaulted his bare chest. He felt that the room was watching him, but that feeling was fading as he heard tiny footsteps thrumming outside the door.

"Water, please." Ted said, but could only croak out a hoarse whisper.

Jill jumped up and moved over to the basin and pitcher, which had two courtesy glasses on a tray. She poured him one, handing him the heavy crystal tumbler, and he drank it in two swallows. She poured him another. He drank that in three. The world returned to him, heart slowed to its quiet rhythm. Jill brought him one more glass. He drank this one a sip at a time.

"We're due for dinner downstairs in about an hour," Jill's voice was soft. "Do you think you'll be up for it?"

Ted nodded. "I think so. I had—I, I don't know—an atrocious dream."

"No, I think it was more than that, Ted. You stopped breathing. I had to shake you awake—you gasped for air just seconds before you woke up."

He looked at her again. Jill was pale and her hands shook when she brought them to her hair.

"That happens sometimes," he said. Though he tried to sound casual, he heard his voice crack, and took a drink of water. "It gets worse when I sleep in an unfamiliar place."

Jill shook her head, lip twitched into a frown.

"It's happened since I was a boy, Jill. But it'll pass. It always does. Trust me," he patted her leg. "It's hard to believe you've never noticed."

Jill sighed. Either in relief or exasperation. Ted shrugged and looked away, working on his water.

"Well, what happened was *weird*," Jill said after a stretch of picking at the bedsheet. "I woke up because you were thrashing, and then you stopped breathing. Then, just before you gasped for air, that cat, Oscar, came scratching at the door. As soon as you breathed again, he stopped, and I could hear him chasing something. It was like—like," she shook her head as she trailed off. "I could have sworn he was chasing something that was in here, or trying to, rather."

Ted stopped drinking and stared at her with a raised eyebrow and wide eyes.

Jill opened her mouth to say something else until she saw the look on Ted's face. Pink circles bloomed on her cheeks.

"It was just a coincidence, Jill." Ted reached out and took her hand in his free one, giving it a gentle squeeze.

"I suppose you're right," she said. "You usually are."

Ted nodded and smiled, then patted the hand he'd been holding.

"Let's get dressed for dinner," Ted said, voice more upbeat. The sweat dried on his skin and his shaking stopped.

Jill got up and showed him the suit she chose from the suitcase.

"It didn't wrinkle," she said. "I must have done something right."

Ted bit back the urge to say *for a change* and smiled with his best party face. "Of course you did," he said.

"Thank you," she patted her husband's arm. He got up and dressed, and she put his empty water glass upside down on a coaster.

They got ready for dinner in silence. Ted, who dressed and shaved well before Jill finished putting on her makeup, sat on the bed and read the evening paper, which had been brought to the door earlier. Once he saw it, he gathered that was what the cat, Oscar, had been playing with.

Jill must have been frightened by him not breathing enough to let her imagination run wild.

He hadn't lied to her about the apnea though. That hadn't happened to him in over ten years, maybe. The last time it had happened, he was in a place similar to this (*there are other places of evil, you know that, Ted*) and he had been alone. Once he started breathing again, awake and frightened, he had sat in the darkness, just trying to get oriented—taking in the time on his clock or watch, feeling his limbs against the bed or his feet on the floor, and rubbing his face and jaw to bring the blood back to his head.

It was just a dream—it was then, and it is now. Dreams like that were rare for Ted, but he wasn't going to give in to a childish fantasy that there was something sinister about the place.

No, this was where they had started their second honeymoon, and this was just a small obstacle in the grand scheme of things. This would be a wonderful trip to Nashton Lake. He was determined to make it that way. If she got pregnant there was no way she'd want to go back to work anymore.

His wife working—now *that* was embarrassing. The looks his colleagues gave him when they found out his wife worked made him feel smaller than a chastised child. As if he couldn't provide for her even on his salary.

Then he'd realized that the reason she wasn't content must have been that she didn't have any children to take care of, and it made her less of a woman when she compared herself to others. That's why she liked teaching high school. There were a *lot* of children she could mold. Once that clicked for Ted, the thought of a second honeymoon seemed obvious. He could give her what she'd wanted in the first place—an extravagant trip to Nashton Lake, and a baby.

That was all ladies needed to be happy—the old ways taught to him by his father had that right. The women who wanted to be doctors or pilots were confused and never attractive enough to land a man. Jill was stunning and didn't have to worry about that. There were men in wrestling matches to get that crown jewel.

He flipped through the evening edition of the paper, to the sports section. "The Grace City Times delivers all the way out here?" Ted said, and then realized that Silver Hollow was likely way too small for any kind of paper other than a periodical filled with local gossip, if that. Grace City was far from here, too. Ted wondered why they chose this one over the closer cities, like Jewel Grove. The owners were from Grace City or Beanton. Their names were long enough. Grace City was filled with elite, pedigreed snobs that kept their family names and just kept adding on, and on, and on ad nauseam to "prove" they were Union royalty. Early in life, Ted tired of Beanton's best and Grace City snobs lording their old money over the Braxburys. Even his father couldn't measure up to their standards. Not really.

He thought about the woman at the front desk. A good looking broad—lean, the way he liked. Kind of like that film star in those mystery movies, the one who retired to marry that prince—only the woman at the front desk was older—by about ten years. The lines around her eyes gave that away, and the dark circles, too. She had pale skin that contrasted her dark hair, and gray eyes. Unusual—they looked like the start of storm clouds. Not dark, but not nonthreatening, either.

Ted reached for his pack of cigarettes in his pocket, then realized the suit didn't have them. Once he found the pack, he lit up, and knocked on the bathroom door. "Jilly, come on, hurry up already."

Jill didn't answer, and he shook his head. *No*, he would not lose his temper over this again, so he sat and smoked, living in his thoughts while he waited.

Silver Hollow—this tiny little almost-town had presented itself to him in the strangest way, like a hand of fate. He'd been plotting out their trip to Nashton Lake for their second honeymoon, but couldn't find a route on his atlas that would allow them to stop and rest for the night.

It was a long drive from their place to Nashton Lake—he wasn't fond of driving, but did it because his father was fond of road trips. Trains made Jill motion sick, so the rail wasn't an option.

So it was driving or nothing. He decided he would just drive straight through, and purchase a more detailed atlas before they left.

A few hours later, while going through the mail on his desk in the den, a brochure caught his eye. It had a lovely picture of the house and the grounds of the Hunter-Kellogg Bed-and-Breakfast (also known as the Dubbs House), and a couple pages about what a quaint and historical bed-and-breakfast it was.

At the newsstand on his way to work, he purchased a more detailed atlas. Silver Hollow wasn't on the map, but the brochure showed where it was. It was right on their way to Nashton Lake.

Ted reached a pleasant sounding, husky-voiced woman (who wasn't the other, husky-voiced woman, Elizabeth), and made reservations. Just for the night.

"How did you hear about us, if I may ask?" she asked.

"I received your brochure in the post," he said, hearing the warmth in his tone and unable to help himself. He was a pushover for a good voice.

"Oh," the woman, Mary, said. "How delightful. I didn't know Elizabeth had started a brochure campaign."

"I guess she did." Ted wondered if she'd be in trouble for casting too wide an advertising net, or exalted for getting business from this far out. *Maybe she'd get a spanking*. Ted grinned at the images built up in his head about the face and body attached to that voice. He finished his business and hung up the phone.

Silver Hollow was a fair point between their home in Leightonville and Nashton Lake—just six hours to get from Leightonville to Silver Hollow, then another three hours to Nashton Lake. Ted couldn't drive nine hours straight, it gave him headaches and tired him out, but six was just fine. Another three hours up to Nashton Lake on the border would bring them to paradise just in time for brunch. Ted thought it was a (miracle) pleasant coincidence that this brochure came to him in the mail the exact day he'd decided to drive straight through.

He hated letting Jill do too much driving. Not that she wasn't a good driver. She was competent enough, making her trips to the market and running errands, never getting a single mark on her car. That didn't make Ted any less grim when she took it.

Waking up breathless and scared in a strange bed-and-breakfast room brought him back to his childhood.

That made him get ugly. Then he would take it out on Jill, and Jill would then ignore him for days.

He couldn't let that happen this time. The last thing he wanted was to wind up a miserable old drunk like his father, with a nagging, bitch of a wife who wasn't even satisfied with her husband building his own soda empire from the ground up. Sometimes, he could see Jill turning out that way—too smart for her own good, not wanting to keep her place—too much like his mother, and that wasn't good for him.

With his cigarette down to a nub, he stubbed it out and checked his watch. It was eight o'clock. Before he could open his mouth to ask Jill if she was ready *yet again*, she stepped out. She was wearing a lovely little black dress with a white half-jacket, velvet piping.

"Excuse me, Miss, have you seen my wife, Jill? The last time I saw her, she stepped into that restroom." He smiled.

Jill waved a slender hand at him and blushed. "Ted, you're so funny. Thank you. I was just about to ask if I looked all right."

"All right? You look wonderful." He stood up and took her arm, jaw aching from clenched teeth.

They were not the last to arrive to the dining room. Elizabeth greeted them with rye and an apology. "Mary is making last-minute arrangements to the menu. Dinner will be served soon. In the meantime, please enjoy some hors d'oeuvres."

The cat was nowhere to be found in the dining area to Ted's delight—he thought that wouldn't be sanitary. The tray of hors d'oeuvres, however, distracted him—he saw caviar, foie gras—but much more than enough for just six guests, eight people in total. It looked like a spread for at least twenty. He thought that was kind of the wasteful for such old money people, but helped himself to plenty. If they served it, he would eat it—dinner was included in their room and board.

Mary arrived about twenty minutes later, and she caught Ted's attention, too—like Elizabeth had. Her blond hair and blue eyes shined, though time had graced her with lines here and there, she looked like a beauty queen.

He wondered what in Perdition these two were doing out in the middle of nowhere. No husbands to take care of them. Old spinsters by choice seemed odd to him. Maybe they were funny—not followers of the old ways.

After dinner, and dessert, Ted felt like he might explode.

"Cigars and brandy are served in the den for those who wish to partake," Mary gestured with a small hand to the other room. "Those who don't smoke, you're welcome to socialize in here, or retire to the library."

Elizabeth stood and showed the gentlemen to the den. There were only three men, and three women as guests. But boy, did these hostesses know how to show a good time. "We get much busier in the summer," Elizabeth announced, looking over to Ted (as if she were reading his mind). "But we never skimp out on cigars and brandy, so long as we have at least one guest to enjoy them."

Oscar greeted them in the den and then left with Elizabeth once she finished doling out the cigars and brandy. The men discussed their businesses, and other things. Ted forgot his strange dream and waking from earlier in the evening. They talked late into the night, and Ted had to excuse himself to ensure he got enough sleep before driving again so early in the morning.

He made his way to the library, to see if Jill was there. The library—an enormous room with books stacked to the rafters in mahogany shelving—was empty. The doors shut with a soft click and he went back to his room, hoping that Jill would be awake, as he couldn't find his key and was sure she had it.

She was not awake when he got to the room, but she had left the door unlocked. He stumbled inside, a faint blue glow of moonlight shining in through the window to guide him.

A sharp, searing pain hit his leg, sobering him. He must have barked his shin on the trunk at the foot of the bed. Ted put both hands over his mouth to keep from hollering and recited an alphabet of oaths in his head. The pain was akin to the time he'd broken his wrist from falling off his bicycle when he was twelve years old.

He took off his jacket and tossed it on the chair, eyes streaming with tears as he held back a scream. Ted bit his lower lip, hoping the pain there would distract him from his goddamn leg. In the morning, an angry bump and bruise would greet him like the sunrise. Had he broken his leg? No, or he wouldn't still be walking.

The effort of throwing on pajamas was too much, so Ted threw himself into bed naked.

His leg throbbed now, and the pain surging instead of subsiding.

After a few minutes of lying there getting tears in his ears, he turned over and felt for the light on the night stand. He found the switch and flicked it on.

The leg was a bloody mass as if it had been chewed on by a wild animal. Ted yelped as his gut dropped. He thought of the weird red cat and fainted. Jill still hadn't woken up, even when he yelped.

***

The clean white walls of a hospital room greeted Ted when he opened his eyes, a sterile smell wafting to his nose, coupled with the scents of bodily fluids. He could hear rustling and clattering, but couldn't bring the place into focus.

After a moment, his surroundings became sharper. This wasn't a modern hospital room by any stretch of the imagination. The walls were white, but they were wood up the bottom half and masonry at the top. He didn't know what it was called, but the place looked like something he'd once seen in a book about The War of East versus West.

Ted sat up, glancing about the room. His heart hammered again, and beads of sweat broke out on his forehead.

"Where am I?" His voice echoed in the room as he looked around, pale face pulled into a scowl. There were other people in beds all around him crying for help, some with lost limbs, some delirious with fever. They were wearing uniforms. Uniforms? Yes, some blue, some red.

"Someone, please help me," Ted's eyes stung with tears.

A nurse in standard uniform for the era—a dark blue dress and white apron—came over, looking just like he'd seen in the books.

It was Jill.

Why was Jill being a nurse? What was going on? Was something in his brandy? Was he dreaming? "Help me, Jill!"

The nurse cocked her head and smiled with sympathy. "I'm sorry, young man, but I'm not your Jill," she said, patting his cheek. "I'm your nurse. My name is Constance. I'm here to help you, soldier, but you need to be calm. You're upsetting the other patients."

Ted looked at her, his eyes wide and lips curled into a deep frown. "What?"

She put a cold compress to his forehead, wicking away the beads of sweat. "You've taken on a fever, Private," she said. "It'll pass. Just let it pass."

"I don't understand." Ted shook his head and coughed.

"You were shot in the leg, soldier, and left for dead. Field rats gnawed on your wound. That's what gave you the fever. But it'll pass. It's clean now." The nurse kept talking, but Ted couldn't hear the rest as darkness took over and the ringing in his ears grew louder and louder. A faint chanting of voices was inside the ringing. Those voices—he had heard them in his dreams as whispers.

"No, no—" he struggled to stay awake, but the blackness took over his mind, with whispers in the dark.

They were a chant in a language he didn't recognize, and the voices were growing, overtaking the ringing. The blackness. The voices.

Then there was only darkness.

***

Jill woke up from her nap. She decided it was time to make dinner and finish packing. They were going on a road trip, in search of their second honeymoon, and they would leave soon.

Dressing the chicken in an aromatic mix of herbs, she thought about having a baby, Ted seemed keen on it. She wasn't sure at first. Jill wanted to keep teaching and go back to school, get her master's degree. Ted frowned upon it. She gave in because it wasn't worth the fights every night. Jill supposed she loved Ted more than getting an education. So she stayed. Plus, she could teach the babies, couldn't she? That was a mother's job.

Just as she put the chicken into the oven, the doorbell rang.

"Oh Ted, did you forget your key again?" She said, smiling. Poor Ted. So forgetful when he was excited. He'd done nothing but talk about their trip for days on end, keen to tell her that this would be a perfect trip. A chance to start over again. Baby or not, they could at least try to be happy.

A police officer stood at her door, face grim. Jill felt her innards go cold.

"Missus Braxbury?" the officer asked.

"Yes?" Jill wiped her hands on her apron. She felt that bit of dread, sure of what his next words would be.

"I'm sorry, ma'am," the officer said, "but there's been an accident, and we believe Mister Braxbury was killed while driving home." He looked at the floor when he said it, then finally met her eyes. "We need you to come with us."

Jill opened her eyes and cried out into the darkness. Frigid air touched bare skin as she sat up, rubbing the grit from her eyes, forcing them to adjust. A silly dream. That was all. She was in bed at the Hunter-Kellogg Bed & Breakfast, crickets chirping and loons screaming in the distance.

"Hard to believe it's spring," Jill said. Her voice seemed to echo, even in the small bedroom. She could see plumes of condensation from her breath and shivered, drawing the covers around her.

The alarm clock—Ted's faithful traveling companion—read six minutes past three. Jill smiled to herself. Maybe she'd wake him with a surprise before they left in the morning for Nashton Lake.

Moving closer, Jill put her hand on Ted's shoulder. He didn't awaken.

The crickets and loons stopped their songs.

A cloud passed over the full moon—or the room got darker. Jill put her ear to Ted's chest. It was as silent as everything else.

She whimpered.

"Help me," Jill's cry didn't echo now—it was as if she'd yelled into her pillow. Was she still dreaming? *Please, let this be a nightmare*, she thought as tears stung at her eyes. A sharp pain on her shoulder told her that no, this wasn't a dream.

Once when she was a girl, Jill caught her tongue on a metal pole and her mother had to use water to get the girl unstuck. The pain of trying to free herself at first was worse than the switch that her mother used to tan her behind afterward. The pain in her shoulder was similar to the former.

Jill screamed again and tried to pull away from the source of the pain. She turned and faced an enormous black shadow. Heart leaping, her skin crawled, and she jumped from the bed, tearing away skin from her shoulder. Whatever that thing was, it seemed to have hooks on its fingertips. They sank into her skin with ease.

From the silence, a scratch. Two scratches. The door to the room rattled and Jill could see light and two tiny paws casting shadows underneath. Scratch-scratch-scratch.

Tears streamed down Jill's face as she clambered for the door, tripping on the bedsheet tangled around her foot.

"Help!" Jill caught herself before spilling onto the floor, but the shadow thing hurled itself off the bed and put its hooks into her trailing leg. *Ice hooks, it has ice hooks.* Jill shook her leg and kept crawling for the door, grabbing handfuls of the rug as she went.

The thing dragged her back, but she kicked with her free leg, feeling her foot connect with—its head? It was enough, and Jill crawled for the door. She grabbed the knob and turned it, but as she pulled, the shadow thing leapt on her, dragging her back into the room.

It was enough.

The cat, the one that intimidated Jill earlier, pushed open the door and ran into the room. He hissed and growled, and the growl grew in pitch and volume into a scream. Jill backed into a corner as the cat with the bright autumn-leaves fur leapt onto the shadow thing, biting and clawing with front and back feet.

The shadow tried to shake off the cat, and Jill backed up to the door, but couldn't stand. Throbbing pain in her leg kept her bound to the floor, but her eyes were on the fight in front of her. The feline—Oscar—was relentless, tearing off chunks of blackness where it fell, sinking into the floorboards with a sizzle Jill could barely hear over the hisses.

With a shriek that rang in her ears, the shadow thing separated itself from the cat, and tumbled onto the bed. Oscar fell to the floor, landing on his feet, and stalked it, jumping back up onto the edge.

It shrank backward from the cat, slipping over Ted's body, and for one moment, Jill's heart felt like it stopped. If it entered Ted's body, what then? Could it enter Ted's body? Its fingers slipped into Ted's gaping mouth and Ted's eyes popped open. But the cat didn't relent. He made another leap onto the shadow thing's face and howled again.

The shadow gave another shriek and hit the wall to the side of the bed, near the open window.

That's where it vanished.

Oscar hit the wall with his paws and made a rebound back onto Ted's chest. He sat for a moment, inspecting. A sniff. Two sniffs. The cat lowered his head, then shook it to smooth his fur.

The cat jumped off the bed and ran to Jill, inspecting her wounds and purring as Jill wept. Oscar crawled into her arms, still purring, and she hugged him to her chest.

Behind her, unheard earlier from the chaos in the room, Mary and Elizabeth pounded on the door to get in, and Jill backed away, still holding Oscar, rocking back and forth as the owners and other guests entered.

"Is it over?" Jill asked. "Is it over? Is it over? Is it—?"

TEA TIME

"Hi Kit. I couldn't reach you on your mobile," Mercy said. Even on the wired connection her voice sounded far away.

"No one can. Mobiles don't work here—it's a complete dead zone. That's why I always email you from work—there's no internet out here, Wi-Fi or otherwise."

There was a long pause while Mercy spoke to one of her children. Kit waited, well-accustomed to those sorts of interruptions from her friend.

"How is Silver Hollow?" Mercy asked when finished answering the children's questions and telling them to stop interrupting her.

"Deadly dull," Kit said, then smiled. "You'd love it. Why don't you come up with the family next weekend—I'm off rotation at the ER—or on your own and get away for a while?"

Mercy sighed, but Kit wasn't sure if it was at her or at one of the kids. "You know what? I'll take you up on that. Just you and me. Old times. If I can arrange it, I'll stay for a week or so."

"Old times. You can stay as long as you want and as long as Frank will put up with the little monsters." Kit chuckled before she hung up the phone. "See you."

Two weeks dragged by, and Kit swore the house was growing in silence with each minute. Kathryn was having more trouble sleeping with how quiet the house—the whole town—was. Without the noise of home—the sirens, the music, the crowds—she was more aware of the silence of the country. It intensified at night, lying in bed with the only sound being her breath, the ringing in her ears, and her heartbeat. The pops and clicks of the house settling didn't help, and when it sounded like children's footsteps running about the floors, that was even worse.

She forgot it when she saw her honey-headed friend pull up the driveway.

"Welcome to paradise," She reached out to take the woman's long-fingered hand. Cool to the touch, the skin dry but soft. "And by paradise, I mean Perdition."

Mercy laughed. "I don't know about that," she said. "I think the quiet will be a nice change of pace."

"Only for a fortnight. After that, it's maddening."

Kathryn kissed her friend on the cheek, noticed the bags on the porch and helped her bring them inside. "I wish I'd brought Faith with me, but I thought I might try my hand at being domestic for a change." The dark-haired woman gestured in the air. "As you can tell, it's not going well."

"Thank you, Kit. Good to see you again," Mercy said, glancing around and repressing a grin. "Perhaps you could do with a maid service."

Kit shrugged. "That's kind of you. I have a cleaner come in twice a week, and he cooks for me now and then, but I should have him visit more often. The house wouldn't be so maddeningly silent, then."

"Why didn't you bring Faith, or Lucy?"

"I didn't think I'd need them—and I've got things at home to keep up with, anyway." Kit waved Mercy off with one hand.

They settled her things into the guest bedroom while Mercy filled her in on her latest exploits and published papers. Then, she moved on to her trip.

"That was quite a drive here from the city. I passed by the town once," she said. "Went right by the exit that leads to Main Street. You were right—not even the GPS app pulls the place up. I knew when I hit signs for Terrenceville that I'd missed my turnoff and had to turn around. Sorry I'm late."

"Oh, it's fine," Kathryn waved her hand in a brushing motion. That was a lie. In reality, she spent the time pacing the floor, clinking the teacups and rearranging the furniture while she waited. "I'm so glad to have company, for a change."

Mercy opened her mouth to say she should have brought her assistants, but thought better of it from Kit's earlier brush-off.

Once her visitor settled in and took a moment to freshen up, they sat in the parlor.

"Scones and tea," Mercy relaxed into her cushion. "I've not had a proper Albion tea since you left Grace City."

Kit smiled. "Eh, you could have—there are only eight different tearooms in a three-block radius from your home. Don't blame me."

"It's not the same," Mercy said. "But I have to know—when did you learn to cook?"

Kit laughed, feeling a faint heat coming into her cheeks. "Well, I didn't. The woman at Haverty's Store baked these scones and crumpets for me. The people here aren't friendly to newcomers, but I helped the family during an illness—so I suppose I won her over for the moment."

Mercy nodded. "There are so many places in the upper Northeast Territory that are like that. The smaller the town, the more suspicious people are of outsiders."

"Agreed," Kit said. "This little place has such a small population—something like forty-five residents in it. Forty-four when I come back to GC—I'm not joking. There used to be hundreds. Anyway, it takes twenty minutes for an ambulance to get here, and that's even worse in the winter weather, you can imagine." She shook her head and brought her hand to her chest. "But I wanted to live here this summer. I felt it was important to do something charitable."

Mercy reached out and patted her hand. "I know. Three years in a row you were off home to Albion again for relief aid and clinics. But I'm happy that this time you picked somewhere closer so I could visit."

"That and a place that hasn't closed its borders, right?" Kathryn said, her tone grim. "To my surprise, they let me back in, but they needed physicians. The dual citizenship didn't hurt, either."

Silence filled the parlor for a moment as they drank their tea.

Little sounds of the house settling—pops and creaks—interrupted the pleasant harmonies of wildlife outdoors.

"The animals are noisy today," Kathryn said, gesturing to the window. "Most days I don't even notice the wildlife around here."

Small talk never lasted long between the two.

"So, Doctor Harris, do you know much about this part of the Northeastern Territory?" Kit asked.

Mercy shook her head. "I'm more familiar with Beanton and the Old Colony Commonwealth than the Empire Commonwealth, with these tiny towns and townships. But I still find it interesting, considering the things I've learned from you about this area."

"It's an unusual place. I mean, I told you about the Historical Society and some of the disappearances. Did you unearth what happened to the Dubbs House—or rather what keeps happening there?" Kit sipped her tea and nibbled at a scone.

"Well, I did some digging with the SHHS in their online archives and noticed there were vanishings after Maxwell-Hunter and Sellers-Kellogg-Watson left. I thought the name sounded familiar, so I researched in my personal library," Mercy said, taking a sip of her own tea.

Kathryn leaned forward, eyebrows raised. "And?"

"Mary Sellers is my second cousin on my paternal grandfather's side," she said. "She was in the middle of a family scandal—refusing to marry a man she didn't love and leaving with Elizabeth. They met in Grace City, but both were from Beanton."

Kit sat back and got comfortable. Further prompting would only cause Mercy to get distracted.

The clink of her cup against its saucer prompted Mercy to continue. "She never spoke to the family again, and they disowned her. Once estranged, they lost track of her, so it was interesting to see what became of the Sellers line. With the records I found from the SHHS, Mary and Elizabeth left with their cat a year after the séance incident—the one you mentioned. They didn't bother to sell the place—nothing more than a cursory listing. The two abandoned it to squatters and the elements. But it was what happened after that—that was what got my attention." Mercy sipped her tea and leaned back, eyebrow raised.

Kathryn's stomach clenched, and she set the saucer down, scone half-finished. "I've almost been afraid to ask, considering the things I've seen at hospital. But you, first. I can't get a word out of the locals and the SHHS has skirted me several times."

Mercy nodded. "I had to badger them for information that wasn't in their archives and bribe their fearless leader," she said between sips from her cup. "Six or seven years after they left, in the early fifties, drifters swept through, brought after the recession. The Southeastern Territory was attracting people from the Northern border—the downturn hit them the hardest. Silver Hollow attracted a few in addition to the migrant workers, mind you—but enough to get the local police to pay attention. Chester Callfield was a young man then and learning the nuances of being a constable from his father."

"A chain of disappearances?" Kathryn asked.

"Forty-five people in a year, here, alone," Mercy pursed her lips as if her scone had gone bad.

"Oh dear—that's just short of one a week, and the whole town's population, myself included—I swear it's no exaggeration." Kit shook her head. Her tea and scone cast aside for a moment, she rose and opened a window, letting the summer air drift in on a cool north wind. She took a deep breath and turned back to her friend. "Sorry, it was getting oppressive in here."

Mercy waved her off. "I understand. But the chain of disappearances was in clusters throughout the year—chains of five to six. Nothing for weeks, with spots of drifters coming in after. They'd never reach their intended destinations, we assume."

Kathryn's brows knit as she leaned against the wall. "Disappearances increase during depressions and recessions. I've seen plenty of transients in hospital. They've lost everything in life and have nothing to lose, so they take risks. More often than not, they're the targets of abuse—of violence. Transients are among the most vulnerable populations out there."

Mercy nodded again. "That's why it went unnoticed for so long," she said. "Most of the townsfolk thought that the drifters squatted at Dubbs House, moved on to their destinations, and be done with it. Since no one was expecting them, it never got reported when they disappeared."

"So how did they discover the problem?" Kit sat back on the couch and took up her tea again. This time she ate more of the scone.

"Seems that the young deputy cared more than his predecessor—his father. Eager to keep the township clean while drifters passed in and out," Mercy said. "He was keen to please, patrolled Dubbs House on his own. One summer evening, he stumbled upon a few squatters outside in hysterics."

"Old Chet Callfield?" Kit's brows shot up for a moment. "He didn't mention this before."

"I'm not surprised," Mercy said. "From reading his public reports, he's terse."

Kit nodded. "Well, that's true. Whenever he comes into the emergency room, the man's all business and only gives me an overview of whatever the incident is, or was." She shook her head and sipped her tea.

"A Northeastern trait." Mercy shrugged. "We have a long history of not mincing words." She took another bite of her snack.

"Sounds like home. Jam for your scone?"

"Please."

"So what happened that night?" Kit asked, trying to reign in her friend from meandering around the subject of the colony days. For someone who just mentioned her culture was circumspect, Mercy had a habit of wandering off-topic.

"Oh, yes, well, Callfield saw three drifters outside in an absolute state. They were babbling in a frenzy that there was something in the house attacking them, and that one of their fellow travelers was missing. He called his predecessor for backup, but the drifters ran, either terrified of getting caught, or terrified of what happened in the house. While he waited for his backup to arrive, he searched the perimeter of the house, and found a man in the back, crawling away from the place. That's when he discovered something attacked the victim, but all the man told him was that 'Evanston was still inside.'" Mercy cleared her throat and took more tea.

"That it is. So who was this Evanston fellow?"

"No one knows. The drifter's injuries were pronounced—he severed his femoral artery—and Callfield tried to stop the bleeding, but couldn't. When Callfield asked him what happened, the only thing he could say was that 'the house did it,' and there were monsters in the basement. The poor fellow died before the medics could arrive. According to the report, his last words were, 'they took Evanston.' When the constable and others inspected the place, it was quiet, and empty. They searched from basement to attic, and nothing," Mercy said with a shake of her head. "If he existed, he either got out or vanished."

"Well, did anyone ever see him? I mean, did he reach his destination, or what?" Kit's face pinched and she held her breath.

"His mother was expecting him in the Southern Territory." Mercy set her cup down and leaned forward. "According to the public record, the Territory Troopers had to pick her up and cart her off to an asylum. She claimed she saw Evanston in a mirror, screaming for help while slithering, slimy things tortured him."

Kit snorted. "No, you're having a laugh."

"I promise I'm not." Mercy put her hand to her chest in an oath, then picked up her cup and saucer again.

Kathryn closed her eyes for a moment, images of the past four patients from Silver Hollow in her ER floating into focus. Phil Hausmann, Paul Ingersoll, Paul Walker, and an unidentified woman still in a coma in the ICU, and needed to be transferred to Grace City once she was stable enough for transport. They came from Dubbs House, except for the woman—she came from the edge of Silver Hollow. Everyone had severe lacerations, what appeared to be pressure bite wounds from various animals, concussions, and every one of them had come near death. Kit had wrestled the Man with the Scythe for the three of them. Three of the victims had business with the house, but the woman was a complete unknown. No one in the hospital could identify her and her matted, bloody blonde hair. At least her brain damage healed, even if by inches. If she woke up, they might find out who she was.

"You're pensive," Mercy said. "Are you all right?"

"Yes. I'm thinking on Dubbs House and this house. This whole town is strange. People go mad, kill their children. It's not just that house. Even this place oppresses me." She sighed. "Do you know anything about this home?"

Mercy nodded. "Yes. Do you really want to know?"

Kit shook her head. "I'm not—you know me, a skeptic—I don't believe in that silly, superstitious nonsense. But no one talks about it, and no one investigates. It's as if this whole place has some goddamn amnesia. But yes, I want to know."

Mercy reached out and patted Kit's hand. "There's a logical explanation for all this. Claims of the supernatural often have a scientific explanation—electromagnetic fields, exposed electrical wires—things like that. A woman in this house went mad and killed her children."

"Damn. This wasn't recent, I hope. They're supposed to tell me and they didn't. I'll sue the whole town." Kit scowled as her stomach tightened.

Mercy still held her friend's hand. "No, not recent. Back in 1868. The widow blamed the Timeworn Order."

Kit nodded and squeezed Mercy's hand back. "Ugh, nonsense. I'm far more inclined to think there's a murderer in Dubbs House and no one's talking or can find him. Maybe he's hidden away in the shed and the townsfolk are too inbred to go have a look." She laughed, a sound that broke the gloom that had settled over the parlor. "But here, in this house, too? What could it be?"

Mercy shrugged. "Mass hysteria and superstition."

"Of course." The black-haired woman finished her scone.

"What sparked your interest, Kit? History isn't your favored subject," Mercy said, refilling her own teacup.

Kit finished her tea and poured another cup as an afterthought. "Well—I've had patients come from Dubbs House, and I overheard that deputy, I think his name is George, say something about how it's happening again. They were there in the emergency department. Callfield told him to shut up because he knew I'd hear."

She took a sip of tea and continued. "Overhear, I did, so thought I'd do some investigating. Perhaps it would help me treat my patients better if I knew what was going on at Dubbs House, or this whole town."

Mass hysteria didn't account for those pressure bite wounds, but Kit put that aside for a moment to ponder later.

Mercy sucked her lower lip while she listened. "Well, that makes sense. I wish I had more information for you. But it's a series of weird coincidences and injuries that lead the locals to cling to their idols in the hope they'll be saved."

"There's something odd going on in this town, and no one will talk about it," Kit said, unable to keep the irritation out of her voice. "But I guess you're right, Mercy. It's easier for them to blame it on woo instead of investigating or doing something."

"Agreed," Mercy said. She raised her eyebrow. "Is the history lining up with what you've seen going on now?"

"Without giving away any personal information about patients—yes. You say that drifter bled out from his femoral artery. Well, I've gotten a few with hypovolemic shock."

"Wait, what kind of shock?" Mercy held up a hand.

"Blood loss. The body can't lose too much or you go into shock—it's a life-threatening condition that requires a transfusion, keeping the patient warm, and elevating blood pressure through restoring blood volume back in the body. Make sense?"

Mercy nodded. "Makes sense. Continue."

"We've had to order a great deal of blood from the Central Blood and Plasma Bank. So much that they asked us if someone was stealing from our stores. Though I don't know why someone would steal blood unless they thought they were vampires or something. When they asked the question about thievery that told me we were using more than usual." A breath of laughter wasn't successful in chasing away the oppressive feeling that had settled over the room this time.

Her eyes narrowed as the smile fell from her face. "I've almost lost four patients in five weeks who came from here, and before that—well, I didn't get the full story right away, but some of them didn't make it. The ones before that, and before I came to work here have died from exsanguination—they bled to death."

Mercy's pale face lost what color it had left in it, and two little red circles appeared on her cheeks. "That's awful. This place seems so peaceful."

"It does—at least at first. It's warm and inviting—a little rural paradise. After a while, though, the people become caricatures of themselves. The citizens put on little shows for the visitors here—pretending they're normal, but they're hiding some kind of secret," Kathryn said. "At first,

I thought it was so creepy here because of the quiet nights, but it's not that. Not at all." She shrugged and laughed again. "I sound superstitious, don't I?"

"A little," Mercy said. "But you've been alone a while. It's instinctual to become hyper-vigilant, don't you think?"

"I suppose so." Kit closed her eyes and sighed.

"Yet if we look at the evidence with an objective eye, the injuries, disappearances, and deaths surrounding Dubbs House are an unusual number, considering the small population of the town. Plus—well—" she shook her head and shifted in her seat.

"Well, what?" Kit's eyebrows raised as she stared at her friend.

Mercy pursed her lips. "The whole town has a history of violence and ugliness. The settlers didn't chase out the indigenous people from this place like in other areas. They moved away of their own free will, but won't say why. I contacted a woman on their council, and she told me that the land wouldn't grow anything, and that was it. That was all I could get from her, and I didn't press her to tell me more. I left it alone and told her she could always contact me if she had anything to share. Sad to tell you she hasn't contacted me since."

"Dead lands," Kit said, leaning back on the couch again. "It seems practical enough." She paused and drank more of her tea. "So—what else did you find when you were digging?"

Mercy set her empty plate aside and finished her cup. "The church-slash-town hall at the end of the circle, in the 1860s, had a preacher who passed through on some mission. Except he didn't worship the same way the townsfolk did. He set up shop here for a while—staying for a year. Once a year had passed, he sacrificed seven women and committed suicide, leaving their bodies on the altar, in a heptagram, with his body in the center. Dumfries was his name—he cut the women open, removed their uteruses and burned them, and then killed himself by attempting to cut out his heart."

Kit's mouth dropped open, but she recovered. "Where did you find that out?"

"I found it in the Union Historical Documents Database," Mercy said. "It was an article in the Nashton Lake newspaper. There weren't many in-depth details, other than what I told you, and the town records offer little insight because the fire damaged many of them. This town has a long history of tragedy, but the citizens don't have the hardihood to contemplate it."

Kit's upper lipped curled. "No. They're a brusque lot—all of them—not just Callfield. The deputy might be loquacious enough to try to impress me, but he's kept on a tight leash."

The two fell silent and Kit rose to open another window as the house was getting oppressive again. She sat back on the couch. At least the sounds of songbirds kept it from becoming unbearable.

"Have you been to Dubbs House?" Mercy asked.

"Only when I first arrived and the overblown head of SHHS took me on a tour of the town as a ragtag welcoming committee of one. I'm positive the society was trying to solicit donations," Kit said with a huff in her voice. "The house is a shambles. The town hall and old firehouse are well-kept, but the house needs renovation."

She shrugged. "I thought little of it and gave them a few thousand to silence them. Greedy guts haven't pestered me since."

Mercy chuckled. "Well, why don't we go see it?"

Kit shook her head and laughed. "After everything we've heard, read, and seen, you want to go exploring like teens in a horror film?"

"Why not?" Mercy asked. "If we see the place in person, it might help us gain insight. It's not like there's anything paranormal about it. Besides, we might find something scientific and logical behind the attacks and disappearances."

"It's trespassing," Kit said, punctuating her pause by setting down the cup and saucer. "What if a—a—I don't know—a woodsy family of cannibal killers with a pack of hybrid wolves hang around the back garden and wait for idiots like us to come along and snoop?"

Mercy laughed. "Are you listening to yourself?"

Kit opened her mouth to retort, but laughed instead. "Right. Ridiculous, I know," she waved her hand as if she were shooing a fly away. "Fine, but I don't want to get caught trespassing. We'll go after Callfield makes his last rounds for the evening—around nine. The deputy is supposed to tour around after that, but I think he spends most of his time at his desk, wanking it or reading primers." Kit shrugged. "Quiet town. Well, it pretends to be."

***

After rest and a late dinner which Mercy cooked, the ladies got dressed for what looked more like a hike in the woods than an outing to a historic site. The pair prepared for any eventuality.

Kit packed up her doctor's bag, and Mercy brought pepper spray and a .38 Special. Kit frowned upon seeing the weapons.

"I hope I don't have to wind up treating you for a bullet wound or a chemical burn," she said.

"Oh hush. You shoot for sport." Mercy brushed a lock of hair from her forehead.

"Clay pigeons," Kit said. "Suppose I should bring my shotgun?"

"Why not?"

"Yes, why not? I'll endeavor not to blow your head off." Kit said. She giggled.

"I should hope not," Mercy said. Though her tone was serious, she smiled.

"We'll need torches—erm—flashlights, in your parlance," Kit said, heading for the kitchen. "I've got a few—power gets knocked out for days during storms here."

Mercy followed her. "Are you planning on coming back here next year?"

"I'd have to leave this place alive, first," she said, opening a drawer and pulling out one large flashlight, and another, smaller one. "Here, take the larger one. If I'm carrying the shotgun, I'll need the smaller because I can clip it to my bag."

Mercy agreed and took the heavy torch from her friend. "How far is it from here?" she asked.

"Only a mile. We can walk. If anyone gets nosy, we can tell them we're going on a night hike—the weapon's for protection. No one will think much about that, I don't think. But I don't believe it'll be a problem. People around here retire at sundown." Kit pulled her bag over her shoulder. She strapped the flashlight to the bag and the shotgun to herself. They left the kitchen through the back door.

"The best way to get there will be through the back woods—keep us away from the main road," Kit pointed to the forest behind the house.

The moon lit up the trail for them better than their flashlights could have, and they crunched their way through the forest. Crickets and frogs trumpeting their songs kept them company in the fresh summer air. Even with the thick leaves from the nearby trees, the trail was lit enough to see where they were going.

Kathryn slowed as they got closer to Dubbs House, and shivered, a pit settling in her stomach that something wasn't right. She stopped in her tracks and felt Mercy bump into her back.

"What's wrong, Kit?" Mercy's voice was not quite a whisper.

"I don't know—it's—too quiet, don't you think?" She looked around as though she might see what was causing the lack of ruckus.

Mercy nodded.

Aside from the gentle breeze rustling the leaves in the tall trees surrounding them, there was no other noise. The frogs ceased making their deep, rumbling croaks—no crickets calling for mates—as though someone flipped a switch to cut off a soundtrack.

Kit stopped moving, but the noise didn't resume. In the distance, there was a growl, then nothing again. She pointed to a bend of the trail, stifling a shiver. "Here's an exit that leads to Dubbs House. Ready?"

"Wait a moment," Mercy said, checking the safety on her revolver. Kit checked a sigh.

Once satisfied, her friend nodded. "Okay, let's go."

Each step closer to the house put five pound weights on Kit's ankles. The air around the place grew heavier. Kit turned on her torch as the moon disappeared behind a cloud, the beam swallowed by the darkness. She carried on in spite of it.

"Battery must be dying. Brilliant," Kit muttered.

A warm blanket of darkness enveloped them and Mercy turned on her small flashlight. The house lit up in a yellow glow reminiscent of stomach bile.

"That's almost better," Mercy said.

"Your sarcasm betrays your nerves," Kathryn gave her a sidelong glance.

"Your projection betrays yours."

"Touché."

The women walked up to the back deck that led to the wraparound porch. "Be careful," Kit said. "The wood is still rotted through in spots." She stepped on a loose board, expecting a creak. Nothing. Kit scowled at it as if she could will it to behave, then shook her head.

Mercy stepped on tiptoe and pressed her face to a back window. "The layout is similar to your place," she said.

"It is. The original owners built it after Dubbs House, modeled the place after it. It has fewer secret passages though—well, that I've discovered." Kit hopped over a hole in the porch and landed on a solid board, standing next to her friend. "Come on, you darling old bluestocking, let's go through the kitchen."

"Won't it be locked?" Mercy asked, grabbing Kit's arm.

"Ha, no. No one locks doors or windows around here—you'd think they would have by now, but they're stubborn—or stupid." She turned the doorknob.

The door opened without a sound which gave Kathryn a start. She glanced at the hinges as if they'd betrayed her.

"Is anyone here?" She cringed as soon as she said it. Letting people know they were there wasn't a good idea.

There was no response. Mercy stepped in front of her with the better lighting.

"You can see where they've finished some of the restoration," the historian said, aiming the beam towards the far wall. "It's an excellent recreation of the original home."

Kit took a look around. The full moon had returned, full beam streaming into the parlor, a half-finished room with coverings still on the furniture. The center of the room had a bare spot, where the floor sagged. "I can almost see all the bodies that've piled up here."

Mercy made a noise of assent. "It started out as a private home after the war, became a makeshift TB and influenza ward, then a private boarding house. After that, they abandoned the place, and after *that*, it took the overflow from the local hospital." Mercy looked up at her. "There was a mix of patients here. TB and mental illnesses. Loads of bodies, to be sure."

Kit frowned. "That's not a proper mix—you can't endanger patients on either side that way."

"True, but remember, this place was backward. Still is." Mercy stepped closer to the dip in the floor and shivered. "This indentation looks like a person. It reminds me of Vitruvian Man," she said.

Kit examined it with a clinical eye. "Except no room for the head. It's a heptagram," she took a step forward.

The floor groaned, and she stepped away as if it had caught fire.

Another groan. It wasn't the floorboard.

"Where did that come from?" Mercy asked, voice hushed.

Kit shook her head. "I think it came from downstairs. The basement." She took a deep breath. "Hello? Is someone here?"

The two women looked at each other. There was no response.

"You want to go see if everything's okay? It could be a squatter," Mercy said.

Kit shrugged. "I wouldn't be much of a doctor if I left someone groaning in pain, would I?"

"I suppose not. A sound like that isn't made by a healthy person."

"True," Kit said. "Let's go, but keep your gun ready, in case it's a squatter who *isn't* injured."

Dust from opening the basement door wafted to Kit's nose, and she held back a sneeze, putting the crook of her elbow to her face. Each step they took on the steep stairs shook and rattled despite the light weight upon them. Both of the tall women had to duck their heads when they got to the last step.

The pain in Kit's chest was growing with her descent. She took a deep breath, hoping it would ease up, and regretted holding in that sneeze.

"Hello?" The rush of air might help ease her discomfort. *If I can yell, I can breathe.*

"I hope whoever it is will be all right," Mercy said. "I don't like that there's no response."

"No, nor do I," Kit said. The pain in her chest had subsided, but the pit in her stomach was heavier than ever. The gnawing feeling in her stomach gave rise to goosebumps on her arms—a sense of someone being around the corner waiting for them was strong. This was the way she felt when walking through a bad part of the city when she was young and stupid. The threat of a squatter jumping out at them and attacking was far more real to her than any supernatural threat.

It could have been wild animals that got inside, Kit thought. "Let's stick together. If we find nothing, we'll head home and I'll give Callfield a call."

Mercy perked up. "Oh, I have my mobile with me, we could call him now."

Kit shook her head. "You can try, darling, but Silver Hollow's a dead zone, remember?"

"Right." Mercy blushed as she spoke. Even in the dimness of the flashlights, Kitas could see it.

They tread into the basement, an acrid smell lingering with must and earth. A thin stream of full moonlight streamed into the basement through a slit of a window.

Kit saw a shadow move.

"Mercy, over there!" She moved her beam toward the noise. "Did you see that?"

"No," Mercy said. "What was it?"

"Thought I saw something move." Kit grabbed Mercy's arm, and they made their way over.

"Nothing," Mercy said. "Damn."

"This basement is enormous. We should sweep through as fast as we can and get out of here."

She turned away from her friend to look where she'd seen the shadow move, cursing herself for doing something this stupid, face twisted with irritation. They should have waited till morning and got permission instead of running in as if they were two teenage girls in a horror film.

The room became dimmer while she was searching. Kit turned back around.

"Did your torch go, darling?" She asked.

Mercy disappeared.

"Mercy?" Kit's brows knit. "Where'd you go?"

No response. No noise to show she'd left. The basement was large, but Kit hadn't wandered far—not enough to lose an entire person.

With a sigh, she grabbed her shotgun and secured her torch to her rucksack. Careful to keep her finger outside the trigger guard (she didn't want to shoot her best friend), she looked around for the woman. Mercy wasn't the type to play practical jokes—the woman didn't have even a sliver of a mean streak.

A scream came from upstairs. It was far away, but sounded like Mercy.

Kit headed up the stairs, smacking her forehead on the crossbeam. She swore and rubbed her head, the skin prickled and grew warm underneath. She pulled her hand away and looked at it. No blood. She breathed a sigh of relief. Since she had no double-vision, and the smack felt superficial, she kept going.

Once in the house, she tried to orient herself and listen for movement—to locate the source of the scream. She didn't have to linger—another scream came from upstairs, and this time, Kit could pinpoint it.

Up the flight of polished stairs, she made her way to the attic.

"Mercy? Are you up here?" It didn't matter to her if other people knew where she was at this point—she'd made plenty of noise already.

The rickety stairs that led to the ceiling opening were locked in place. Someone had to have been up there.

Realizing she shouldn't run up there as if she was head of a cavalcade, Kit got quiet, waited, and listened.

The sick pit in her stomach threatened revolt as she noticed the house was silent. No settling, creaking, or any of the sounds Kit had grown so accustomed to living in an older house. Silence and darkness spread like cancer over the room. Her own heart pounded in her ears, and took a slow, deep breath to quiet it.

Kit crept up the stairs, peeking into the attic, expecting to see Mercy and trouble.

There was nothing there.

Her beam of light spread as she turned a full 360 degrees. "Goddamn it."

A little girl giggled. She turned again. No one was there. The attic was filled with boxes, more dust, old toys, and knickknacks. When she turned back, the corpse swinging in front of her made her yelp and she bumped into it. CLANG. Her flashlight hit the ground and she stooped to pick it up, heart pounding in her ears. If it was a body, she had to investigate. She stood back up and pointed the beam at the corpse.

There was nothing there.

"What's going on here?" Kit's teeth clenched so tight she felt her eardrums pop. *I'm spooked. That's all. That's all it is.*

Mercy screamed for help. Still, the sound was faint, because now it was coming from the basement.

"Mercy, I'm on my way!" Kit ran down the stairs when something caught her ponytail, then let go. Kit fell the rest of the way, catching herself with the butt of her weapon a fraction of a second too late. She gasped for air as the floor connected with her stomach.

Rolled over onto her back, Kit saw a shadow move in the attic, but discarded it as imagination. *Something pulled my hair.*

Nonsense. My hair got caught on something.

She pulled herself up, caught her breath, and ran back to the basement, mindful of the crossbeam this time.

She saw Mercy off to the side of the stairs.

"Are you okay?" Kit asked, still winded from her fall.

"No, something's got my leg and I can't move," Mercy said. "It's pinned. I think my ankle's broken."

Kit saw her friend in the dying light of her torch and went to her. A cylindrical object the size of a large man pinned Mercy to the ground. There were cuts all over her friend, and her hair was no longer a dark blonde from the blood. The scents of copper and iron hung in the air, and something else. Something akin to spoiled meat. It left a greasy, metallic taste in the back of Kit's mouth.

"You have a head injury. I've got to get you to hospital." Kit said to her, rummaging through the first-aid bag. "Here, press this to your head, hard. It'll stop the bleeding."

"I'll be okay," Mercy said. "I need to know if my ankle's broken."

"Yeah, hang on, let's get this—whatever it is—off of you," Kit said, putting the weapon back in its scabbard. She leaned forward, bending her knees. The object shined back at her.

When she grabbed it, it was cold and wet, and the odor of fetid meat and something musky, like a skunk's spray, hit her nose. It felt sticky under her hands. Her lip curled.

The object moved, dragging Mercy with it.

"Help! It's got me!"

Kit stepped back and grabbed Mercy's arms to pull on her. Whatever had grabbed her wasn't letting up, and Kit saw that the large cylinder wasn't some kind of furniture. It was attached to something.

Like a tentacle to an octopus. Kit's eyes widened. That would have to be an enormous octopus. For a moment, all she could envision was a giant sea creature, bigger than ten blue whales. But where was it coming from, anyway?

The darkness. It came from the darkness.

She let go, grabbed her shotgun back out from its scabbard, and took aim. This was nothing like shooting clay pigeons. While whatever-it-was dragged Mercy away,

Kit took aim. The shotgun slid in her sweaty palms. Hands shaking, heart pounding in her ears, she pointed the sight as far from Mercy's body as she could and still hit the beast-thing. Mercy reached out, clinging to whatever she could hold. She grasped at a support beam, putting her arms around it as the thing pulled her in the other direction. Mercy cried out in pain as the tentacle stretched her in the other direction.

The gun went off and there was nothing but the resounding ringing in her ears from the shot. Her face and hands felt sticky, and she looked at them, discovering a thick, amber goo left behind. It was cold.

The thing let Mercy go, and Kit rushed to holster her shotgun, and check Mercy for bleeding. She pulled her doctor's bag off her back and put her stethoscope in her ears. It didn't help—her ears were ringing too much to be useful. They weren't in a safe place—and though it was risky to move her, and drag her up the stairs, it would be better to get her out of the basement.

She put her instrument away and slung the bag back over her shoulder. Mercy slipped from Kit's sweating palms and she gripped her friend harder. "Hey, stay awake. I'm going to get you out of here."

Mercy shook her head. She said nothing.

Kit got a better grip under Mercy's arms, careful of her neck. She slipped her arms under Mercy's legs and carried her up the stairs.

The ringing was subsiding as she brought Mercy out of the house to the front porch. She laid her friend down and gave her a better assessment.

"Can you stand?" she had to shout to hear herself.

Mercy shook her head and pointed to her ankle. Kit looked at it. It was swelling, and would need an x-ray.

"I'll carry you home," Kit said over the ring in her ears. There were screams coming from inside the house—they echoed in her head, sounds that were either an animal being tortured, or something that wasn't human.

No, that's your imagination, Kathryn, stop it.

"Come on, darling, stay with me." Kit lifted Mercy off the ground and cradled her as she walked towards the main road.

"I'm here," Mercy said. "What happened?"

"You have a concussion, I'm sure, and your ankle might be broken," Kit said, puffing out air as she walked. "I need to get you home so we can drive you to hospital."

"I'm in no condition to drive," Mercy said.

Kit chuckled. "I didn't mean you, dear, I meant I'll drive you, okay?"

Mercy's breath shook as she spoke. "Oh, I hit my head when I backed away from—erm—something. I don't remember."

"Keep talking, Mercy. Tell me where we are." Kit said.

"Silver Hollow," she said.

"What day is it?" Kit asked.

"Saturday. We were at Dubbs House looking for something. I think we found it."

"What's your full name?" Kit asked. The ringing in her ears was still steady, but at least she could make out what her friend was saying.

"Mercy Evelyn Endicott Harris, PhD. I'm a professor of history at Veritas University," she said.

"Excellent. Stay with me and keep talking. Tell me how you feel." Kit asked, still walking down the road. She wobbled as she walked.

The quick whoop of a siren and flashing of lights got Kit to turn around and sigh with relief as the old prowler pulled up behind them. She turned around to avoid jostling Mercy.

The deputy got out of the vehicle. "Doc? Is that you?"

"Yes, and we need a ride to Mercy Hospital," Kit said.

"Well, what were you doing to get all banged up like that?" He asked, jaw slack.

"I'll explain later. Get us to hospital," she said, barking at him.

Postman. His name is Postman. She tried to still her mind. "Deputy Postman, we need your help."

"Yeah. Let's put her in the back," he said, coming over to relieve Kit of the lightweight burden.

He kept the lights on and Kit tried to check her irritation to avoid slapping him. If he ran the siren, she'd hit him hard. He sped along as she buckled herself in, catching a glance of the small bruise threatening to erupt on her forehead, and the amber goo splatter pattern on her face.

"What happened, Doc?" Postman asked the three-quarter profile as she stared out the window.

"We were taking a night hike when we heard screams at Dubbs House. I couldn't call for anyone, so I said we should investigate and go to the station to report what we saw. If anyone was injured, well, I wanted to provide aid, first."

Postman handed her a handkerchief and Kit wiped sweat and goo off her face and neck before speaking again.

"Thank you, Deputy. Anyway, we found nothing and Mercy fell down the stairs. I thought someone in the basement grabbed her. When I followed, I guess in the chaos I didn't pay attention and my weapon went off. Lucky for us all it didn't hurt anyone."

She pocketed the handkerchief, attempting to hide the goo.

"Yeah, Doctor. You don't strike me as the gun-carrying type, and accidents like that are bound to happen," he said. If he saw the goo, he said nothing, and Kit noticed from previous encounters he was a man who announced his observations. She might bring that goo over to pathology and have a look at it.

Kit checked a sigh of irritation and looked out the window. "You're right. I should be more careful. It's not like shooting clay pigeons, is it?"

It wasn't. Kit didn't need him to tell her that. She saw the coiled tentacle wrapped around Mercy's body again and shuddered inside. She focused back on the deputy.

"No, ma'am," he said. He paused for a moment, seeming to consider something. "But what was that yellowish stuff on you?"

"Sap," Kit said without a moment's hesitation. "I don't know where I ran into it out in the forest, but I'm sure one of those trees got me with something. What do you think it might be?"

"I don't know, but some of those trees are sick. Seen none of them running sap so heavy, though," the deputy said.

He was young, eager, but far from stupid, and Kit realized she'd underestimated him. Instead of trying to continue the deception, she turned her attention to her friend in the backseat.

"How are you feeling, Mercy?" Kit asked, checking the wounded woman's pulse. It was strong and steady.

"I'm feeling okay, just a headache," Mercy said. "Fogginess, too, like early in the morning, before coffee. My ankle hurts."

"We'll run a CT scan and x-rays tonight after I do a full exam," Kit said. "Then we'll check you later with an MRI to make sure there's no bleeding or complications." She smiled. "You might not recall this conversation later, so I'll explain it again if you need."

"That's okay. I don't even remember how I fell," Mercy said. "Or what I was doing before it happened."

Kit looked into her eyes. Mercy winked. Kit turned around in her seat and stared straight ahead.

The doctor would run the test just the same. She didn't have to tell the deputy anything about Mercy's care, except that she had a concussion and situational amnesia. Then her friend could return to Grace City, out of their reach, protected by her lawyers. Not that they could do anything to either of them. Kit had her own army of attorneys. She was sure that would be the end of it. It was never a good idea to get on your town's doctor's bad side—plus, it might get them unwanted attention. The townsfolk never liked much attention.

    Kit flashed back to everything that happened—not just the tentacle thing in the basement, but the hanging body in the attic. It was there, in front of her—tangible enough so she could smell the rotted flesh—and then it vanished. She went down the stairs, and something grabbed her ponytail. She examined the memories with skepticism, even as the screams echoed in her mind.

    Perhaps something they'd eaten had contained psilocybin. Or something outdoors got into their systems, causing hallucinations. She refused to believe it was anything other than that. There were no giant tentacle creatures waiting inside houses, posing as people to bait outsiders into entering the house. It was no enormous Venus fly trap. There must have been something around the house they inhaled, and the inhalant had been a hallucinogen.

Satisfied with that explanation, she decided that later, she would bring it to SHHS so they could hire someone to check and decontaminate the area. They would be wont to make fun of her if the recommendation came with another fat check.

"Something's wrong with that place," the doctor said.

"Everyone says it's haunted," Postman scratched his nose and watched the road.

"No, it's not supernatural, it's likely something like a plant or fungus that's causing a kind of inhaled hallucinogen to be released into the air," she said.

"Really? I didn't know that could happen," Postman said.

"It's rare, but it occurs," she said with a shrug. "I'll be certain to raise Doctor Langelier, and I'm keeping your handkerchief to examine the amber stuff. It might be in the sap."

That seemed believable enough, she gathered, because Postman didn't skip a beat. She believed it herself. It was a logical conclusion.

"I think they'll be grateful for that, Doc; and don't you worry—you won't get in trouble for trespassing. You were just trying to help." Postman gave her a grand grin, pleased with himself for this magnanimous decision.

"Indeed," she said. "I'm certain Langelier will be cooperative."

She sighed to herself. To point out that a ten-thousand-dollar donation to SHHS was a surefire way to keep from being arrested for illegal trespass would have been gauche.

But Langelier's cooperation was the only thing she was sure of—nothing else about this evening made sense. What if there wasn't any hallucinogen? Her scalp still ached from the hair pull. The sticky substance all over her—that *wasn't* sap. Then there was the hanging corpse in front of her she bumped into, and that felt as real as its odor still clinging to her nostrils.

The cold, sticky tentacle that wrapped around her friend and pulled—how could that be just her imagination? A rat settled into her brain and gnawed away at her logic.

"Do you believe in Alastor, Doc?"

Kit started at the deputy's voice and looked over at him, scowling. "Of course I don't. Those are old tales and superstition. Absolute nonsense."

"Me either, Doc." He shrugged. "It'd be nice, though. To have a kind of savior to rescue us from the bad things."

Kit's scowl softened, and she raised an eyebrow at him. "What bad things, Deputy? Like the things that've happened here?"

Postman swallowed, making a series of clicking sounds in his throat. His voice warbled when he answered. "Well, I guess all the bad things in the world, Doc. If Alastor was real, then maybe—I don't know."

Kit looked out the window again, and the deputy said nothing else. *If Alastor were real, then maybe that house wouldn't be standing*, she thought. *What nonsense.*

Something happened, though, didn't it? Doubt crept in once more, smothering her till she had to open the window for fresh air.

They pulled into the cul-de-sac of the emergency room, and Kit ran inside. She grabbed a nurse and a gurney, then fetched Mercy out of Postman's patrol car.

Summer couldn't end fast enough.

ELLA & HER CHILDREN

1868

Constable Platt surveyed the crime scene with an indigo handkerchief over his nose and mouth. The coroner sent from Jeffries gazed up at Platt, unaffected by the copper tang and rotten meat in the air.

The five bodies of the children were laid out side to side, holding hands. Palms missing fingers.

"Never seen a butchery like this," the coroner stood up and mopped droplets of sweat away. "The three boys and two girls have been disemboweled, intestines are missing in places. Looks as if they've been—well—chewed out."

That's when the constable vomited. The coroner just stared, face dispassionate. As the constable wiped off his mouth, the man from Jeffries stood back and waited.

"The intestines were removed postmortem, and the hearts are missing. But those were cut out." Jeffries shrugged. "The bodies are butchered and eaten in places, and none of the bite marks look human. The teeth marks are serrated, and unlike any animal I've ever seen."

Constable Platt's mouth popped open, eyes widened. "What?"

"Don't know what else to say, but that's what it is. She set an animal to rip them open and feast." He shook his head and looked back at the bodies.

"Cause of death? The stabs to the chest, most likely," the coroner shrugged. "While sleeping, as there are no signs of struggle. This happened about six to eight hours ago."

Turning gray as a storm cloud, the constable muttered thanks to the coroner for his time. As the man left back to

Jeffries, Platt remained with the crime scene, which included the mother, Ella Smith.

Ella was a small, thin woman with sallow cheeks, hair the color and texture of straw. Dirty, matted, caked with blood now, but most of the woman was bloody—her hands, dress, and body covered with spatters of the red mess, congealing as the minutes passed.

Huddled up in the chair, she'd been that way for several hours until a neighbor came by to visit. Ella stared out into space, whispering things that just sounded like nonsense to Platt.

The neighbor had come to Platt screaming. The constable had to shake her to get the woman to calm down and say what happened.

"Dead—all the children, dead—Ella—," tears rolled in fat drops on her cheeks, a runner of clear mucus falling from her nose. Platt ran and found the mess. Despite the strange November heat, Platt shivered.

That frigid hand over his heart crawled to his eyes as the constable stared at the madwoman. Five children, dead, because of one crazy woman. No sympathy for Ella. Not from Platt. Not now.

Platt wasn't a killer at heart, even getting upset when eating meat, if he thought on it too much. But this time, for this woman, Platt would see her hang. He'd bring Ella to the courthouse and turn the murderess over to the marshals. *Good.*

He moved forward to get Ella and go to the holding cell at the constabulary. This would be her chance to tell what happened, if possible. The woman was in pieces—not like the children, but a babbling mess of a person. Ella's whispers in the gloom of the house gave Platt a sick feeling, stinging his gut with tiny needles.

"You're under arrest, Ella." Platt's voice didn't sound real to his ears.

"There are stars in my eyes."

The constable shook his head. "What, Missus Smith?"

No response. Platt sighed.

"Well, you're coming along to the jail." Platt leaned forward and the odor of rotten meat got stronger. The constable's stomach churned and curled as if punched from the inside.

Ella wasn't hearing him. Her head cocked to the side as if listening to something far away. Her eyes were distant—looking beyond the constable and out the window to who-knew-where.

"Jail? Why am I going to jail?"

She looked down at the blood on her hands, face contorted in horror, eyes widening. Platt smelled urine as the woman's bladder let go.

The woman's screams would keep Platt awake for years after.

***

Platt locked Ella Smith up in jail for the night, sure the marshal would arrive in the morning to take her into custody. She stopped screaming on their return to the office. The faraway look had returned to her face, and she obeyed Platt without protest. She sat on the bench in the back of the cell, staring at nothing.

That night, he stayed, and Cora brought supper, a tray for Platt, and one for Ella. Cora brought the trays over to Platt's desk without missing a beat, though Platt could see her face was graying from the amount of blood on Ella's hands.

"Thank you, Corie, but I'm not so hungry tonight—and how did you know to bring two trays?"

"That's fine—eat when you're ready." Cora shrugged as she headed for the door. "Word travels fast."

His wife returned with a bucket full of water, apron soaking inside. She walked up to the cell and motioned to it with her head. "Open the cell. I'll help her wash so she can eat."

"Corie, what that woman did makes sure she doesn't deserve to eat."

Cora shook her head. "I'm not the one to judge that. She'll get what she deserves, but for now, she's in my care, and a meal is in order."

Platt nodded. Cora would get her way, and the constable opened the cell door.

She took in the bucket and cleaned Ella up, speaking to the woman the way she spoke to a distressed child.

"Miss Ella, I'm washing your hands and face. Get you cleaned up so you can have supper," Cora said. "Roast chicken and stewed carrots from the garden. Eat with your hands and wipe up with the napkin."

Ella said nothing to Cora. Platt stood at the door of the cell, just in case.

Once the constable's wife finished and left Ella her dinner tray, she let her husband lock the cell back up. Her face changed from its soft, pinkish tone to ash. She watched him, standing by the desk, bucket and apron at her feet.

"Now I remember why I married you," he said, putting the keys back on his belt and walking over to Cora.

"Oh? And why's that?"

"You're a kind and tender woman—sweet and gentle as a summer day is long."

That brought a small smile to the woman's face. She stopped shaking for the moment. "I'm going back to the house. I'll see you when you're done with this."

Cora left with the bucket and apron.

Platt checked the cell to see that Ella hadn't eaten, either. She was still sitting in the corner of her cell, whispering things he didn't understand, rocking back and forth.

He went back to his desk and picked at his tray of food. The roast chicken had a crispy skin and juicy meat reminiscent of last summer's town barbecue. Carrots were a garden favorite for Platt, and they were less salty this time.

After a long stretch of doing nothing, stomach settling from the meal, Constable Platt decided it was time to coax the woman into a real confession. The whole story.

Platt was not a cruel man, but not one for nonsense, either. He could take things in stride, but anyone who back-talked found their hides in a sling in a hurry. Like that Murray kid he ran out of town—found him stealing from the farm where he'd worked. Platt took a hand to him and

Murray split, knowing his choices were a beating and a ride out of the town limits, or stay for worse.

"Ella Mae Smith, it's time to talk about what you did."

Ella looked up at the constable and looked at him and past him at the same time. Eyes the color of tobacco smoke bore into him. He swallowed, but held her gaze.

"It's time, Ella."

The woman looked at her feet from between her knees and said nothing.

Platt's tone changed, the way it did when coaxing a child to take his medicine. "Ella, it's a pus-filled wound. You've got to get the pus out so it can heal."

He didn't believe the words he spoke. She would never heal from this. She would hang for this if justice prevailed. He would bring her to the courthouse, himself. She would swing—there was little doubt.

Ella's tear-stained face glistened in the jaundiced, yellow light of the lantern, pale skin absorbing the sick glow from overhead. "You won't believe me if I told you," she said. Her voice was scratched, gritty, irritated from the screaming, most likely.

"I don't care. I want to hear it. What got into your head that made you do such a thing?"

The constable didn't believe in gods, demons, ghosts, or any of that. Though he didn't doubt there was a creator, he didn't think that it involved itself in the minutia of mankind. Those things weren't logical.

He sat on the bench just outside the cell, running a sepia thumb over his opposite hand. A nervous habit from ages ago.

"They, *they* got into my head, Timothy," Ella's voice croaked, not looking up from her new fixed point, fascinated by her bare toes. "Once they were there, I couldn't stop. It was me, but it wasn't me."

She continued talking, and Platt became more grayish as the story progressed. By the time she finished, he thought he might wind up as white as she was.

"We weren't a happy family to start. Sure, since Russell died, it got easier without him yelling and beating me, but we struggled. Couldn't send the oldest to school anymore because he had to work. But at least he could read and write. Yes, sir, he could do that much. Smart child, too, but we needed the money to survive. What we grew in our vegetable patch wasn't enough to cover our debts.

"I wasn't sleeping much this summer on account of the heat, and when I slept, I woke up with hands touching me, and inside me. Long, black hands. Slick, deep black, the way ebony wood looks. Real shiny, freezing, and all over me.

"I thought I was just dreaming. Just missing having a husband. Because I had needs. No matter how much he hit me or hollered, he still fed those needs.

"At first, I liked it, I admit. But after a while, the *voices* spoke, offering me more. Offering me a husband proper, and a good life.

"I never doubted those voices for a moment—never thought they weren't real. I had no one to talk to so I believed in them. They told me I could be free and revered if only I sacrificed something important to the Timeworn Gods.

"Well, that was when I tried to stop listening. I mean, I didn't like the kids much, but sacrificing them to the Timeworn wasn't something I was ready to do. In particular my little Christopher, the youngest. He wasn't Russell's. No one knew that, till now, and no, I won't tell you the father's name, on account he was a drifter. He's long gone, and it doesn't matter anymore.

"Well, maybe Russell suspected it, because the beatings got worse after I gave birth to little Christopher.

"I'm glad that Russell drank himself blind and fell down the stairs. That was one of the best moments of my life when I woke up and saw him through my swollen eyes.

"I fought it for a long time, I admit. But those voices, those touches—they were persuasive. They tormented me with promises of something I always wanted. Night after night, they were relentless."

As she paused, Platt cleared his throat. His tongue was far too big for his mouth now, and it was dry as sand. He nodded to show he was still listening.

"You know when you're desperate and want something in your heart, no matter how deep it's buried, you'll find a reason to have it. No matter what it is or how much you fight doing something bad, if you want it enough, you'll make up reasons. Well, this was something I wanted in a way.

"To get where I wanted to be, to be free, I was glad to do it, Constable. I was glad to do it for my freedom and the promise of pleasure, though at first, I wouldn't admit that. But it's the truth, even though it wasn't me, but it WAS me. I—"

"I don't understand how it could be and couldn't be you," Platt said. He grimaced.

Ella ignored him. "Well, as long as the voices were with me, then I was happy to do it. I'm not happy, now. I don't believe it was I who did it. Somehow, it was and wasn't me, and I don't know how to say it otherwise. The voices, they were overwhelming with their promises and their demands. To be with the Father of the Timeworn as a husband? I felt compelled to take that offer."

Platt sighed.

Ella talked past him. "For a while, I resisted. I knew killing was wrong, and they weren't asking to borrow the children. They told me they had to be sacrificed by the flesh, and they told me it was the only way I'd be free to be with them. See, they are the True Gods—they are One God. I guess it's hard to conceive, but they're akin to leaves and branches on the trunk of a great tree.

"Those leaves whispered every night, and then all day, during the day. No one else could hear them. I became short-tempered with the children, and they became sullen. They cried more often. They became gray. Docile. I grew to hate them. Not just resent them, but hate them because they stood in my way to happiness. I'd be happy with the Timeworn Gods.

"I gave in when the voices got more forceful. With my permission, they took over my body, and they knew what to do. They led me to the supper table with my stew. They put that rat poison in it, right in the stew pot. I ate none. The children did. Even my youngest. I put them to bed. They didn't even complain with their stomachaches, Timothy. They were too frightened I'd become cross with them.

"Soon their breathing stopped, and I laid them out in a chain. *We* laid them out in a chain, and *we* cut them open."

Platt's mouth dried up even more. He tried to swallow, but the only sound was a series of clicks in his throat.

Ella took this as a signal to keep talking. "The strangest thing happened then. That blackness I was telling you about? Well, it flowed out of me. Not a trickle, but lightning. Slick and fast, kind of the way a person vomits when they're real sick. It formed a tall person who didn't have a face—just an ebony wood man.

"I sliced the children open, *it* cut out their hearts and intestines and ate. Ate, ate, and ate. Oh, it was joyous for the things, and I remember clapping my hands in delight, and even bathing in the blood. We would be together, the Timeworn and me. Together."

Platt stared and felt something slither through his stomach and wrap around his heart. Beads of sweat broke out over his forehead, and he licked his rough lips with a dry tongue.

"But then, it left, and the voices left with it." Ella brought her hands up to her face to mime the action, splaying out her fingers near her ears and wiggling them, then spreading her arms out and upward. "Oh, how I cried. Not just for what I had done to my children, but because the Timeworn deceived me. Near as I can think, they'll be back for me, but not the way I thought.

"I don't expect you to understand that. Now it's quiet and I'm not sure I understand it. But they were there, they were real, and I did what I had to do for the Timeworn! They'll be back for me, you'll see. Maybe even greater than I imagined—I did what they wanted."

Ella's face bloomed with a fervor that Platt associated with the madness of religious people when they think gods are speaking to them. She moved toward the bars, and Platt took an involuntary step back. The woman reeked of blood from her clothing, piss, shit, and something else he didn't recognize. Akin to rot, but too sweet, too sickly smelling. Not as sharp as death, but dying. He supposed that was how madness smelled.

Platt was quiet, beads of sweat standing out on his brow, his heart pumping into his ears. She was mad and deserved what she got for what she had done. He turned away and went back to his desk, writing up everything she had told him, without personal commentary.

By the time the pen ran out of ink, the constable regretted eating his supper. Stomach a tight ball, the constable stood up and retrieved Ella's tray, putting it outside for the hounds. The fresh air on his face kept him from losing supper.

***

Dumfries wasn't a smart man, and he wasn't a kind man. He was a man who loved trouble.

This, too, was trouble. News of the Smith woman traveled fast among the residents of Silver Hollow, and a fever poured over them, which Dumfries loved. He knew there'd be trouble, and that's where he wanted to be—right in the center of it.

Twenty-two people showed up to his little emergency meeting at the Church of The Benevolent Alastor, and that was enough. That put a smile on his rugged, pale face. Well, an internal smile, because he couldn't present such grim news with a huge grin on his pate. No, this had to be done with somber but commanding tones and mien. He could only use his chiseled jaw and bright green eyes to charm people. The rest was pure substance.

Bloodthirsty trouble was always the best kind.

"We're concerned, here, that justice will not be served because Ella Mae Smith is a woman. There's always a chance the judge will feel sorry for her and let her go," he said to the crowd. He was a loud, barrel-chested man who towered over the tallest person there by a good foot. He used his height to his advantage, and his stentorian voice echoed in the church halls as the weeping God Alastor watched them from the altar.

The crowd murmured their agreement, and someone—either Aggie or Maggie Grimshaw (they were twins so hard to tell which one)—spoke. "Think of the children! Who will bring justice to the children?" She cried out, wiping at her forehead as though she were to faint. The other brought her hands to her heart.

Dumfries, not wanting to be overshadowed by the pearl-clutching hysterics, spoke up over her, slamming his fist into the pulpit for emphasis, hard enough to rock it forward and bring his greased, bottle-black hair into his field of vision. "We will. We will bring justice to Silver Hollow!"

The crowd got more feverish with their murmurs and cries, and Dumfries roused them further.

"I say we go to Platt and demand she be released to us, so we can serve up justice."

"Justice!" The crowd's noise reverberated off the walls.

It was Eugene Bayless who gathered the rope and swung it around as if it were a lasso to round up a calf. Others brought their shotguns, and still others brought clubs and lanterns with them.

They marched on to the small constable's office where the jail was, and as they gathered, more joined the twenty-three. Some out of curiosity, and still others who just wanted a show. They weren't as feverish as the original set, but Dumfries didn't care. As long as they didn't get in his way, they could enjoy watching the old bitch swing.

The constable was outside with empty dinner trays when they approached, Dumfries leading them—a shepherd of strange, rabid sheep. Every step, crunching the packed, dry dirt beneath his boots excited the leader of the mob, increasing as he approached. His mouth was near slobbering with fervor.

"Hold on here, Dumfries," Platt said, holding up his palms toward the crowd. Dumfries halted, but he had no intention of leaving without getting what he wanted, and that was a swinging Ella Mae Smith. He wouldn't be happy till he saw her hang, tongue lolling, with her neck rope-burned so deep it about took her head off.

Now, *that* was intoxicating. Better than any spirits he'd ever had.

"We don't want to hold on, Platt," Dumfries's voice was full of reproach—a stern father figure, even though he and Platt were close to the same age. The townspeople respected Platt, so the man was careful at first. Best to put Platt in an enemy position—an obstacle to be removed. "We want justice, and we don't think a judge in Cartston or any of the towns nearby is gonna do it."

Platt shook his head. "That's not your call, Dumfries. That's not anyone's call here."

The constable was calm and lowered his hands. Dumfries watched with wary eyes while he spoke.

"It *is* our call, Constable," he said, and the crowd voiced their assent. "We're the residents here who let that—that—*witch* into our township, and *we* are the ones who will see that justice is served. Step aside, Platt."

Dumfries tried to push past the constable. Platt might not have been as big, but he was just as strong. He dug in his heels and refused to move.

"Now, calm down, everyone," Platt said. "Everyone go home."

Dumfries could tell by the look on Platt's face that the constable was unconvinced the crowd would disperse. The bigger man tried again to push past him, and that's when Platt reacted. Platt reached out to take Dumfries by the neck and then to the ground.

Dumfries moved faster, and whacked the constable with the club he'd been carrying. It connected to the other man's head with a dull thump, and Platt fell, prone.

"Sorry to do that to you, Constable," the man said, kneeling and patting him on the back as if he meant it. He moved to Platt's belt and hoisted the cell key off him.

"We had to do it," he said to the transfixed crowd. They gaped for the moment on the constable's limp body. "Platt will be fine. Bayless, you're with me. Carmont, you make sure Platt's all right. Take him to that bench."

He wasn't a complete barbarian. Dumfries would not kill the man if it wasn't necessary. Kill the witch. That *was* necessary.

With force enough to make the bars clang, Dumfries opened the cell door, and a look of utter, bitter *hate* crossed Ella's face. "Don't you get near me," she screamed, backing away and scratching at him. It was all the leader of the lynch mob could do not to burst out laughing at her.

"Oh, see, everyone? She's not so brave now she's here alone," he said, crossing his arms. "I see you can kill children with ease—now let's see you try to stop us."

He reached out and tried to grab her, but she scratched him hard in return, drawing blood from his arm. Then she laughed and chanted.

For just a moment, Dumfries thought he saw her eyes go from that strange, icy blue to black. He wouldn't have admitted it, but for just a moment, he thought his heart would stop with fear.

"The TIMEWORN GODS are on my side!" She finished her strange chant and barreled through the crowd.

She only got so far, however, before Dumfries snapped out of the trance that took over his body. Now burning with ire, he leapt on her. Hands grabbed at her, holding her down. Whispers of *witch*, *vile woman* and *whore* escaped the voices of the crowd.

They kept pulling until her struggles ceased to matter, and they dragged her to the back of the church.

There, an old willow tree stood, its branches thick and huge. Bayless and Krueger brought up the rope and made sure the noose was secure. Ella was babbling now, and thrashing against those who held her. They struggled to tie her wrists tight and took time securing the noose around her neck.

"Last words?" Dumfries asked. He was sure he didn't want to hear them.

"You're already in Perdition," she said, eying as many of the people as possible. The gazes back at her were mixes of defiance, shame, and desire.

They pulled her up until she was five feet off the ground.

She swung, gurgling, kicking, body stiffening, and noose tightening. She lost her bowels and urinated, and Dumfries consoled his erection with a quick, soft tug. If anyone noticed, they said nothing. It was tempting to take care of it and see if anyone joined him. At that point, he was so feverish throughout his whole body, he didn't care. His mind saved him with a reminder—there were other things that needed attention in this town.

He didn't think he'd get away with it, though he was almost certain there were two ladies—Aggie and Maggie—who saw it and liked it. Maybe he'd attend to it later with them both, on top of the cold, dead body of Ella Mae Smith.

They watched her swing from the old willow tree, the stars in the clear black sky as silent judges.

JOURNAL SCRAPS

2 September

Thoughts of friends and this journal are the only things keeping me sane. It's been four months of living in Silver Hollow now. Summer is over and soon I'll be returning to Grace City—what a relief.

This place is a tiny little township. The residents call it both a town and a township here, depending on the age of the resident, and the two terms are interchangeable. I'm not sure why, and I've never asked. I don't care.

Cities. My life has been set in cities. During the summers, Father would bring Phillip and me to Albion's countryside. The bitterness of sweltering summers that left me itching in my starched dresses. The smell of horse manure lingered in the air and left me with a distaste for the countryside. When Phillip wasn't pinching me or using me as a target for his rock launcher, covering me in bruises all over my back, chest and legs, I was either getting strains on my inner thighs from horseback riding, or coping with ringing in my ears from shooting clay pigeons. Only later did I learn that Phillip was removing the foam hearing protection in my kit. The nights were quiet, but I never noticed, passing out from being exhausted and understanding how a pin-cushion felt. The city always made me more comfortable—a lifelong theme for me.

  The heavy, metallic air of the city is more appealing. Watching skyscrapers glisten in the morning sun over breakfast and tea on the penthouse balcony is the best way to wake. After a fortnight in the clean, open air with fresh-cut grass and glistening dewdrops on the verdant fields, hearing animals chatter and birds singing their songs, it's time to go home. Take me back to the sounds of horns, sirens, people chattering, and the smell of freshly baked bread and spices from the bakeries. Fresh-cut grass makes me sneeze.

This town, or township, is small, and that's an understatement. One church of the Timeworn Order or Alastor (or both, I don't care) now just a meeting hall, a constable's office, a general store, and perhaps about forty-five people separated by at least two or three acres of land each. Except near the roundabout, where there is a small cluster of buildings.

The locals are right out of a horror film. They stare until I look back. Then they avert their eyes. At six feet tall and one who doesn't shy from wearing heels, I gather by the gaping maws that I might seem interplanetary. There are people here who still use old wives' tales as medicine, putting grapes on cuts to heal them, and other such woo.

A look around the general store, and one can find old liniments for arthritis and cod liver oil for irregularity (which isn't unsafe, just dated). From the dour looks on their faces, the oil wasn't working.

At best, the reception was lukewarm—they saw me as an outsider with my Albion accent and tailored suits. Although when I saved the old man who runs the general store, they moved from active disdain to distant tolerance. The man had pneumonia, and they were treating him with herbs and such. I paid no attention to what they were using because their witchcraft wasn't working. They might as well have brought in an ancient priestess to dance around in a tutu or whatever it is the religious superstition requires. After taking a sputum culture, I treated him for bacterial pneumonia. Three days later, he was well enough to get back on his feet (still taking the course of antibiotics). After that, he smiled when he greeted me, and offered me free items when I came in to purchase a delicious treat or something for my dinner.

I'm a horrid cook but living alone has given me opportunity to burn plenty of things and learn how not to bake something, and how grease fires can be put out with baking soda. Once I tried to make cupcakes but had no eggs. Since eggs are a binding agent (I didn't fail chemistry), I thought to use applesauce instead. Too much applesauce (this was obvious in retrospect). When the timer went off and I opened the oven, six puddles of chocolate and flour-flavored applesauce stared me in the face. Lots and lots of chucking dinners in the bin and discovering curse words I'd forgotten existed. Still, a learning experience.

But the poor cooking skills are another issue. There's a much bigger problem in this part of the Northeast Territory, and treating the elderly gentleman who runs the general store highlighted this greater matter. My presence here is because the area is lacking in physicians, and I volunteered to help. That meant that I had to bring equipment with me. (They will see the out-of-pocket expenses on my next tax return—I gave them to my accountant.) I brought a portable defibrillator, EKG, sonogram device, etcetera, along with a slew of antibiotics, sedatives, and epinephrine. I brought everything I might need for an emergency to keep at home, because with the exception of a simple first-aid station at the constabulary, they have nothing. That's how backwards and isolated Silver Hollow is.

Mercy Hospital is stocked and equipped due to the new health regulations. It's also a twenty-minute drive. It's in Terrace Lake, and it services several neighboring towns. The place is nestled among other areas of industry—an enormous laboratory facility for the Center for Health Assurance, a steel mill, and several other factories. The people who live close by are mill workers and those who make no decent compensation for their work. Yet it's one of the richest areas next to Nashton Lake. It shows in some of the bigger homes and manors on the water.

Near the lake, the sprawling homes and yachts in the slip enhance the outskirts where dilapidated and decaying small houses with three or four cars out front rust and rot alongside.

They don't pay their physicians much, either. I took this work as my personal required outreach, in fact. The highest paid physician here doesn't make enough to support a family—it's "not in the budget." It's sad, when one looks at how much they spent going to medical school, only to wind up struggling to make out a life. It's getting better, so the economic reports say, but it will take time.

So while Terrace Lake is a 'rich' town, and Mercy Hospital is well-equipped and well-stocked, they are overburdened. Because the budget of the territory goes into other projects and making sure the hospital is prepared, there isn't much leftover for salaries (they line the pockets of the administrators first). Once these hitches are resolved it'll get better, I hope. After my tenure this summer, I will contact our legislature and prove to them that better funding for this section of the Northeast Territory is needed.

For now, I'm stuck here, gathering information. I didn't bring my personal assistant or any of my staff and I regret that decision. It's most painful when I have to throw out a whole chicken because the skin isn't supposed to turn to ash when one cuts into it (note: do not fall asleep while something is in the oven. Also, check on fire insurance policy.).

It's so quiet here, even in the daytime. At night, stillness settles over the house like a heavy blanket. With the windows open, a cool breeze comes through, and the songs of crickets, cicadas, and little peep toads come through—nature's chorus. Most nights. Sometimes it gets far too still here. As if something smothers the property into silence. The house pops and creaks as it settles, but that never lasts. Or worse, sometimes I hear the foundation settle and it sounds as if tiny little feet are running across the oak floors. Then the silence impregnates the room and I can't get back to sleep.

It's not like the place I come from—Great Smoke City. Great Fire City was what they called it when I left and moved to the Union. Those were terrible times. I hate to remember them at all.

Mercy Hospital is almost a nice escape from the house, but it would be better with two or three servants to help. They're all back home, taking care of things there until I return. I'm a fool for not bringing Faith, because at least she can cook. The nearest restaurant is a twenty-minute drive from my rental home, in Terrace Lake. Most of the time I'll get takeaway and bring it home with me, but I've learned how to cook noodles, omelets, and steak. They're nothing compared to what Faith can make, but once I found recipes, I discovered it was easier than trying to guess around it and winding up basted in flour, looking like a fat-lipped ghost.

Takeaway it is five times a week.

I have never experienced this much isolation in my entire life, and this isn't a developing country. I've seen better communities in impoverished nations. That's an exaggeration, but only by a bit. The dilapidated farmhouses with thin, bony dairy cows, dirty-faced men with holes in their pants, broken down cars and rotting barns, and people who can do nothing but sit on their porches and stare into the air—either too disabled to work, or they've given up hope—are a testament to what's called "First World poverty." There are no children here. None. Everyone here is in their twenties or older—and they're considered the young ones. None of the youth have seen a university. The town hobbles along with support from Jewel Grove and whatever's leftover in the territory's annual budget. There is no surprise that this place doesn't show on modern maps. This area is forsaken.

    I found it through a mailer which came from the Historical Society. Faith (or maybe it was Lucy, I can't recall) said she didn't see it in the mail she sorted, so by lucky (?) coincidence, I got to read about this forsaken place. Langelier must have taken my name from one of the Grace City Historical Society functions I've attended for my friend Mercy. Otherwise, this place might be the gateway to Perdition.

    If that place existed, this would be it.

They have a sense of community from person to person though. Around here, everybody knows everybody. Except me. They don't trust me because I'm an outsider.

I don't trust them either.

They're cordial enough, but they never say much—at least not to me. They have plenty to say to one another in whispers and pointing when I turn away. I'm that 'damn city doctor.' Except for the owner of the general store and his wife, who seem to be grateful, I am alien to them. At least the two of them give me free apple pies to show their appreciation.

Silver Hollow used to be a bigger town. That's what the Historical Society tells me—the population was in the hundreds. There have been several attempts over the years to breathe life back into the place, but all seem to fail in spectacular fashion. Children have been murdered here by the dozen, perhaps hundreds when the town was thriving, and that doesn't sound inviting on a tourism pamphlet. The town began to rot after the first incident (there was more than one, I'm told), and people left.

Well, perhaps it was already rotten, and that was just its death knell. Attempts to revive it have been futile.

This place is full of strange history. I'm not good at history. That's my friend, Mercy— she's got her PhD in the subject and knows a lot about small town development over the course of the Union. But I've been trying to piece together the strange pull of this town—it attracted me too after I received the brochure from the SHHS. (I didn't realize when they said 'secluded' that this what they meant.)

According to local lore, the allure of Silver Hollow "pulls" people here and then things "go funny." Those were Langelier's words in quotes. (Mercy will visit soon, which reminds me I need to pick up a few things at Haverty's.) He is skeptical as I am about these stories, but mentioned it just the same. It was so comforting I might vomit.

The man is, without peer, the most egocentric, narrow-minded pragmatist I've ever met. He never stops speaking about either himself, or the Historical Society. He's the only one who will spend time with me because he's greedy for my money and for sex. Though I've donated already (money, not sex—I'd rather drink bleach), he'll be back to solicit more money from me. He's not a person I would put in my diary for a visit in Grace City, but company is needed sometimes. Even if it is a bit obnoxious.

I am hopeful Bryce will be back from his business soon and will pay me a visit. I like the independence, but I would enjoy more-than-friendly company now and then.

After Langelier told me that little story about Silver Hollow going mad at a stranger's presence, I gather I'm the one who will make things go funny by existing here. I assume that's what he was driving at, though I don't understand what was the motive behind telling me all this. Except to enjoy another snifter of brandy and keep me asking questions.

The old bastard left after that brandy and without a check in hand. I went to bed with a smug sense of satisfaction I'd annoyed him by not caving (on the money or his hand on my knee).

Well, it's been four months, and nothing. So far, the only funny things that have happened are weird incidents at the hospital. But that's normal when working in A&E, or rather the ER or ED (Emergency Room/Emergency Department) as they call it here. That and the psychiatric cases that come in with some frequency. There are certain ones who stand out with their madness.

These people stand out because there's a pattern—almost like a mass hysteria, but not enough of them at once to qualify. These are the ones who blather on about a darkness consuming them, their place, and their lives. It sounds as if they're trapped in a black hole and can somehow communicate what it's like. They come to the hospital, terrified, jumping at every shadow, looking at me as if I'm not there—looking past me.

I put them on a seventy-two hour mandatory hold, sedate them and send them on to the psych ward. It's all I can do. But even when I sedate them with the most powerful drugs, they still appear to be disturbed by the things they claim to see. The never-ending darkness, which some claim is full of stars, and others say it's filled with unspeakable horrors—it's all they can talk about. They don't even try to describe the horrors. If they do, they fall into gibberish. It sounds like a foreign language.

There's a pattern. It's obvious.

Fatigue has taken over, so I will come back to this later. Mercy is coming, and she's real company, so I want to be rested so we can enjoy a week together.

K.C.

***

3 September

Mercy sleeps tonight at Mercy Hospital, and I'm not leaving her side. I'm just sitting here with my tablet, touch-typing this out as a steady stream of beeps from her monitors tell me she's still alive.

This is awful. She's a little worse off than I thought, though, more than just a mild concussion and amnesia. The amnesia is something she's faking so Callfield and company won't ask too many questions, but her ankle is broken and she lost more blood than I'd initially thought. She's hooked up to three units of whole blood now, and her BP is climbing.

I sent a message to Langelier a few moments ago:

Francis, wanted to let you know there may be a fungal issue at Dubbs House, in and around the area. I was at the house with my friend as we were walking through the woods and heard noises. Chose to investigate and once at the property heard what we thought were cries for help. There was nothing inside. Suspect spores and suggest sending in inspectors. -Kathryn

I left out the details of the tactile and visual hallucinations (I'm not giving him more ammunition than necessary), but there are some kinds of fungi spores which, once inhaled, cause people to hallucinate. Monsters don't exist. It's fairy stories—and I don't give in to tales of the supernatural.

Father was a geneticist, and he taught us the hard facts of science. When I was a girl, and the governess brought me no comfort, he came into my room and sent her away. His presence—a tall, foreboding man was enough to frighten away any of my imagined and uninvited guests. The stentorian boom of his voice helped, too. "Your fears are natural, Kitty. Through millennia, our ancestors had to survive predators in the wild. Right now, you're experiencing what every primate does—you're keeping watch for them. But since they don't exist, and you're safe in the house, your brain's gone into overdrive and making up stories to justify your vigilance. I assure you, my kitten, it's not real."

Father's explanations brought me greater comfort than that of my playmates', whose explanations included belief in a savior saint name Alastor who chased them away with his supernatural powers. Twaddle. That was all it was.

It was easier to tell myself that my brain was reacting to a wild imagination and that I was safe. Nothing was there in the dark that wasn't there in the daytime.

Mercy told the deputy she remembered nothing. Earlier she winked at me in the patrol car—she was more with it than she was letting on. That was because she didn't want us getting into trouble for trespassing. She'll be fine, I'm 99.9% certain. I told her of a possible hallucinogen in the air. She hasn't commented on it. Instead, she looks at me like I might belong in the mental ward, complete with straight jacket and padded walls. I've known her for years.

Does she really think a tentacle monster tried to kill her? I'm not asking. Doubt runs about in my brain like a hamster in an exercise wheel.

The adrenaline has run its course through my body, and my heart has slowed into a quiet rhythm, but I have enough nausea to account for three people. My legs stopped shaking and my knees have become water. All I can do is have a lie down in the doctor's lounge for now and check on Mercy to make sure I didn't do any permanent damage.

I hope she'll still want to stay the rest of the week and not return home right away. I would return with her, but I have to stay till the end of my promised contract which means I'm here through mid-October.

People in town will talk, I'm sure. Let them. They do little else with their lives. As soon as we go home later today, I'm taking a shower, sleeping for twelve hours, and spending the rest of my time with my best friend.

***

9 September

Mercy stayed with me for the week, and she is quite a trooper. During her recovery, she asked me for a glass of Braxbury Cola. When I brought her a glass, she looked at me with a puzzled expression. "That's not right, Lucy. I asked for a Braxbury." It took me a few heart-skipping moments to reorient her.

"I'm not Lucy. I'm Kit. Remember?"

"Oh yes. Where's Lucy?"

My brows raised. "She's at home in Grace City. You're in Silver Hollow."

"Right. Oh! Right. I'm visiting Kit. You're Kit."

"Yes, I'm Kit." Looking into her eyes with my penlight, she roused to full consciousness and her pupils reacted. She looked at me, aware. I breathed a sigh that shook my lungs.

I've scheduled a follow-up MRI to ensure no permanent damage. I'm sending her to a friend of mine in Grace City—a neurologist and lovely person. She'll take excellent care of Mercy, I'm sure. Someday (I hope) we can look back on this week with some fondness, or at least a laugh or two.

Now I'm alone again, though, the house seems ever more ominous and dark. Because that visit to Dubbs House may have affected my endocrine system, I ran some blood work and checked. All normal. My norepinephrine and serotonin levels? Normal for someone who's experienced a fright. So, I'm blaming an ever-growing imagination and group-think along with a potential hallucinogen in the air. The town's belief in the supernatural is leaking into my head.

I am crossing off the days on my calendar, counting down to the day I get to leave this ridiculous town.

***

15 September

Things this week were getting a little better for me. Now I've around a month left in Silver Hollow. I miss home. I've been in touch with Mercy, and she is recovering, although shaken from her experience. She tells me she had nightmares about it, but that in her dreams, her children are the ones in danger. The dreams sound bizarre—telling me of her little brood of six laid out dead in a heptagram with her husband as the crown. Yet she says they're dreams that will fade over time.

She and Frank are planning to pick me up in October and bring me to Grace City so we can have a proper celebration, and they're going to bring Bryce with them if they can get him to arrange his schedule. Frank loves road trips and has since he first got his license. Something to look forward to instead of dwelling on this empty house.

I'd rather fly from Terrace Lake (I can fly my plane or charter one, for goodness sake), but this seems like it's something special to Frank and Mercy, so I've given in and am letting them come get me. The drive will be full of leaves turning and the sights of animals by the roadside grazing to fatten up for the winter. Then it's back in the city, away from all this—whatever it is.

Once again, thoughts of home and my friends are keeping me sane. So is this journal. I need the anchors because I'll spin off into my babbling madness without them. I'm not so sure that's an exaggeration, either—not after the stress of playing paranormal investigator and putting my friend in danger.

I'm writing this now because everything seemed to be at a nice lull until the end of the week, and then a slew of madness at the hospital started up again. Babbling insanity, injuries—ghastly injuries, and a death from hypovolemic shock. I checked with Langelier, and he said that the agency he hired to check for hazmat found nothing. Then he suggested that it may have cleaned itself up or that the heavy rainstorms did the cleaning.

The bullshit wafting from his mouth—overpowering.

Arguing with that pompous tit is futile. If Langelier tries to weasel more money out of me, forget it. I'll report the incident to the CHA and let them take care of it (I have friends there). See how that git enjoys having a bunch of

CHA agents in hazmat suits hanging around looking for the problem, fining him thousands for infractions along the way. Brushing me off is a mistake, he'll soon learn.

I've never been the nicest person in the world. Except for those who are close (there are four people I care enough about to check on with frequency), I'm a human glacier. I don't change it—it protects me from users.

The end of this week has been trying for me, and I am ready for a fight.

Well, perhaps tomorrow I'll fight. I need to rest.

-K. C.

***

Didn't sleep very much. Napped for about an hour. I have a patient who's been weighing on my mind.

I've recorded our interactions with her permission, and will call her 'Wendy' to ensure confidentiality. She came in with a severe scalp laceration (forty-three centimeters long from forehead to occiput), claiming that something had scratched her, and speaking gibberish. It sounded familiar as if some other patient was fluent in this made up language. After sedation she became coherent again, unlike the others. This one was a fighter.

I stitched her up but if that was an animal scratch, it must have had knives for claws. The 'scratch' looked like an attempt at an old-fashioned scalping. It took around seventy-six stitches to get it sewn up (I have the exact number in her records I'll pull later), and we had to shave her entire head. Pity, because she had long blonde hair that didn't come from a bottle.

"How are you now?" I came in to see her while on my rounds. She gave me a wan smile.

"Well, at least it'll grow back," Wendy said with a hand pressed to the side of her head. "Been trying not to play with it."

"Yes, not touching it is a solid idea," I said.

"After everything that's happened, I don't want an infection." Wendy adjusted how she was sitting and I reached out to arrange her pillows.

"Would you be willing to do an interview with me, recording you?" I waved the small recorder at her.

"Is this for a psych evaluation?" she asked, picking at her cuticles and biting her bottom lip.

I nodded. I wasn't about to lie to her. "It's part of it—I prefer to keep a verbal record for my transcriptionist—and I find it helps me stay on top of my interviewing skills. As part of the evaluation, if I determine you're a harm to yourself of others, I'll keep you here for a mandatory hold. Why don't we chat for a while and see what happens?"

The patient shrugged. "I'll wind up here for a few days, I'm sure."

I said nothing to that and turned on the recorder, then asked her for her consent. She agreed.

Her story began at the old bed-and-breakfast—as many of them did.

"I'm working on my PhD at Grace City University," she said. Her voice was shaky at first, but gained strength as she continued. "My specialty is ancient languages and translations. It's a hybrid degree, though, because of the narrow scope I chose. I cross over into the history department, so I get the pleasure—or displeasure, of having to defend my dissertation to professors of both departments. On the bright side, I work with some of the brightest people and learn from them, and they from me.

"Part of my studies led me to Dubbs House to help them with some translations of an old book they'd uncovered in the basement. They found it in between the underpart of the stairs and the storage area." She fell silent for a moment and shrugged. "It's a little tough to describe but there's a crevice between the staircase and the little cubby."

"That's clear enough to me," I said, familiar with the basement but not about to admit it. "Go on, please."

I poured her a cup of water and handed it to her. She took a drink before continuing.

"When I drove up to Silver Hollow, Doctor Langelier was all too glad to see me. He was just happy for the free work."

I repressed a laugh. "I know who he is, and perhaps you're correct."

Damn right she was correct. That man was a leech.

Wendy gave a faint smile and nodded. "Oh, then you understand. He was eager to show me the exact spot where they discovered it, and then took me back to the Historical Society where they kept it.

"It was old. The pages were thick, likely vellum, and the words were a dark red but legible. When I examined it further, I discovered it wasn't vellum. It was human skin, and the ink was blood."

Years of practice listening to bizarre things patients say helped me keep a straight face when she told me this. Also being from Albion helps as we're supposed to be famous for our deadpan expressions (I fit the stereotype). But I dismissed what she said.

The experience traumatized her and building things up in her mind, she may have fantasized about was her way of coping with it. People have strange, fleeting thoughts and when coupled with a traumatic event, she was likely exaggerating things in her mind.

"I told Langelier I would need to bring it back with me to Grace City, but he was immovable on that point," she said. "But he offered me first publishing rights if I stayed and translated it, so I rented a house on Maple Street just outside of the town limits. A fair compromise."

I nodded, and she coughed, so I offered her more water. She sipped several times and then reclined again. I waited as the lighting grew dim from the sun hiding behind a cloud. For a while, the only sound was the ticking of my watch, the beeping and tones of monitors, and the distant busy murmurs of nurses as they went about their business.

"The first thing I did when I was home—well, at the rental home—was try to put a date on the find. This is where my undergraduate dual degree in history and archaeology comes in handy." Wendy chucked, then turned serious. "Dating the document was foremost in my mind because that would help me with the linguistics. This piqued my curiosity. The pages, as I've said, were thick, like vellum, but not as elegant. The color and variations of each page told me I wasn't looking at hide, either, but in fact human skin."

Though she did have the air of authority I recognize in experts, I balked internally with disbelief. There have been such gruesome tomes in history, yes, but for it to be here in this place was a surreal idea I pushed away for the moment. That being said, I have kid leather gloves and leather-bound books, so perhaps I'm just being stubborn. Humans are animals, too (I have no illusions we're any better than the so-called lower primates, and likely we're something worse).

Wendy kept going, some color returning to her cheeks as she spoke. "The ink resembled dried blood—a dark reddish brown, but mixed with something else. I don't know what, but it was vibrant and easy to read. It wasn't fresh, that much was obvious. I decided to get it to GCU for proper dating as soon as possible.

"Anyway, I had luck while looking at the pages. Some of it was in Albionian. By the style of Albionian and the use of calligraphy and artistic style of the drawings, I narrowed the age of the book to be from somewhere between 1050 and 1080."

What Wendy was saying was akin to her speaking a foreign language—I was never a fantastic history student, as my friend Mercy would attest. I switch dates and forget details about wars and politics. I can retain information about diseases all day long, and even quote history of the diseases, but for other items like that, I lose interest. Her education and area of expertise was enough to convince me it was fact. At least the date part of it.

Wendy was a master linguist even before she went to graduate school. She didn't state that outright. I speak some languages other than Albionian—Francian, Alsatian, and Nipponese (enough so that I can get around Nippon without a translator), but this woman claimed to be fluent in *ten* different languages. It wasn't possible to verify it at that moment, but I'd seen it before.

I didn't hide my shock—my jaw dropped and my eyebrows shot up my forehead. "Ten languages, *fluently?*"

Wendy laughed and raised a weak hand to wave it at me, dismissive. "It's not that impressive. My father was from Thule, and my mother's from Rus Soyuz, and they spoke several languages themselves. I enjoyed speaking three languages before age six—Albionian, Rusyan, and Thulish—and children's brains are sponges. I picked up languages with relative ease and loved speaking and reading them. Now I've incorporated Union Sign Language into my languages—speaking with my hands."

I nodded. "USL is a good language. Useful," I said. "I've been meaning to pick it up when I get the chance."

My upbringing was similar to Wendy's. Father spoke Albionian and Alsatian, and mother spoke Francian and Albionian. Those languages learned early in life made it easier to learn more as I got older though Nipponese has been a challenge.

Wendy rested a moment, though physically tired, her eyes were glinting with excitement. She took a sip of water, seemed to gather herself, then continued. "By the time I got to college, I spoke six languages, and by graduation, ten. I'm just glad I put my talent to work in linguistics." She shrugged and gave me a soft smile.

I would say the woman was a genius.

"But this language was odd. There were no base similarities to any language I knew from which I might extrapolate." Wendy frowned as if the memory was aggravating her. "Nothing close to Shenzhouan, Rusyan, Thulish, Alsatian, Albionian, Mashriqic, nor any other one

I spoke. The Albionian wasn't helpful, either, as it contained just random words such as 'wheel,' or 'reach.' Just enough to give me a clue to the dates due to the spelling. Some of the longer sentences were Albionian translations of events that came before and sometimes while the book was being written."

"That must have been frustrating," I said, unsure if she wanted me to react or was just taking a break. When I spoke, she nodded and relaxed. She was checking to see if I was still listening. I sat forward.

"I was getting frustrated with it and wrote it off as nonsense," Wendy said. "Just a hoax or something that a historical joker wrote."

She sighed and shook her head. "Tired, and feeling as if I might have been the butt of a thousand-year-old joke, I took a break from it for a while and contacted fellow linguistic gymnasts for a consultation. I gave three of them different pieces—copies—of the work so that none would claim it as their own discovery. Many people would say that's just paranoid, but I've seen it happen before. I was being cautious. You know how it is."

I nodded. "The more competitive the school, the more they would steal from each other and claim as their own. Healthy paranoia, in that case—you won't have to stay for that."

She chuckled.

So she separated out the scraps. Now when I say they're scraps of a journal, that's my Albion tongue and gift of understatement. I've lived in The Union for many years now, so I've changed the way I use grammar and spelling. I still retain some of Albion's quirks, though, and my accent remains unaffected. That won't change. I have to hang onto something of the place that once was.

These scraps were, according to Wendy, quite a tome with over two hundred pages.

"Although several were missing and looked as though they'd been cut out of the book," she said. "But rather than take that as a setback, I took it in stride and was even more determined to translate the pages. That would help me figure out what the missing pages might have said."

I sat back again and rested my chin in my hand, chewing on my lower lip. As she was talking, I decided to take down some notes while the recorder caught what Wendy was saying.

This isn't a fanciful woman. Now that she's coherent, I can observe just how intelligent, driven, and well-grounded she is, in spite of her excitement. She is a tenacious spirit, unfettered by even this harrowing setback that landed her in hospital. She seemed to suffer from some mania when she first came in, with flight of ideas and pressured speech, but she is unlike the other manic patients I've seen in my career in the emergency room. She became grounded faster and doesn't seem to have difficulties keeping to one subject after sedation. Many I've seen still have those problems even after sedation.

I looked back up at her and put my tablet away. She kept talking.

"I set to work deciphering the language once I did a little background research and found comparison words to Aramaic. My colleagues found comparisons to Sanskrit and Thracian. When they returned their findings, I could translate quicker. As I worked, it appeared to be that these were spells, chants, and recipes of some sort. Dark and cruel, by far some of the worst things I'd ever read that weren't fiction."

Wendy leaned forward to take another sip of water. For a moment, her hands shook, but she took a deep breath and seemed to steady herself.

"One was a spell to raise the dead," she said. "That was one of the tamer ones. It reminded me of the horror movie about the Necronomicon."

I must have made a face at that because she sighed, slumping her shoulders. "You don't believe me."

I shook my head. "I do, but it's foreign to me. The book—I know it exists—it was at the Grace City Museum before someone stole it, but what it claims is outrageous."

Wendy's face went from pinched to relaxed, more confident I didn't dismiss her belief in it, rather it was my personal reaction to the book's concept. I am a scientist and have seen many dead people. They don't just come back. Sometimes they sit up during rigor mortis, but they're not going anywhere.

Nothing brings back the dead. Perhaps I've brought people back with CPR, but they weren't far gone, and there was still something to resuscitate. This spell, however, brought people back from underground, their half-rotten, embalmed corpses sloshing their way through six feet of dirt and soil, somehow without breaking their rotted fingers off. I could laugh at it but only because it's impossible.

"So you said that there were other spells that were worse?" I asked. My interest was in her story rather than the tome, but it was up to Wendy how to tell it.

"Yes," she said. "The other spells, I found, were more unusual and unnerving. One of them had illustrations along with instructions on how to bring down the powers of the Timeworn Order with sacrificial children." Her face was a little pale again.

"Do you want to stop for now? Take a break?" I asked, shifting in my chair to get up and give her respite. She shook her head.

"No. I need to tell it. I can't keep this inside any longer." Wendy punctuated each sentence banging a weak fist against her leg.

I called in the nurse to bring her some food and coffee, and gave her some money to get me a snack from the vending machine. The break would do me some good, too—I could feel the inner quakes of low blood sugar.

It gave me time to reflect. That anyone believed it in the first place was unnerving. How many children were murdered because of a belief? The images my mind brought forward—of little innocent bodies piled up while believers worked themselves into an orgiastic frenzy to raise deities who didn't exist made me want to take a power drill to my skull. Even the mind's eye wants to stop seeing such things, and yet, the more one tries not to pay attention, the more those images flood the mind. The brain is a cruel thing sometimes.

Food services came, and the RN came in with my snack bar. I thanked her and told her she saved me from passing out on the floor.

Wendy picked at her meal. "I have to say I didn't believe it, either, and it made my stomach clench thinking that people would do something so horrific. But I continued to translate, and as most translations go for me, I was getting better and faster at it as I went along, finding more and more commonalities among each spell, chant, incantation, and some gruesome recipes that made me want to vomit."

I didn't ask. I ate my granola bar and checked the recorder to make sure it was still working.

Wendy kept going after looking at me to see if I'd say anything. "One 'recipe' required severed baby fingers from a newborn. That disturbed me the most."

In the ER, I have witnessed some of the worst child abuse imaginable. I wished I could go back in time and take this tome with me so I could shove it sideways up the author's arse. I put down my half-eaten granola bar and tried to hold what I'd eaten down. The gore didn't upset me. What upset me was the thought of long-forgotten infants and bereaved mothers. They must have been beside themselves when the feverish believers cast those spells. In my mind's eye, they tore at their dresses and wailed over the dead newborns with their missing fingers, faces twisted in gray grimaces.

Wendy wanted to move along. "One chant was to be done to get money, fast. Seemed innocuous enough," she said. "It promised riches without consequence, in exchange for a night with Undaga. Undaga of the Underworld. I didn't know who that was. I can only assume it's one of the Timeworn Order, but I'm no cultist and I never studied religions of any sort. So I laughed it off. Spend one night with that guy for untold wealth without consequence? Too funny. I kept working through the translations."

She took another bite of her food, finishing the tray except for a few bites, and set it aside. I put my re-wrapped granola in my lab coat pocket and gave Wendy my full attention.

"I made a dent in the translations—about fifteen out of two hundred different passages, when I call from Grace City General back home. My mother had fallen down the stairs and broken her hip."

I gave her a grim nod. "At an advanced age, that can be a death sentence."

"True. Mother was eighty-seven, and her prognosis wasn't good. I left for a short while, with the tome in a safe at my rented place. I'd had gotten far enough into the translations to be obsessed with it, but not enough to take it with me and risk losing any of the pages."

Obsession was her word, not mine, although I would agree that it was accurate.

"I spent all of my waking hours with it, and there were times I forgot to eat. I lost weight—twenty pounds in, well, I don't know how long. Even when visiting my mother in the ICU, it was all I dwelled on and talked about to my brothers. I mean, I was concerned about her health and her care, but my mind would travel back to the book and everything it offered—to further my career and helping me advance in academia."

"I'm glad you said that," I said. "For a moment, there, it sounded like you meant you obsessed over the spells and what they offered."

Wendy gave a chuckle that sounded more like a resigned sigh. "Oh, no, not exactly. The spells were fascinating—I was a bystander looking at a pile up, I suppose."

I nodded. "Gruesome, but fascinating. I understand."

"My mother recovered, but needed a great deal of physical therapy and home health care. The bills for the whole family were piling up after the long hospital stay. Union Care only covers so much and there are several extras that can only be covered through private insurance or out-of-pocket. She had extra coverage, but you know that the in-home services she needed were huge and they didn't cover everything. The co-pays are insane on some of them."

"Union Care is getting better now, but it takes time for things to change, and for costs to come down," I said. "But that hurt you when you needed it."

Money was something I never worried about, coming from a fortunate family. That didn't mean I was oblivious to the struggles of others though.

Wendy said the amount owed was in the hundreds of thousands. That was for ICU, surgery, ER, the physical therapy, all the pharmaceuticals from beginning to end, and the visiting nurses. Unsurprising—the costs pile up so fast.

Her mother was distraught, not knowing how she would afford the payments and be able to stay in her home. At that point, she couldn't afford to go into a convalescent home, either. Not on her daughter's meager stipend.

"My poor mother was recovering, but she was worried and depressed. My brothers tried to help with some of the bills, but their jobs didn't pay enough to support her and their families. You know Grace City's expensive. So, while at home with her, a pile of bills, and my stress mounting by the minute, I decided that spending a night with Undaga and getting money might not be a bad idea."

I held back a laugh and kept my face neutral by taking in a deep breath, turning my head, and swallowing hard, which hurt enough to keep me in line. Wendy seemed so sincere in her storytelling I couldn't laugh. With her stress as it was, it was understandable.

Crazy ideas come to people when they're desperate, and the whole family was getting desperate. They weren't rich—just a middle class family on a downward slope. It was that fact which kept me sober, along with the pain in my throat.

Things like that are the reason I donate to charity. I work because I enjoy it, but I realize that so many people hit rock bottom through no fault of their own, and that's where Wendy's mother was. It was only natural that her daughter would want to help.

"I laughed at myself for believing in the tome's power in the first place, and moved on when it didn't work," Wendy said, upper lip curling into a snarl. She looked out the window of her room, then back at me, eyes glossed with tears. I handed her the box of tissues in case she needed them, but she set them aside.

"I was bitter about it. It wouldn't have meant anything to spend a night with whatever it was to save my family, and I suppose it was a childish fantasy, but I needed it to be real. I needed magic."

She sounded like a child pleading for food and I fought the urge to whip out my checkbook and ask her how much she needed.

Wendy took out a loan on her house in Grace City. After contacting the bank back home, she filled out an application and took a second mortgage out on her place. That raised about half the money she needed. She paid what she could and negotiated with the accounts receivable departments to cut some of the charges to get the bills to come down.

"I was lucky to have a house." She slumped over again and took a deep breath. "Most people don't even have that. But Dad left me some money for a down payment, so I'm glad I went for it."

While the bills went down, they still owed more than they had. The collection calls stopped for a while.

Days passed, filled with disillusioned translations, but not much else. No sign of Undaga. Where was he? Why did he not come when summoned? Did she actually believe he would show?

That's the human condition, or at least part of it—to get caught up in magical and fairy tale solutions. It happens to everyone. Even to a hard scientist (now and then). I even wonder about the divine sometimes—in the pantheist sense. That kind of god makes much more sense than a bevy of ancient gods or a saint that interacts with human beings. Then I realize it's just my mind trying to make sense of the world, seeing patterns in chaos. That's all.

No, I won't lie. I've prayed to any Gods that might be listening. 'Please, nothing else is working, save this patient.' Desperation forces our hands, and makes us try things we've never dreamt.

Sometimes my prayers are answered with such an exactness I almost can't write it off to coincidence. Perhaps the Universe is intelligent, but I doubt it. I still think I'm just a primate seeing patterns where none exist.

While all that philosophy and theology is a fascinating exercise in futility, Wendy had real problems on her mind with no real solutions on the horizon. The collectors calling and harassing Mother Willow weren't going to go away. They loomed over the mother and daughter. Wendy needed a way to pay her mother's remaining debts.

"So while I'm translating, I discovered that the money spell was only half finished." Wendy looked over at me with her mouth half-turned up in a grin.

"First, you have to gather some different ritual items," she said. "Chalk, black powder, and blood, and then gather a small amount of the common currency. The chalk is used to draw a kind of ritual circle, and the black powder forms a sigil: a circle with four compass points and a dot in the center. From there, five drops of blood are placed in the middle of the sigil.

"There is then a chant to be repeated three times while walking clockwise," she said, but didn't describe the exact words. In fact, she hesitated so long when she came to that part, I leaned forward to see if she was beginning to have a seizure. But her freezing hadn't been for medical reasons. Wendy did not wish to repeat the words. I don't understand why—it could be they intimidated her, or she did not want to share them with me for other reasons. As if I might try them.

In the dim light of the bedroom, I sit here, still thinking about her story as I type out this journal entry. The silence of the house, interrupted only by the pops and creaks of a settling foundation might give someone more superstitious reason to be unnerved. Why she would think I'd try magic is beyond me.

"The money spell," Wendy said, tracing one slender fingertip across the rim of her cup. "That fell on its face, and I was about to write it off when I discovered a page shoved into the back of the book. It was the other half to the spell. Because of this, I didn't know what to do with the currency." She paused. "It only appeared in the ingredients section."

"I'm assuming it's like some strange recipe book," I said. "That's sort of what it sounds like; and a rather morbid one, at that."

"Yeah," Wendy said. "It does kind of read like a recipe book. It lists the tools and ingredients needed, and then the instructions to carry out the spell." She shrugged. "But the currency—I thought it was a mistake. There it was on the list, but no mention on what to do with it when I finished. So I left it aside the circle and continued the ritual. I knew nothing about spells, so I never suspected it was incomplete. What a difference a missing page made."

I held up my hand to halt her for a moment. "How did you find the missing page in the back? I mean, did you skip to the end or something?"

Wendy shook her head and chuckled. It wasn't a joyful sound. "No—it was just an accident. I was picking it up before going to bed. See, with the special collections, you have to handle these things with respect—dry hands or while wearing white cotton gloves. When you wear the gloves, you have to watch out not to put too much pressure on the pages if they're paper. I was tired, and I grabbed the book by the spine which I shouldn't have done. Anyway, that's when the back opened and the page fell out. I could have slapped myself for my carelessness, but it was undamaged. That was lucky."

She heaved another sigh. "'Lucky,' I say. At the time I thought it was lucky. Just the same, sleep was no longer an option once I made that discovery, and I translated the missing page."

Wendy discovered that one is supposed to create a small fire in the circle, and burn the currency once the chanting is done, then invoke Undaga to come and take the exchange. Untold riches for one night with Undaga. That was all.

"I felt recharged by my discovery and that magical thinking crept back into my head. I had no expectations it would work—except for that little voice of false hope inside. You know, it was almost just for fun, and hey, if it worked, so much the better, right?"

"We all give into superstition and wishful thinking when we're pushed into a corner," I said, putting as much sympathy into my voice as I could. My voice is often cold and unfeeling, and Wendy didn't need that from me. So I tried to soften my edge as best I could, and when she didn't recoil, I saw I had done well enough.

"Right. That's what I thought it was, just wishful thinking. Well, nothing came about for about three days," she said. "The weekend passed, and Monday came, and I figured whole ritual or not, it was worthless. Perhaps a long time ago, these incantations meant something, but now, the old magic meant nothing. I put that foolishness away and made plans. Although this time, I didn't know where to get more money. There were only so many things I could do to raise funds."

She'd translated about half the tome by now, and Wendy's mother was in need of more hospital care. That meant more bills, and the bill collectors were harassing the poor old woman again. Things were getting worse, and I suppose that's why Wendy gave that old spell another try.

When people are desperate, they do things that are mad. Some people make deals with the devil, in a manner of speaking. I don't know if I believe in all that—but before I tread the waters of theology once more, it's important to explore what Wendy told me and what I could confirm in reality.

Wendy stopped thinking about it and went on about her translations that Monday night. After a grueling day trying to work things out for her mother, it seemed almost a welcome break, to play with her new favorite obsession.

She stayed up most of the night, going to bed at around 5:30AM. She slept hard until a loud knock at her door around 10:00AM woke her up.

Fuzzy-headed from being stirred, she went to the door and looked through the peephole. No one was there.

Opening up, she looked down to see a rather large package. It had her name and address, but no return address.

"The box was huge, and I didn't think about what could be inside it—I was so groggy. There was no lifting the thing, either, so I had to drag it inside. Made it all the way into the living room before I gave up and went off to the kitchen. Before I did anything else, I needed to clear the cobwebs from my brain so I made myself some coffee. I'm a dimwit in the mornings—there could have been a bomb in that package and I wouldn't have given it another thought."

That made me laugh. "I can relate to that feeling. It's why I prefer night shifts."

"Me, too. I'd rather teach evening classes and work all night, myself." Wendy raised a hand to her shaved head, then stopped, putting her hands in her lap. "Where was I? Oh yeah. I went back to the living room and opened the package."

She mimicked the activity with her hands. "Inside was a beautiful wooden box. Looked like a cherry wood, and it smelled like roses. It was a heavy box, and large. Perhaps the size of a large dresser drawer. On the lid, there was an intricate carving. It was the sigil I'd drawn for the spell was in the center of it. There were additional symbols

I thought looked familiar, but I couldn't quite place. I bubbled with excitement to see it. I giggled when I touched it."

As she contemplated the carvings over the lid, she realized they were not just doodles, but words written all over it, and one of those was Undaga. Another was the word 'gift' and yet another was two words, put together, and Wendy could find no direct translation. She wrote it down and referenced her notes. She discovered, the first word was 'friend'—which is what her first name means. The second word was her last name's meaning (which I am keeping confidential, it wasn't Willow).

"Sounds like the box was made just for you," I said. She gave me a narrow-eyed look.

"You sound like you don't believe me."

I shook my head. "It's not that I don't believe you— it's just that it sounds incredible, Wendy."

She sighed. "Yeah, I know it does. I have moments where it doesn't seem real. I wouldn't believe it either if it hadn't happened."

"If you think it's true, then that's good enough for me," I said. Anything else might shut her down, and I needed to hear what she had to say.

That seemed to be the right choice because her face relaxed and she slipped back into her story.

The box was not something she could remove from its outer packaging due to the weight, so she had to cut it apart to remove it.

"I dragged it to the center of the living room and opened the top. In it was—as I'm sure you've guessed by now—bundles and bundles of money. All in large and small denominations."

I held back a huge sigh because I promised to be opened minded—but it was almost too predictable. It had to have been an elaborate delusion. I couldn't accept it as anything else. Scratch wounds or no, this woman must have had an encounter with a wild animal while in a manic state, and her mind invented an elaborate story to protect her. Any other explanation would have been supernatural, and complete nonsense.

That had to be what it was. Those who experience mania, and bipolar disorder, are just as bright, and as stupid, as those who don't have those problems. They come in a wide variety of intelligences and backgrounds. Wendy was intelligent. I confirmed she could speak all those languages with some doctors and nurses I found who spoke the languages she claimed to know, and she was a fellow of the University—a quick internet search revealed her affiliation.

Another point of interest I confirmed, however, and found rather disturbing was that she had no history of mental illness. This bothered me because at her age (she was in her thirties), bipolar and/or depression have shown up by then (in most cases). It can happen late—but that's rather rare. There are often hints at it even before an official diagnosis.

That fact still disturbs me at this writing. She claimed no family history of mental illness, either, and though she might have been prevaricating, I can't imagine what she would have thought to gain by doing so. Perhaps more credibility to her story, but I cannot say for certain.

"So what happened?" I asked. Even though I remained skeptical, there was more.

"I felt like my heart had stopped and couldn't catch my breath. The only sounds in the room were the sounds of me gasping for air and the grandfather clock ticking behind me, which seemed like it was louder than ever. I've never seen that much money in one spot. I mean, we weren't poor when I was growing up, but there were piles of it in there."

Here she paused and looked out the window again, eyes glassy with tears she blinked away. I sat in silence.

She took a block of funds out, closed the lid, and examined it. It was a bundle of $20,000.

On a whim, a crazy whim, she'd said, she bought herself a bunch of new clothing. That suggested a late onset of bipolar disorder had occurred, due to the impulse spending. Then, she went home, and checked back in the box to see if it was still all there, minus her block.

It was. She had about eight million dollars; somewhere around that amount. It was all legitimate currency, as far as she could tell—FDR on the hundred-dollar bills, and Woodrow Wilson on the fifties. The threads of blue and red fibers in the paper and the hologram on the back all intact.

"That's a huge amount. No wonder you couldn't lift the box." I guess I must have sounded less skeptical because she remained relaxed.

"I know." She brushed an imaginary hair from her forehead and shook her head. "It was insane. I couldn't believe my good fortune."

Her demeanor wasn't excited, as I thought it would be, but that could have been an effect from the sedative.

"I was about to faint from hyperventilating," she said, then took a drink of water. "But I stayed conscious and thought about what I needed to do with the money."

She contacted her mother's debt holders, paid for her expenses, and set her up with a private nurse. The elderly woman's health care came to a little over a million dollars.

Wendy bought the home outright, donated a large amount of money to her favorite charity, and spent the rest on herself, paying off her mortgages. The sum of the money in the crate was around five million dollars after she settled her and her familial debts.

How could I believe her?

"I consulted an accountant," Wendy said. "I wanted to pay my taxes on it like legitimate income. He helped me through the process, citing things that I didn't understand as the source of my income—related to unclaimed inheritance, blah, blah. I paid my taxes, and he set up accounts for me to use at my discretion."

There was one thing I could fact check now—the money.

I have a good friend (former companion) who works for the Tax and Revenue Service. I contacted him. After a few minutes of banter about how he never got to see me anymore, and how we must get together some time, he was happy to give me the information.

Her taxes the year before reflected a graduate student struggling to pay her bills. She made around $58,000 that year (which in Grace City, isn't enough to afford anything). The following year—the year she was telling me about, saw an increase in her tax bracket. She was a millionaire.

"Where did all this money come from?" I asked my friend.

"According to the paperwork, she made all of this money in 'investments—after a found inheritance,'" he said. "That was quick. Should I go in and audit?"

As much money as I have, I know better. You don't invest a few hundred dollars and become a millionaire overnight. This isn't cinema. It takes longer than that unless you invest a lot more money into it, or hit something that booms, which is rare. At any rate, it takes thousands to get to that level. Hundreds of thousands depending on the market. "No, darling. I'm sure it's legitimate. Behave yourself."

He laughed. "Only for you, Mistress."

"Ha-ha." We parted with cordialities and I sat there, gathering my thoughts.

So there was a hard fact to support her claim—something legitimate. I suppose it could have been a gift from a benefactor and admirer (a real one, not a mythical beast), but that's just speculation on my part. Perhaps she received an inheritance which she invested. That could happen. But why concoct such a story?

I figured a psychotic break was to blame. Yet she seemed lucid in every other way. This tale seemed to be the exception to the reality rule.

So in the harsh fluorescence of Mercy Hospital, the smell of antiseptic and the steady beeping of monitors in other rooms, I sat by her bedside and listened to her tale continue.

"Doctor Cross?"

"What is it, Wendy?"

"You seem like a lady who has a lot of money. Like your accent is from the nicer part of Albion, and your clothing is expensive. I mean, I know it's rude to point out stuff like that, but I can just kind of tell when people were born into money. You were. You carry yourself like it."

I shifted in my chair, tensing up in my shoulders. "I guess so."

"It's not a bad thing, Doctor," she said, sitting up a little. "You can't understand what it's like to struggle and then, well, just not have to anymore."

I nodded. "No, I've never experienced it myself, but I have empathy for it."

"I'm glad. But you must know how it feels to have pressure on you if you're from Albion."

This was territory I didn't wish to explore. "Right," I said. "But enough about me. Tell me more about how things changed for you. How you got here."

Wendy nodded. "I wanted to let you know that I get where you're coming from, and that I'm glad you get me, or are trying to, anyway."

"Well, that's kind of you." I shifted around in my seat.

"I was living the high life. Without having to worry about finances, I could devote all my time to translation of the tome. All that money helped, and I was obsessed even before that happened, but having things come to fruition just fueled me forward. I don't know what's worse than obsession, or greater than obsession, but I had it."

There was that feverish look in her eyes again. Just for a moment.

"I was comfortable enough to get rid of the second job and focus on my duties as a lecturer at the University and on my dissertation. Now I one of the lucky ones—and I invested a large chunk of the money, kept the rest in bonds and savings, and lived off the interest. I got to do what most people in my position can only dream about, and I didn't take it for granted. This opportunity let me dedicate myself to my passion, and I immersed myself in the tome."

But she kept some of the pages to herself. The useful spells like money spells. She also continued to treat it as if it were a work of pure fiction and myth, written by magi who believed the spells to be true. At least to the outside world.

That seemed almost a hint of reality peeking though. She knew it was a ridiculous notion, this supernatural nonsense, and I believe that perhaps she recognized she had gone mad, and knew to hide it from others.

"Did your mother or siblings ever question you on your sudden windfall?" I asked.

"Yeah, they did," she said. "I told them the same story we did with the Union Revenue Service. I'd taken a 'nest egg' of vague origins and invested it. Then I gave them gifts and helped paid their bills. That stopped their questions."

Denial is a powerful tool for people. They can sit there with something obvious right in their faces, but if they don't want to see it, they won't. They'll construct an entire reality around that denial. All of us go to great lengths to deny objective reality when it doesn't fit into our comfortable scheme of things. Even me.

Now, back to Wendy's tale.

"For a long time, I carried on with my life, forgetting having to spend a night with—with him." She swallowed hard and let out a deep breath. "The texts had led me to believe it would happen soon after the money, but since it didn't happen, well, I figured that part was just a myth to scare people from using such a powerful spell. If that was the case, people must have feared that god, or demon, a great deal."

Wendy shrugged. "After nine months and no Undaga, I relaxed." She winced at speaking his name. "I went back to my translations and got to an entire chapter of the tome dedicated to these demons mentioned throughout the many spells and incantations. One section was devoted only to Un—Undaga." Her breath hitched on the name again, but she spoke it without wincing so hard this time. Her hands shook, and she gripped her cup of water to steady them.

"I laughed when I read his description. The pages described him as a tall, slender man with no face—just like the modern Slender Man urban legend. You've heard of that, right?"

I grimaced. "Yes I have," I said, trying to cover a shudder. I had a terrible encounter with two children in the ER in Grace City who got carried away with the urban legend and one stabbed the other multiple times. The kid survived, and his 'friend' went to juvenile detention. "He's quite a popular made-up figure. Something awful."

Wendy nodded. "Terrible, even. The translation also described how many times he had shown up throughout the history of the lost culture. This guy was like every other urban legend—told by the friend of a friend of a friend who saw him firsthand. That kind of thing. I shrugged it off. This was just a simple, but ancient, folk legend used to scare people into obedience, keep thieves away, and protect secrets."

She shrugged. "I knew it had worked, the spell came to fruition, and there were no signs of the demon."

After a few weeks, things got harder for Wendy.

"Nothing good lasts forever, right?" Her brows knitted, and she put one hand to her forehead. "About a month later, my mother died. This wasn't unexpected, you know? But it was a difficult time for me. I still had a chest full of money and provided a good service for her. That was the normal part. That was the only thing that was normal, but I grieved too hard to think about it in any depth. The weird part was the phone call from Grace City Coroner I got. Well, that's where the weirdness started. And yeah, weirder than what had just happened."

I nodded, trying to show her I understood and was sympathetic. The GC Coroner—another fact I could check.

She told me his name. An old colleague of mine, in fact. That made it easier.

"He called to let me know that my mother had died clutching a piece of paper and pencil, and when they wrested it from her hand, they discovered it was a note for me. The coroner said he had read it, because it was his job to investigate, but he knew it was a personal note devoid of meaning to anyone else but mother and daughter."

A single tear slipped down her cheek, and Wendy picked up a tissue. I sat. There is nothing that a person can say to comfort a grieving person. The only thing I could do was listen.

He sent her the note via courier, hand delivered that evening.

After a long space of silence, I gave her a little push. "What did the note say, Wendy?"

She closed her eyes and I thought she might not answer me, but after a moment, she opened them again, and in a shaking voice, recited it as though verbatim. "Wendy, I have met Undaga. He will collect his debt soon. Love, Mother."

I felt my jaw drop and snapped it shut. I shivered. Despite my disbelief, it was still a chilling tale.

"Yeah. That was my reaction, too," Wendy said, pointing with her chin in my direction. "You can imagine this gave me the shivers, too. I just about pissed myself, in fact. How in the world could Mom have known about Undaga? I never mentioned him, not even once. I still hate saying his fucking name. Even then I didn't like it."

"It sounds like an exotic disease," I said.

"Huh, I suppose it does." Her tone was cold. "But I told no one about him. That'd just make me look like I was bonkers, and would cause a scare for nothing. I talked about some of my translations, but naming any of the demons? My family wouldn't have given a shit. Excuse my language."

I waved her off. "I've heard worse."

"The more I told them of my discovery the more they wanted me to shut up about it, anyway, so I know I didn't mention him."

I nodded. "Why would you?"

"Right."

But this wasn't something the woman could shake off with ease. This was her mother having knowledge of something she shouldn't have, and to let her know—to warn her, of an impending collection. A night with Undaga.

"All that week, I couldn't sleep," she said. "I kept the lights on and tried to figure out ways to protect myself—brought a knife from the kitchen and put it on the nightstand so it was within reach at all times. I slept in jaunts—just an hour at a stretch. It would exhaust me and I'd fall asleep, only to pop up an hour later with my heart racing and feeling like there was something in the room with me. I'd stay that way for about ten or twenty minutes, then crash again."

"Sounds like a classic nocturnal panic attack." I should have kept that to myself so she wouldn't think I was doubting her story, but Wendy nodded.

"I'm sure it was. It felt like *he* was around every corner just waiting for me."

She fidgeted, tapping the side of her cup, then poured herself more water. Tap, gulp, sip. Tap, gulp, sip.

"Well, I forgot all about doing the translations, called out from my obligatory lectures, leaving it to the TA to take over for me. Since I had plenty of money in the wooden box, and I used that to my advantage, and became a shut-in. I had my groceries delivered, and I never ventured out, I didn't even answer the door. Not until I was sure it was just the delivery guy and all that. I took a leave of absence from work and hired an attorney over the phone to do all the paperwork for me. My mentor tried to look after me, but I gave him the brush-off. I told him I was grieving and needed time to myself. He was sympathetic and told me to contact him whenever I needed something. I promised I would."

There wasn't much I could offer, so I nodded for Wendy to continue.

After a moment, she did. "I didn't care and had no plans to call him," she said. "I wasn't going to let this demon get me. At that point I was beyond doubt. I was in danger, and there was no other explanation for it."

"How did you know you were in danger?" I asked. "I mean, I know you said all that about his appearance, but it was just spending a night with him, right?"

"Would *you* want to do it?"

I gave her a wry chuckle. "No. I guess not. He's not sounding like my type."

"Well, that was part of it, but when I read that chapter about him—about what he does—what he was—I knew it was a threat."

Right. She said nothing specific, and she didn't talk about that part any longer. I wouldn't push her further.

"So after everything I'd studied I was sure that leaving my house would be the one way he'd get me. So it became my sanctuary. The safety zone. My fort."

"Supernatural or not, you thought it was some kind of safe ground," I said, just to show her I got it and she needn't keep repeating herself.

In my career, I have seen agoraphobia develop with patients in short periods of time, and if allowed to continue, it can become a lifelong problem. Wendy seemed to develop multiple mental disorders from this incident. Checking the locks on her doors and windows to excess, pouring saltpeter on all access points to the house, and blessing herself with holy water she ordered online from some cult store. I didn't ask. These were all the activities she did five times a day to keep herself safe. Check, pour, bless. Repeat. It was OCD brimming on the horizon.

"How long did this continue?" I asked.

"About three weeks," she said. "I'd never been a shut-in before, and even though I was still paranoid and fearful, I had cabin fever. You know it's bad when you go online and stare at a blank page for five minutes. I couldn't amuse myself and I wouldn't leave, so I negotiated."

At this point I asked her if she wanted a break, but she shook her head.

"I'm good for now. Anyway, I tried taking a shower and cleaning the house. That didn't help. I played spider solitaire. Got bored after a few hands, and didn't feel like playing any of the other games. I looked at the tome, but I couldn't put my head to doing translations. I compromised by opening the patio door out back and letting fresh air inside. If that worked out, then maybe I'd venture out into the yard for a while."

"That was brave of you," I said. "Most people who are that scared wouldn't have dared."

She shrugged. "I wasn't good at being that scared. This was the worst I've ever been."

I checked the recorder to make sure it was still working. Satisfied everything was in order, I told Wendy to continue.

"The air was cool but not too cold, and there was this gentle breeze wafting in from the wide-open door. I set myself up with a sleeping bag, a plush futon mattress from my guest room, and a bucket of ice to hold my sodas. With some soothing music playing on my sound system, I just sat there, enjoying the summer air and watching the sun set—the light in the sky changing from bright blue to washes of gray, lavender, pink and gold. It looked like there were gold bars against layers of cotton."

"Sounds poetic."

"It really was. One of the best summer nights, you know, where the North Wind won't let you burn."

I sighed out of contentment at the mental picture. Wendy did, too.

Then her face turned from relaxed by the memory to a pinched expression again.

"So I closed my eyes, trying to regain my sanity. I knew this wasn't normal behavior, even though I couldn't seem to stop myself. I was losing *me*. Reality slipped away. Once when I was a little girl, I was out west and there was an earthquake. That's how my mind felt—swaying out of control and the earth was opening to swallow me whole."

Another tear trailed down her face and she brushed it off with a hasty hand. "All I wanted was to go back to the translations and get my dissertation ready. It would feel normal to be standing in front of a class of a hundred people, discussing the various linguistic procedures used to translate ancient texts. I would love to feel normal again, not a prisoner in my living space."

She cleared her throat that was threatening thickness with tears. "That's when I felt as though something was watching me."

Her hand moved to her chest. "My heart hammered, and I figured I was freaking myself out over nothing. So I dared myself to open them. The world came back into focus, and—there he was."

Wendy closed her eyes again. She didn't want to look at me and see the skepticism reflected there—which I'm sure it was. My eyes are a light shade of blue, and they look hard and cruel, some (brave) people tell me.

She continued talking, avoiding my gaze. "This man—no—this thing—it had a face, but he fit the description of Undaga otherwise. The face was the worst part. I'd almost rather he'd looked like Slender Man in the face than this creepy thing. That *face*."

Wendy shuddered and she stared at me. I kept my face neutral. "He was peeking around the side of the door at me. His face was thin. You know the Jester on the playing cards? Thin like that, with jutting cheekbones, hollow cheeks. He had a mop of floppy, curly brown hair. His nose and chin were long and thin, like dagger points"

Her eyes widened as if she were seeing him right in front of her. "And his eyes—a mix of blue and green with hints of brown in them. That was the most normal thing—the color." She hesitated, hands shaking again. Wendy stopped and took a drink of water.

"They—his eyes were open wide, as if he had no eyelids. But I knew it couldn't be because he had long, curly eyelashes. Yet he didn't blink. He just *stared.* He stared and stared, with a huge, wicked, manic grin spread across his face."

There were beads of sweat breaking out on her forehead, despite the room being cool.

"I thought I should run, but when our eyes met, I felt frozen in place—I couldn't move, scream, or even speak. All I could do was gasp and keep looking into those eyes. I blinked, and that stopped my paralysis. Then I backed away a little, still entranced but not helpless, I guess."

Wendy fell silent again, but not for long. "That's when he crawled into the breezeway, his movements sleek and slow—a demonic humanoid bred into a walking stick. I know that makes no sense, but that's how he moved. Insect like—like his joints were on him the wrong way. He continued with his staring, and that god-awful wide grin, moving in one stick limb at a time. But even as I backed up, I couldn't take my eyes off of him. Not just because he was unusual looking, but his eyes—they seemed to hold me in rapture, unwilling as I was. There was no struggling against the web."

Unblinking and intent as he entered the house, Wendy felt tears stinging her own eyes as she continued to gape at him.

He took her drinks, and then he ran off into the back yard. "Skittered was more like it. He snatched the sodas and dashed off."

She looked at me and chuckled. "Would you believe it?"

I shook my head. "He—took off with your sodas?"

"Yeah. I came out of the trance in a hurry when he did that. I was just stunned and staring at the ice bucket for a minute. I breathed a sigh of relief and my face felt so hot, but my tears felt hotter. Was that it? Was he going to collect something of mine and leave? Did he just want my sodas and nothing more? If that were the case, I'd just leave him cases of soda to take every night."

"No kidding," I said, but her expression changed as she went on, no longer recalling that sense of relief.

"I was shaking all over, and I felt like that couldn't be it, but it seemed to be. I looked outside and couldn't see a sign of him at all, then slammed the door shut, locked it, and went to my bedroom to lie down—I thought I might vomit."

It occurred to me that Wendy could have made all of this up, but I was leaning toward a great delusion and hallucinations. I had some of those myself when Mercy came to visit, though not as elaborate as this.

Wendy kept talking. "I hadn't cried myself to sleep in ages, but that feeling like I might puke was just me holding back tears. I crawled into bed and pulled up the covers, and just let out all my fear, grief over losing my mom, and the relief it might be over."

She shook her head. "I was a fucking idiot. Drifted off almost feeling safe, but in the middle of the night, I heard this weird clicking sound. It was like when a dog's nails aren't trimmed and they run on a hardwood floor. I woke up with his face staring into mine, unwavering grin and stare in place. And he was nude."

I expected her to be tearful again, but she wasn't. She fixed her gaze on me and kept talking.

"I tried to reach for my knife, but that feeling I couldn't move washed over me—it was like gripping a live wire. It was painful but I couldn't let go. But somehow, I *wasn't* paralyzed. Not all over my body. It was more like I felt really weighed down. I could move, but it was like moving through tree sap. A mix of the two. It's—it's hard to explain. I backed away a little but that backfired in a hurry. All it did was give the creature room to leap into my bed and help himself under the covers."

Wendy kept looking at me, her face expressionless, delivering a report rather than telling me about a trauma. I'd seen this before with rape survivors when they're too shocked or they have to tell their accounts so many times. Part of them shuts down so they don't have to feel it again and again.

"The creature—Undaga—had these long, talon-like fingers with razor-sharp claws at the tips. He ripped at my nightshirt, shredding it to bits like you or I'd shred a tissue, exposing my body to him."

She swallowed hard, but not out of excitement or enjoyment, and her eyes looked away from me. She hung her head. I've seen that look in many rape survivors in the ER, too. Shame.

Still, though, Wendy gathered herself and looked up once more. She wasn't looking at me so much as beyond me.

"He eyed me with greed, aiming that repulsive stare at my breasts, stomach, hips, and pelvis. Never taking that grin off his face, and drooling. I felt the hot slime of him fall on my stomach, and I whimpered. I tried to scream, but that small whimper was the loudest noise I could make. The creature paid no attention to my protests— just hovered over me, silent and smiling. He forced himself on top of me, and fighting back was useless. It seemed when he didn't look into my eyes, I could move. It didn't matter though. He was stronger than those stick limbs should have been. He overpowered me with ease. The more I struggled, the harder he got."

I've seen so much aftermath of rape and violence in the ER that her description didn't faze me. She seemed to look at me again as if to check and see if I was being judgmental. I spoke up.

"You don't have to share anything that makes you uncomfortable, Wendy. That being said, Many rape survivors find catharsis in sharing their histories. Whether that's true or not seems to be up to the individual. But whatever you tell me, know that I don't judge you."

That seemed to be enough to give her the power to continue.

"Once inside me, he thrusted, looking into my eyes. I froze again. When I tried to close my own eyes, I couldn't. Couldn't even look away. Something inside me just—I didn't give in, but I sort of relaxed and let it happen. Is that—is that wrong?"

I shook my head and put up my hand in a 'stop' gesture. "No, no it's not. It didn't mean you consented, and it doesn't mean you wanted him there."

Now I think on it, it may have made it worse for her, because she seemed to give up. Her tears fell, and here, as I told her this, she reached out and took my hand. I held it, losing my words. Touch isn't something I do often and I don't get touched often. Here in the Union, it's different, so I try to be good about appropriate pats on the back or a reassuring hand squeeze. I forget though—it's just not part of my particular culture, to touch strangers. Even patients. But I gave her hand a squeeze and let her decide when to let go.

"He drooled on me while he worked at my body, same smile still on his face. I wore his saliva with my tears.

It was—I can't even describe it. Horrid scent, like—like something rotten. And the act seemed to go on forever. I don't know how long he stayed on top of me. I was numb. I didn't even notice he clawed at me. That's weird, right?"

"You were in shock," I said. "It's not so weird. The pain from being entered by force may have distracted you from the other injuries. That, coupled with the amount of adrenaline from the fear you had could have dulled your other sensations."

I had stitched up her scalp, neck, and shoulders myself while she was unconscious—she had to have been in shock for her not to realize what was happening to her at the time of the assault. There were also puncture wounds on her breasts and near her areola. Another centimeter, and he would have punctured straight through, perhaps removing her nipple.

"When he finished, he came inside of me. That took a long time, too. I don't know if that part was in my head or in reality, but it seemed like forever."

Wendy kept talking when she saw there was no judgment from me. "Then he collapsed on top of me. Grinning still. Satisfied with himself. He grabbed the tatters of my nightgown and wiped off his—his junk. I laid there, shivering and bleeding. That's when his face came away from that grin, and he said just one sentence."

She took a deep breath and her voice changed to imitate him. It was a scratchy, low-toned voice. *"You're mine for eternity, now. Speak my name."*

Wendy twisted the bedsheet in her hands. "I managed to squeak out a weak 'Undaga,' and that was it."

Grinning once more, he left her bedroom. She could hear the tap, tap, tap of his footsteps as walked out the back door, closed it, and disappeared into the night.

"After, I looked down at myself and saw I was bleeding. Blood running down my face. I still couldn't scream, but I could talk, so I called for an ambulance and they found me. Now I'm here. And you're here." She gave my hand another squeeze and let it go. "Thank you for listening."

"You're welcome. I'm grateful you shared this with me," I said. "But I'd like to do a pelvic exam and rape kit if that's okay with you. You don't have to make a police report—that's up to you. We'd hold onto the evidence until the statute of limitations ran out, which here in the Northeast Territory is seven years. In case you change your mind and file charges."

She agreed, but wasn't sure about the police report—she thought it would be impossible to prosecute a supernatural creature.

For me, this was a chance to show her a human being raped her and her mind had fabricated this tale to protect her psyche from the reality that another person was capable of such barbarism. I didn't believe her story—for all I know it could have been a man in a mask or costume of some sort—but *she* believed it.

Once I completed the rape kit, I made a gentle suggestion to her she stay for a psychiatric hold. I wouldn't commit her, because she wasn't a danger to herself or others (she didn't make those wounds by herself), but I thought it would be wise, just in case. To my relief, she agreed. She checked herself in for a psych evaluation, but not because she thought she was crazy.

"I'll be safe here, from him. You don't quite believe me, but I'm okay with that," she said, offering me a wan smile.

"It was real to you. What I think on that subject doesn't matter." That's something I've said more times than I can recall.

Most of the time those who have experienced hallucinations and delusions of this nature are intent on getting other people to believe them. She was calm, accepting of the fact I doubted the veracity of her claims.

After this encounter, I began fact-checking. This wasn't for treatment. I'm not a psychiatrist. I was just curious.

The vast majority of her account is true. I cannot say that Undaga exists anywhere but in her reality, but everything else has proved true. She was translating an ancient text, she took a leave of absence, her mother died, and, as I mentioned before, Wendy handled all of her expenses and more with a sudden upsweep of income.

I'm still waiting on a call from the lab about the test results.

***

3 September

I have the results now from Wendy's rape kit.

Pak from Pathology came up to the ER to see me in person, all apologetic and sheepish looking.

"What's this, then?" I said, unsmiling. "Do you have news for me on the kit?"

Pak nodded. "I—let me first apologize and tell you how I regret it when something goes wrong."

My face pinched to a scowl. "Oh? Walk with me. I need coffee."

We went into the physicians' lounge and I poured myself a cup and sat down. "What happened? And don't mince words. I can't stand it when people just dance around a point."

Pak gave me a small, knowing smile. "I know. I've been working to figure out what's going on but I think we're having a system-wide malfunction. The sample you gave me from the rape kit? It wasn't human. It was spermatozoa, for certain—but the DNA is unlike anything in our database. So—not human or any known animal."

I almost dropped my coffee cup. "What's in your database?"

Pak described it but I was only half-listening. My mind was racing over everything Wendy had told me. Could it be true? No. Not at all. The equipment was faulty. Or we'd made an advancement in zoology.

"So I can tell you only that the sample was contaminated at some point, or our equipment's borked."

I shrugged. "Test your equipment," I said. "The kit could have been faulty, too. Check that. I'm sure I took a clean sample."

"Well recheck everything," Pak said. "I wanted to apologize in person if you were waiting on good results."

I took a sip of coffee and checked a sigh. "It happens."

He left, and I sat there for a while, just sipping my hot drink and trying to reel in my imagination. The sample was bad. Had to be. There was nothing of it left, either. Otherwise, I would have sent it to Father, since he's recovering and looking for things to do. His genomics research and vast knowledge could have answered the question. That's not just familial bias. His two (count them, one two) Nobel Prizes backed up he was the foremost expert in genetic research.

But that's of no consequence now. I can't do a thing about it.

The pathologist blamed the equipment at the lab rather than naming some kind of crypto or mythical creature, or jumping to a conclusion that we were looking at a new species—which made sense. It's what I would have done—made the most logical assumption, given that science tends not to jump to a cryptozoological answer. In training, we're taught that hoof beats mean horses ninety-nine percent of the time, not zebras.

There are plenty of questions raised. The immediate response, from me, was that an old boyfriend or someone she knew attacked her and she couldn't cope with it. She invented this Undaga story (or, more to the point, her *mind* invented the Undaga story) to protect herself from what happened. The machines that tested the semen and fluids in pathology were broken. All of them though?

What if those machines weren't wrong, and something from another world attacked her?

There are just some questions I don't want to answer. I have evidence staring me in the face, don't I? Yet here I am, twisting the facts to fit my reality rather than twisting my reality to fit the facts, right?

No, I'm committing myself to rationality. It's far more rational that a power surge or similar damaged all three machines. I have to be a skeptic. Fall for this, and I could fall for anything.

They need new equipment down in pathology. I'll petition the administrators for special attention their way.

It's late, and I have early morning rounds. For now, I'll try not to think about Wendy, her story, and the dreadful demon from an ancient world.

If I can.

Signed,

Kathryn Cross, MD

***

18 September

It's evening again, and I can't sleep. I wound up pulling a double shift in the ER because one of the other doctors had to attend to a family emergency. Underserved is an understatement around here. It won't improve for a while, I don't think. I'm giving up on hope they'll attract more staff. Also, where is all their funding going? I won't worry about it right now. Perhaps I'll put in a call to a friend at Central Health later.

When I got home, I poured myself a glass of wine and sat down on the couch. Soon, sleep decided it was the most important thing, and I drifted off with the empty glass in hand. There were no dreams. I fell into the void and the glass clattered onto the floor. I heard it, but the soup that my brain and body had become refused to let me get back up to take care of it. The dreamless void soon swallowed me whole.

A loud crack from a thunderstorm woke me up about twelve hours later. For a moment, I felt as if I'd slid off the couch and into a pool of slimy water. But it wasn't water, it was sweat—all over the fleece throw and myself. The place came into focus. I wasn't in my penthouse in Grace City. Lightning flashed, casting heavy shadows on the walls. My stomach complained of hunger with such force it hurt, and I was nauseated.

Or perhaps I drink too much when I'm alone.

I ate a small meal of leftovers, and found there was little else I could think about but ancient texts, demons, and Wendy. Though my body settled, my mind was not so satisfied.

Becoming rather enamored with Wendy's story as of late, I've done a great deal of digging during lulls in the ER (and every break I could finagle). I'm tempted to try the spell in its entirety, but wouldn't dare. Does that mean I believe? No. I'd just feel like a fool doing it.

I've brought my research on Undaga to several scholars, universities, and even Wendy's mentor. There is nothing known about him outside esoteric references, and Wendy uncovered one of the exiguous translations available. He's not mentioned in other texts at all, and those other translations discuss other members of the Timeworn Order, but no mention of that one. At first, I thought perhaps Wendy's imagination invented him in a desperate attempt to save herself from whomever the real perpetrator of that rape was.

Wendy's mentor was next on my list of fact-finding. He was perhaps the easiest to track down of all her connections save for her immediate family.

"I've had a long look at the translations," Professor Alan said. "Undaga would be the closest translation we could make into Albionian for his name, so, no, it's not fabricated. Was Langelier saying that was the case?"

He didn't know why I had paid him a call, other than curiosity about the current work he was doing.

"No," I said. "It was just a personal curiosity as I'd never heard that name before I encountered the SHHS."

I told him my interest was due to my connections with the Silver Hollow Historical Society because I didn't want to give away any of Wendy's confidential information. As far as he knew, Wendy and I weren't acquainted.

He knew Langelier was quite a wind-bag, so he concluded that the man had been gabbing, and I wouldn't correct him. I heard him mutter something and the name Langelier, but what he muttered I couldn't make out. It didn't sound pleasant, though, as little connected with that man is.

"This is an exciting discovery as it's the earliest work that mentions Undaga," Alan said, a tinge of hurriedness in his voice. "The student who made this discovery will go down in history for its significance."

"No doubt."

"There are few later texts that mention him. Only two I've ever seen, and I've been studying the Timeworn Order for almost forty years. Fifty, if you count my fascination as a boy."

I chuckled as he continued talking.

"Both are about a hundred to two hundred years younger than this text. The student found a gold mine."

"Incredible," I said, biting back that he really didn't know the whole story. We said our farewells and concluded our business.

So Undaga is there in the texts. There is no question whether he appeared anywhere else because he did. That still didn't mean he was real, or he somehow came to life to terrorize Wendy.

There's something a little strange about the recording I made of Wendy, too. There was nothing wrong with the recorder at the time. It's a small, digital recorder that I can upload to a secure cloud service we use for medical records. While I was uploading, saving it by patient code, I took a minute to listen to it on my laptop.

Any time Wendy mentioned Undaga, I heard a noise I couldn't identify. The hospital is a noisy place, filled with electronic beeps, boops, and voices over the intercom. The room that Wendy and I were in was a private room, and though I can hear a hiss of ambient noise, this isn't related to anything found in a healthcare setting.

It's a growl, covered in a layer of static.

I have no idea what it is, and I'm not sure how to go about investigating it. But I have other things to concentrate on, rather than some electronic disturbance that may or may not be "unexplained phenomena."

I'm going for a walk and will stop by the Historical Society. I'll write again when I have answers. Or rather, when I have good questions that are worth answering.

-Kit

***

29 September

This past fortnight (short of a fortnight), I decided to dig more, and went back to Wendy. She is still at hospital receiving treatment and doesn't wish to leave just yet. Again, not because she thinks she's mad, but because she believes she's safe.

The patient refuses medication, but is showing no signs of mania nor depression, and is only upset about the attack. She is like any person who has faced a crisis, other than her story of Undaga.

"Do you have a moment?" I asked before entering her room.

Wendy motioned me in, but she seemed more distant this time. I haven't spent all that much time with her, being busy in the ER and all that.

"Sure, as much time as you can spare," she said.

I took a seat. "Would you be willing to tell me more about this Undaga?"

Wendy shook her head. "Why do you keep asking about him? You don't believe me."

"No, I don't believe in the Timeworn Order. They're fairy tales from long ago that people in authority used to control the populace."

She scoffed. "Yeah, that's what I thought, until one of them raped me."

I opened my mouth and closed it again—scrambling a moment for what to say. "I'm sorry, Wendy, that you went through that. I think your mind changed a human being into this demon to cope with what happened to you. I can't blame you for that. It's terrifying to think that a person would do such a thing."

"I can summon him, you know," she said. She was giving me a scathing look. If she'd had something sharp, she would have stabbed me.

This was not going the way I'd envisioned. Wendy was bitter about the incident now that the shock was over. I should have seen that coming. I should have left her alone to grieve what happened to her.

Instead, I pressed. "Is that so?"

"Yes. The text translations told me how."

If Undaga existed, I wanted to see him. Not that this would happen. I tried to hide a scoff at her and instead put one hand up to the back of my neck and gave it a squeeze.

"Perhaps I should just go. You don't seem like you're in a good place right now and I'm not helping."

I stood up to leave. Her therapists would do a better job than I would, and, my curiosity overrode what was best for the patient. The only solution was to get out of there and stop bothering her.

Wendy shrugged. "Tell you what, Doctor Cross. When I'm discharged, I'll send Undaga your way."

I froze and turned around to look at her, raising an eyebrow. "Did you just threaten me?"

She barked a laugh. "No, Doc. You want to see him so much; I'll send him to you. That's all. I'm tired of people not believing me."

I got it. But what did her delusional mind mean by sending him my way? Did I *want* to encounter such a creature? Was she angry enough to summon him and send him to harm me? She thought I didn't believe her, and I suppose she was angry about the incident, so she turned to a target convenient and safe as an outlet—one of her doctors.

"If it's that important to you, Wendy—that someone believes you, then please, send him my way."

"Sorry, Doc—I'm tired." She put her hand to her forehead and rubbed the area between her eyebrows.

"I know, and apologies for disturbing you."

Wendy nodded, and I left.

I'm not a psychiatrist. Right now, I am an ER doctor in a small township who has to clean up messes in my department. I don't have the time, patience, or inclination to work with psych patients other than to toss them in the rubber room when they get out of control. The lot of us are overworked (normal for doctors but double for us). I can't wait to go back to Grace City at the end of October at the latest and never return. I promised myself I'd stay committed to charity work, and help in a rural area with an underserved population. Silly me. The next time I leave, I'm going to Albion to serve the still-struggling country. It will always be my home.

At any rate, I've left Wendy alone for a while, checking up on her through my colleagues and taking peeks at the case notes on her. Been doing that for a while now.

She recovered to where she decided she would be safe. We could no longer keep her in the hospital, despite her insistence upon an ancient demon rapist that assaulted her. That's not dangerous, just delusional. She threatened me for a while, though. When I reviewed the case notes, I found that out. That alone could have been enough to keep her hospitalized, because even though none of us believed her, she could be delusional enough to hunt me down, then blame the demon. Then the threats to send him my way stopped. It's okay to be out of touch with reality these days, so long as no one gets hurt. I won't even start that whole political hornet's nest.

Time for bed. I can't think about this anymore for tonight.

-K.C.

***

3 October

None of this matters anyway, because now I'm one of the nut cases, too. Except I don't believe what happened was real. My mind made it up out of fear and generated by a night of having too much to drink and being alone all too often. Not to mention a possible fungus that has infected my rental home.

Maybe.

Ever since I moved to Silver Hollow for the summer, I have had difficulty getting to know people and making friends. All of my friends—Mercy, Frank, Bryce—they're all at home in Grace City, which is a bursting metropolis in the Northeast Territory. Mercy's there, recovering after her incident. I still feel guilty about that—that I put her in such danger. Perhaps this is my comeuppance.

Life here consists of long walks, visiting the general store (Haverty's) to be stared at like a medical curiosity, workout, and work at the hospital. Bryce was planning to visit, and I was planning not to let him get any sleep.

This is off track but I'm getting around to explaining what happened—whether in my mind or not.

My injuries were real.

I was sitting up in bed awhile after Wendy's discharge, alone with my near-empty glass of red wine in one hand, and in the other, my favorite detective, Sherlock Holmes. Holmes comes to bed with me as often as possible these days. Near the end of *The Hound of the Baskervilles*, I heard a noise outside my bedroom window.

Stupid is not a word I use to describe myself. One, we have wild animals around here, and I've heard them make human-sounding racket outside my house, so I won't just fly off the handle with my shotgun. Two, I didn't bother to inspect it, because it would likely turn out to be a large animal, and what did I care? If it tried to come in the house, I'd shoo it or shoot it if I had to. Simple as that. Unlike some city dwellers, I've never feared animals. I suppose that's because of my summers in the country in Albion. My brother and I encountered so many wild animals there. We knew to keep our distance and observe them.

After Mercy's visit, I wasn't shy about using my shotgun. Plus, if any of the residents got it in their heads it was okay to break into my home, I was ready for them to be surprised. I hate having to shoot a person, but I will if it means protecting myself.

When I looked up, the noise stopped. I strained to listen. No noise. I went back to reading the last three pages.

As I looked back down at my page, the noise started again.

Fantastic.

I got out of bed, grabbed my shotgun off the wall and loaded it (as a woman living alone in a rural area that still gathers a transient influx, I don't think this is paranoid). Then, I walked over to the window and pulled back the curtain, calm as always.

But there was nothing there. Just the bins for refuse and the enormous oak tree that bent in the breeze.

Not stupid enough to open the window's screen and stick my head out of it, I put the curtain back in place, and crawled back under the covers. I set the shotgun down onto the floor (within reach) and picked up my book.

As I finished my reading, I heard the noise again.

I sighed and shrugged my shoulders. It was just a large animal—a deer wandering around looking for a garden to graze or a bear on the hunt for berries. There are black bears around the area but they're people shy unless they're starving. Then they'll march right into one's garden or home and help themselves to the kitchen. In the summer here, Haverty told me, wild animals appearing in people's yards was not a to-do. Though I'd spent time in the countryside as a youngster, I didn't know this was so prevalent (it never happened to us). After a few weeks of being in Silver Hollow, I'd gotten accustomed to the country. Wild animals in the Union still gave me a bit of a scare (the worst we had in Albion was foxes), but I learned that if one leaves them alone, they will return the favor.

    I reclined back on the bed, dimmed the lights, and just listened.

A few crunches, and then silence—not even crickets chirping. But it was getting colder at night, and I supposed the insects and amphibians wouldn't be as active.

I switched on some classical music and settled.

That's when the creaking noise happened.

Just a soft creak as if someone had stepped on a floorboard and disturbed it. Again, living alone makes one vigilant, so I snapped my eyes open and grabbed my shotgun. This wasn't a normal house settling sound. It was just one footstep. Not the little kids noise either—as I mentioned before, sometimes the settling of the foundation sounds like small children's feet pattering across the floor. That wasn't it. This was a deliberate footfall.

The cats are back home, so it couldn't be that. Besides, it had sounded too heavy to be a pet-sized animal. It was more like a man walking in my house.

The thought made my stomach tense up and my flesh tighten, a sensation of little bugs crawling all over my arms and neck.

I sat up and listened for a moment, shotgun in hand. Nothing. When I checked the hall from my open bedroom door, I couldn't see anything.

I turned on my side and raised the lights, then double-checked to make sure my firearm had shells loaded and ready. Paranoid? Yes. But what if I wasn't?

Looking out the bedroom door from my seated position, I kept my gun at the ready. I didn't ask 'who's there?' or say anything aloud, because why give away my location? No. Instead, I waited in silence to see if I would hear it again.

I did. More than once. Creak, creak. Stop. Creak. The noise sounded as though it had reached the top of the stairs.

That was enough to make me come close to weeing myself. My heart rate picked up. I felt the first prickles of fear touch my scalp and work their way down my body, steeling my spine and making my stomach drop.

Weapon aimed at the door, I heard the footsteps get closer. "I have a shotgun aimed right at you, so whoever it is, you'd better get out of here!"

Then, a laugh. A soft, low, deep voice laughing. "Don't shoot," the voice said. It sounded like Bryce.

I got up off the bed and hollered again. "Where are you?" It was far too dark out there and the light from my room was obfuscating the hallway.

"I'm at the top of the stairs. Can I come in?"

I went to the door and saw Bryce standing there. Tall, handsome, black-haired, blue-eyed Bryce. He and his man-jaw and sexy prominent cheekbones. Stupid git.

"What are you doing here?" I said, coming over to him and giving him a hug, my sigh of relief audible. He hugged back and I could smell his cologne, like burning autumn leaves. I inhaled my fill of him as he squeezed me.

"I wanted to surprise you, so I let myself in with my mad lock-picking skills," he said. "But when I got here, I saw something funny hanging around the back window, so I went to look, but there wasn't anything there. Sorry if I scared you." He gave me one more reassuring squeeze back.

"It's all right," I held him close, then backed away and pointed at him. "But you could have been shot, you know."

"I should have known better, but I trust you not to be a hair trigger," he reached out for me and snickered. "I wanted to be spontaneous."

My frown from admonishing him turned back into a soft smile. "Well, I suppose I can't fault you for that."

I forgot all about my earlier grievance. I put the safety on the shotgun, then back on the floor next to the bed, and hopped in, giving Bryce an open invitation. He was enthusiastic. It had been a while for me, and I think so for him too. I didn't care if not, but he's selective about his companionship. Judging by his repeat performances that night, he had been living a monk's life during my absence.

A natural sleep aid, I drifted off in his arms in a matter of minutes after we were uncoupled.

His heart's rhythm carried me off into the darkness. Then, the rhythm changed to a kind of drumbeat. Bryce was not the man in my bed. It was that god-awful monster my mind had built up to be demon from Perdition—Undaga. I was paralyzed underneath him, much the same way that Wendy had described. He tore into my flesh, the pain not registering at first, and then searing and burning came, enough to wake me up.

When I turned over, I expected to be face to face with Undaga, but it was Bryce, his chest rising and falling in a deep sleep. I huffed out a sigh as I relaxed.

I put my head on Bryce's chest and listened to his heart rhythm. The slow, steady, and strong beat of an athlete's heart. It helped to calm my racing one, and still my breathing back into its own quiet pace.

I closed my eyes and took a deep breath. Another. An echoing laugh sounded in my head and I saw a wide grin with crimson lips stretched too far to be human, revealing sharp, serrated teeth, a runner of drool trickling out of the corner. My eyes snapped open, and the image faded. I stared at my lover for a while, watching the rise and fall of his broad chest, the smoothing of his brow, and the tiny twitches in his face as the muscles relaxed. My eyelids drooped, and images of our earlier pairing soothed me back to slumber. Then, on horseback, chasing my brother through the sloping fields of the summer home as we rode towards a lighthouse. The great tower loomed at the edge of a cliff as waves crashed against the rocks, and I was on foot then, running, cutting the bottoms of my feet on jagged rocks as Phillip laughed, pointing to the sky. The sky turned red, and the towering lighthouse caught fire, raining stones down on us.

    A noise cut off my dream and I snapped awake, too accustomed to waking up for emergencies from double and triple shifts at the hospital to be disoriented this time—and perhaps the wine wore off. It sounded the way bones pop when they're broken, or surgical rotation when I cracked open a chest for a quadruple bypass. POW!

I had turned away from Bryce while sleeping and saw my clock read 3:33. When I turned over again to look at Bryce—my gaze met with the smiling face of a beast.

It was, by Wendy's description, Undaga. That appalling, comical grin that stretched out too far across his narrow head. The wide eyes that could almost be human, but were too large. I could make out the tendrils of blood vessels in the whites that looked like cracks of black (not red) lightning running to the bright green irises. His praying mantis, walking stick-like body moved in an insectile way—not human, yet with all the human musculature. The air filled with an odor of decay—old decay, the way it smells when an animal dies in the walls during winter.

The creature was wearing Bryce's clothing from earlier—for a moment. He was far too thin to be wearing his outfit, and slithered out of the clothes with ease, still holding onto me, as if this was a simple task for him. While one spider-like hand (foot?) gripped at me, he shed one side of the clothing, then the other. It was a freakish display of flexibility.

I shrieked and hit him, trying to get him away from me, but he kept hanging on. I found I could struggle against him, not paralyzed as Wendy had described, but he was so strong I couldn't fight for long without getting drained.

"Where's Bryce?" I asked, hollering at him as I tried to push him away. My muscles shook with the effort. No answer. He kept smiling *that smile* at me. Was Bryce dead?

He didn't answer, and then he was inside of me, biting at my chest rather than scratching. The bites were far from love bites, and I was bleeding runners from the wounds, wondering if that decaying smell from his mouth would turn my wounds septic. The pointed teeth were smooth rather than serrated—it was like being bitten with large-bore needles. I squirmed, trying to reach the gun on the floor, but it was no use. Undaga held me fast, and his legs felt like sandpaper against mine. He was unbearably hot, trickles of slime running down onto my body as he moved inside of me. It bit into every nerve, and the only thing I could do in protest was to stare at the clock and count the minutes while he held and bit me. Had he not broken eye contact to bite, I couldn't even have done that. Two minutes became six minutes. Six minutes became ten minutes. I lost track as the smell of decay overwhelmed me and I realized he was coming. My stomach rolled and clenched, and my body filled with a thick, hot slime that was thicker than any male seminal fluid. I gagged, but nothing expelled from me.

When he finished, he put Bryce's clothing back on and left me lying there. I grabbed the shotgun. "Undaga—face me."

He turned those huge round eyes on me, and I fired, the blast from the shotgun making my ears ring. The adrenaline in my body went into overdrive, and I could see every detail of his face as it contorted into something like shock and betrayal. The jaundiced face with the too-wide mouth going pale and turning into a deep frown—the round eyes narrowing into slits of hate. I took my finger out of the trigger guard to resist firing again. He collapsed, bleeding from the chest wound—and I was surprised it wasn't black. Instead, it was just as red and iron-rich as any human's. I turned on the lights and went to the door. The lump of being that was there was in Bryce's clothing, and far too big to be Undaga.

It was Bryce.

The horror of what I had done made my knees turn to gel and I screamed. Well, more like made a horrible choking noise that was something between a sob and gurgle. My heart pounded in my still-ringing ears and I sobbed, trying to pull myself together. The strings of my sanity were frayed down to a thread, but I held to it, lest I fall off the cliff into the ocean.

Running to my bed, I called for an ambulance and the police, trying to tend to Bryce at the same time. I reported that I'd mistaken Bryce for an intruder. I decided I would just tell them the bites were from rough sex. *That might blow their little country bumpkin minds.*

When I hung up the phone, I ran back to Bryce and resumed medical treatment right away. Stop the bleeding, take his pulse, supportive care until the paramedics came. While I worked, I couldn't stop crying. The sirens were getting closer, and they sounded strange, like a pulse.

I opened my eyes to see I was safe, in bed. An empty bed, but still—a bed. I looked down at myself. No bleeding. No bite marks.

What was even better, even Bryce had been a dream—well, not better, but he wasn't dead, so while I didn't get to have a pleasurable night, I thought that was a more than fair trade. I slapped the alarm off and sat up, rubbing my eyes. Was that a dream? My hands were still shaking and I felt like I would vomit at any moment. I looked down to see the shotgun by the bed and picked it up.

As I put it away, I heard a moaning noise. Maybe Bryce hadn't been a dream. Confusion settled in fast as I worked out the difference between dreaming and reality.

I had nightmares as a child, and Father taught me to become a lucid dreamer. My dreams are often as detailed as anything I experience when I'm awake, and as a consequence, I have to work hard to tell wakefulness from dreaming. After being taught how to lucid dream, I have a sign that tells me differentiate my sleep/wake state. A literal sign that reads: YOU ARE DREAMING. It's written in red ink on a black background. That's the only way I can tell, and if I don't get that sign, I wind up disoriented for a while.

"Bryce?" I raised my voice to be heard outside the bedroom.

"Yeah?" Came his voice from the bathroom across the hall. I breathed a sigh of relief. Okay, so only *part* of my evening had been a dream. At least I didn't shoot him.

"Nothing, I wasn't sure where you'd gone," I said, climbing back into bed for a while. Why my alarm clock had been on was a mystery—I was sure I'd shut it off earlier. It didn't matter. I set the shotgun down again and snuggled up under the covers.

I was dozing off when I heard Bryce come back in and get in with me. He cuddled up against me, and I noticed how cold he felt; how thin he was. My eyes snapped open, and I turned around to see the horror that was Undaga in front of my face again.

No, not again—this couldn't be happening. My heart dropped into my stomach and my stomach dropped even further. Hot tears stung the swelling rims of my eyes. My body tried to curl in on itself, but couldn't. My mind tried to shut down and I came close to blacking out, but the tightening grip on my arms and the sandpaper scratching on my thighs brought the world back into focus.

The monster repeated every action from my dreams—the biting, the unwanted sex—all of it, wearing that ludicrous smile of his.

And I *couldn't* look away.

When he finished, he got off of me, and I lay there, bleeding and sick to my stomach. I didn't know what to do. I held still and looked for the sign to tell me I was dreaming or not. It never showed up. Not a dream, then.

That's when Bryce came in, and I wasn't sure if it was him or not, because it seemed like Undaga had been able to disguise himself. I couldn't say a word, but I grabbed my shotgun, and I cowered from him. I aimed it at his center mass, and he put his hands up.

"Kit? What's wrong, honey?" He asked. "You're injured. What happened?" His voice was gentle, tinged with concern, and he held up his hands in a gesture to show me he wasn't up to anything untoward.

"Get away from me. I can't be sure if you're Bryce," I told him. That sounded nuts, but after what had just happened, with Bryce right in the house, how could I be certain it was him and not another trick?

I took a deep breath to steady myself, and Bryce stepped back. "Kit, you're bleeding. You need help." His voice was soft. I kept the sight trained on his chest.

"Kathryn, just relax. I'm going to call for the paramedics. You're bleeding a lot, and I'm worried," he said. I stared at him, hard, trying to decide who he was.

This is insanity, I thought. *It's Bryce. You know it is. That's his gentle baritone, his manicured (talons) fingernails. Stop this.*

But what if it wasn't Bryce?

He got out of the room and dialed for an ambulance. Though he kept his voice hushed, I was still flushed with adrenaline, and I heard him speak. "She's bleeding a lot and won't let me near her—it looks like animal bites—and she's acting unusual."

Bryce never saw Undaga and had no clue what had happened—or what I thought had happened. I doubt Undaga would have called the authorities. It couldn't be Undaga, then. I dropped the shotgun and ran to Bryce, who remained Bryce. He tried to help me with the bleeding wounds. I talked him through it.

"I think I'm hallucinating," I said.

Bryce looked up at me. He was pressing hard on a wound on my thigh. Tiny beads of sweat were breaking out on his forehead. "It's okay. You're safe now. Just stay calm."

"I'm calm." That was a lie. "But I'm not safe. I'm going into shock and I need a blanket to keep me warm. Also, you need to elevate my legs. Don't give me water no matter how much I ask for it."

"Okay. But hang on for me, honey. Keep talking."

I kept talking.

Perhaps I was hallucinating again, like I had on that night with Mercy, and this time, I had a story of Undaga in my head. I could have scratched myself or had another injury that looked like bite marks.

Was that a stretch? Could the fungi that was in the air have spread, or blossomed in my system the way poison ivy does? I wasn't a botanist, but it was the best answer I could muster for the moment.

The Constable—Chet Callfield, came into the house (Bryce left the door open so the paramedics could come through) and helped Bryce tend to my injuries. I had warmed up, and the shock was subsiding because of my companion's careful ministrations.

Callfield, not terribly unfriendly to outsiders but suspicious of them, had an accusatory look in his eye every time he glanced over at Bryce, who was oblivious to the scrutiny. He was far too busy tending my wounds and making sure I was lying supine with my legs elevated.

"Are you able to answer questions?" Callfield asked me. "I mean in here. Mister—"

"Bryce Gansen," he said, and I saw he took no offense to Callfield not recognizing his name, even though the Gansen family owned just about every commodity in the Union. His humbleness made my heart soften. I loved him even more in that moment.

"Mister Gansen, would you excuse us?"

Bryce looked like someone had goosed him for a moment, then nodded. "Oh, yes, that's fine." He gave my hand a gentle squeeze, and I saw his torn shirt where he'd used it to tie off a direct pressure tourniquet on my arm. "If you need anything, just have Callfield come get me."

His hand lingered, and then he left for the other room. I could hear his footfalls growing more distant.

"You want to tell me what happened?"

I shrugged and bit back the sarcastic answer that came to mind. *Not that you'll do anything about it.* "I'm not sure. Bryce left me alone to attend his night habits, and something attacked me. I don't know what it was, and I think I was seeing things."

"Like what?"

"Things that couldn't be there because they don't exist. But I can tell you one thing, Callfield—these bite marks won't match Bryce's impressions. He didn't do this. I know you're thinking you've got a domestic on your hands, but you don't. I don't know what kind of animal attacked me, but these bites came from mouth larger than my boyfriend's."

Chet's mouth became one pursed line, and he grunted his agreement as I showed him one of the bite marks. "They look human."

"Almost, don't they?"

He sighed. I could see he believed me, but there was something else. A resignation I didn't understand and at the time was too unwell to ask him about it.

"We still need a forensic dentist to take impressions," Callfield said.

I nodded. "I know. Bryce will cooperate, I'm sure. But expect him to get an attorney if you intend to question him further."

"Right." Callfield said.

The ambulance came, and I told them I needed blood and fluids. Then I attempted to sit back and let them do their work without my interference.

Bryce and Callfield followed behind.

I came in via a gurney ride to see Tom Patrick—my colleague on duty in the ER that night—greeting me with an ashen face, but stitching me up just the same. He gave me all my jabs and made sure I started on a prophylactic antibiotic.

"Those bite marks look human," Tom said. "Mouth's too big to be your partner's." He was sitting on a rolling stool by my bedside. "What in Perdition happened?"

I told my story to Tom, and then to Gina, the psychiatrist on duty. I said I was likely having a lasting effect from the hallucinogen that had caused my previous issues. Both knew me and they knew I wasn't in any danger to myself or would become a source of danger to others.

We agreed that there must have been a plant or spores that invaded my house, and it would be vital to bring in someone to do a thorough cleaning, and getting an air filter.

While I stayed in the hospital for my injuries, I had Bryce take care of that. They found nothing, but thought a certain plant called *soma aculeatus* (around here they call it stinging weed) was active. I'm getting tested to see if I'm a slow metabolizer of the enzyme that attaches itself to the 5-HT2A receptor. In people who are sensitive to it (slow metabolizers of the enzyme), it can cause hallucinations, among other symptoms, including a rash that resembles bite marks. When scratched, it tears the dermis enough to bleed so much so that they look like deep bite wounds. At the time I write this, I'm still waiting on those test results, as they have to send them out to Grace City. The joys of being overworked and understaffed (not to mention underequipped) in the path lab.

They treated me, and I recovered.

I'm home now, resting—Bryce took me back to the house.

"Callfield gave me a colonoscopy," Bryce said while he drove back from the hospital. "Had to tell him my family history back to the 1100s and provide my kindergarten photograph."

"Stop exaggerating." Even though I was weary, I laughed. "I wouldn't worry about it," I said. "He's got nothing on you."

"I know. I think he cares about you, but doesn't know what to do. Do any of us? If you hadn't told me about that company that came into Dubbs House to clean up, I would have thought a monster attacked you, like a wood ape."

"You? The day you believe in that stuff is the day I grow a beard."

"Too late," Bryce said, then laughed. I punched him in the arm. It was a weak tap.

"Don't kick a woman when she's down." I grinned and fought the urge to check my face in the mirror for beard hairs.

Under the volunteer contract I signed, I go back to work in two days to finish out the obligation. It'll be a relief to return to Grace City. I have one more week, and I can bear it. I can't stand the thought of leaving with them having last seen me in such a vulnerable state, either.

Yes, I know it's ego. If I could stop myself, I would.

-Kathryn

***

10 October

Bryce has not left my side since the incident. He is staying with me in the house until I'm finished with my work here in Silver Hollow.

He makes me breakfast, and dinner is on the table when I come home. It's strange. I didn't know he could cook. I mean, he can cook well, too. Every bite is a trip to a Michelin Star restaurant. Someday, with cooking lessons and luck I might be able to return the favor.

Who am I kidding? Meal planning is the extent of my food knowledge.

There's something weighing on my mind. I'm five days late from my menstrual cycle, having nausea and vomiting in the mornings, and my void frequency has increased.

Symptoms shouldn't show up this early, and I haven't taken a test yet, but also haven't mentioned a word of this to Bryce. When he asked about the vomiting, I said it would take me some time to recover from the *soma aculeatus* poisoning.

I'll take a test before I start my rounds tonight at Mercy Hospital, but I can't bear the thought of this right now. Not after what happened.

It nags at the back of my mind — the incident that was so vivid, so real, and not a dream. A hallucination, I suppose. But I still can't help asking: whose baby is this? Do I want to carry it to term to find out? I'm terrified to tell

Bryce, not because he'll be upset, but thrilled. He'll ask me to keep it—and what do I tell him if it isn't his?

Ridiculous thoughts, I know. It was all hallucinations. Yet I don't know what to do. I'm not ready for this. Not at all. I have no time to devote to a dependent human being. Plus—what if none of that was a hallucination?

I get sick to my stomach for multiple reasons—one of them is that I might buy into that garbage that Wendy believed.

Bryce will want to keep it. I know it. I should tell him, but it'll take every ounce of courage I have.

He is a kind and gentle man. I am making excuses. I could pay for an army of nannies. But I don't want it because of the—incident.

I believe it, I just don't like admitting I was wrong.

No. There is no such thing as the Timeworn Order. They were nothing but a fantasy concocted to keep people in line. Wendy thought so, too, but now?

This is the thought that keeps me awake at night. Maybe I should go back to the hospital and get this sorted out because these things aren't real.

They just feel real.

I may argue with myself forever as to what I've experienced. Bryce is my companion, my lover, and my best friend. Why would I doubt that? Just because of a terrible hallucination?

Although, every once in a while, I look over at Bryce when he isn't aware I am looking. I see that gleam in his eyes that looks like a caricature of himself, and sporting a foolish, wide grin.

-K.

GHOST TOWN

Doctor Francis Langelier enjoyed long walks around the township. A bit heavyset, he rather fancied himself pleasantly plump, but always stayed in the best shape possible. The old hip would act up occasionally, but he paid it no mind.

Old Esther Standish stood on the steps, sweeping the mottled brown leaves away. She was lonely, even though Postman and Callfield would visit, it was never enough.

Standish lost her entire family. One of her own had fallen victim to The Incident.

That's what they called it, the ones who were left. The Incident was living history. 1968. Though Langelier found it interesting, he had no compassion for the situation. Nothing more than a simple, defining moment for the township.

The death knell. The final blow to a dying town that was so vicious that the remaining residents never spoke of it, unless in reverent whispers spiked with dread.

Langelier could fake sympathy, though he was certain it wasn't quite right. But Standish appreciated the efforts. Otherwise, why would she be sure to come about during his walks with some performative chore? And how was it she would always bring him his favorite lemon bars to supplement his energy on his evening constitutionals?

Lonely older woman, solitary mature man. The few people left in this town surely believed he and Standish were carrying on.

Let them. He just wanted the lemon bars.

"Hello, Mrs. Standish," he waved back to her as she approached, broom in hand, a small smile on her face. The formal greeting was intentional. In the Northeast Territory, neighbors of 20 years still used surnames.

"Langelier, you're looking well today," Esther said. "Time for a short visit? I've made extra lemon bars and my kettle is almost whistling."

Langelier heard the hope in her voice. It was the same every time she invited him in. "Of course. I'd be delighted."

She opened the gate and motioned him inside.

They sat at the kitchen table in the farmhouse, and Standish served the lemon bars.

Langelier waited for her to pour the tea and sit before diving into the dish.

"How are your berry bushes coming along?" Langelier asked.

Esther gave him an extra lump of sugar. "Better'n I expected," she said. "Nothing really grows around here, but I think there's some magic in the compost. Those blueberries are almost ripe or will be in a week, and the raspberries will be ready come October. After the first snow, they'll be done for."

"You should be proud," Langelier said. "The lemon bars are delicious as always, and for quite some time, your gardening efforts have met with success."

"Pride never did much for me," Standish said. "You wear it better than I do."

Langelier laughed. "I don't find anything but pleasure in my accomplishments," he said. "And you should, too."

"They're just berries, not a PhD like yourself." Standish said.

"Ah, stroke my ego a bit harder and I'll think you're sweet on me," he said.

This surprised a laugh out of Standish. She gave him a bashful glance. "Now, don't tease. Tell me, do you like blueberries? I make a mean blueberry buckle."

"If your blueberry buckle is half as good as your lemon bars, Mrs. Standish, I'll take a pirate king's share." He gave her his best magnanimous grin.

They fell silent for a moment, and Standish clutched her teacup to keep her hands from shaking. Langelier couldn't tell if it was a palsy trying to develop, or if her nerves were worn. He made no remark on it—best to avoid appearing too nosy on one hand, and on the other, he didn't care.

"I'd like to talk a bit more about the town history," Standish said. "I have a question only historians can answer—well, only you can answer."

"You're flattering me," said Langelier.

"Not at all. You're intimately familiar with this township and its grim history. Even more so than the other Silver Hollow Historical Society members." Standish raised the cup to her lips. The shaking was worse.

"Ask whatever you like—and you can say 'SHHS,' I'll know what you mean," Langelier said. He tried to put some warmth into his tone, unsure if it sounded sincere.

"Why does something ghastly happen every hundred years in this place? I don't understand it. This township has always been a shithole, but it seems like every hundred years something big happens. Big and ugly." Standish's eyes started to shine, but no tears fell.

"To answer your question, we have to pick it apart, I'm afraid," Langelier said. "It's a lengthy answer. Would you have time for it?"

Standish nodded. "Yes, sir, I would make time for it."

"There are suppositions in your question that are false. First, something ghastly happens everywhere, all over the world, every day. Historians review news from everywhere at many points in time, and most of us narrow down to a specialty. But a broad overview is necessary to understand that narrow era that draws our attention. Since the first written words of the Polidorites and the Oshini peoples, tragedy befalls societies almost daily." Langelier took another bite of his lemon bar and followed it with a sip of tea.

"You specialize in Silver Hollow, though," Standish said. "Don't you think tragedies happen here more often than, say, Terrace Lake?"

"It would depend on how one defines 'tragedy,' I suppose," Langelier said. "This town has its equal share of sadness, possibly more so, but there are towns all over the continent that suffer the same. Besides, Mercy Hospital is at Terrace Lake. I dare you to spend a day in their Accident and Emergency ward and tell me our town has more tragedies."

"I suppose. People say the place is cursed," Standish said. "I reject nonsense like that, but there have been days that make me wonder." Standish glanced out the kitchen window at her garden, then back to Langelier. "What can you tell me about 1868 in this town?"

"If you mean about Ella, I can tell you most of it. Are you asking me if I suspect what happened back then is linked to The Incident?" Langelier kept his face neutral, perhaps even showing concern.

"I lost my family in The Incident. I was a young mother then. The following forty years have been … so … long." She shrugged, her jaw set, blinking fast to avoid tears shedding. "I want to ask, because I want to know. Could they be connected?"

Langelier paused for a moment. If he ever wanted to be invited back for more lemon bars, then he had to play this gently. His normal urge to mock that sort of ignorance pocketed, he took another sip of tea before continuing. "If you'll allow me room for a bit of philosophy, I would say that everything that happens in a town is interconnected. So in a sense, yes, Ella's tragic outcome is connected to The Incident."

Standish lips pursed tight as though she might vomit, but she forced her tea down despite the subject. "That's not what I mean," she said. "What I'm saying is, I wonder if the influences were the same."

"I believe I understand. Specifically, the nature of the two tragedies are interconnected by a tenuous theme, but there's no apparent direct line between them," Langelier held in a sigh. "But towns have a societal connection. They absorb what the people put into it. The reason that Silver Hollow is becoming a ghost town so fast is because we're all old, dying, and no one is moving in to replace us. No children returning to the township, and with the rocky and difficult-to-farm soil, no one wants to invest in agriculture."

Silence fell again. Langelier waited.

"Ghost Town. There are a lot of those all over The Union, and for a lot of different reasons." Standish sighed. "I wish I could leave here, too, sometimes. Thought about it on and off for the past forty. But where would I go? And I—as foolish as it sounds—I don't want to leave my family."

Langelier smiled. "It's not foolish, my friend. In fact, that's the spirit of a historian—to want that connection to the past."

"Even if it kills you," she said.

"Even then." Langelier nodded.

"I have something I want to give you. For the historical records. A couple of things. Something for the Silver Hollow Historical Society, too." Standish got up from the table and left the room. She came back with an ornate wooden box. "Here. My family memories and as much as I remember of that day are in there."

Standish set the box down with a soft thud, then sat back down, nudging it over to him.

Langelier first examined the box. It was old, about the 1860s, when gold inlay was all the rage and jeweled handles were so delicately placed. This one was a blue opal. Rare and valuable, it hung on the handle, looking like a teardrop. "This box and everything in it? Are you certain?"

"Yes. Never had any use for it but to keep my stuff inside it. This box may be pretty, but it's full of pain." Standish refilled her teacup. "Please open it. Maybe there's relief inside if another person looks."

Langelier understood the gravity of her words and held himself back. He didn't want to appear like a greedy child at Winterfest. Instead, he opened the box with the expected comely restraint.

Inside, there were several photographs. One was a 1968 class picture with children around age nine and ten. One was of a young Standish and her husband, Solomon. Another was of the family, the two children seated at the very steps Esther had been sweeping not forty-five minutes before.

"Are you sure you want to part with these?" Langelier asked. Best to ask and not face an angry call from regret.

"I have copies of each one somewhere in the attic. I can find them if I want. But these are the originals." Standish said. "There's more."

Langelier put his hand in the box and pulled out a roll-up of pages. Unrolling them, he discovered they were her handwritten memoirs in her impeccable penmanship. She'd signed and dated them and marked them with a fingerprint for authenticity's sake, he supposed. "The Incident, I see," Langelier said. "You wrote this last year."

"Thought about killing myself," she said. "But changed my mind. I decided making you lemon bars was a better idea."

He paused rummaging through the box to give her a surprised stare. "Really? That's what stopped you? I—I'm touched."

"I like your company. Besides, I've lived this long without them, what's forty more years?" Standish shook her head. "Damn good genes letting me live till I'm over a hundred."

He wasn't sure what to say to that and went back to the box. A copy of her Last Will and Testament. He scanned through it until he saw the SHHS mentioned. "This is a generous gifting, Mrs. Standish."

"Well, I don't have children, and while Postman and Callfield come to check on me, you're the only one who spends a lot of time with me. I've picked up new hobbies because of you." Standish gave him a small smile. "The Society should have the house and the money when I'm gone."

Langelier put the photos and documents away and closed the box with a quiet click. "You are too kind, Mrs. Standish. This is most generous, and I hope you do live another forty. Perhaps we can develop more hobbies together."

"Or maybe I'll make good on offing myself someday and make you all rich," she said, then shook her head. "But I'm not young and I can't live forever."

"Indeed, none of us can," Langelier said, finishing his tea. "Well, I hope you'll stay with us. I'd like to go over your memoirs in depth. Perhaps conduct some interviews with you and draw out more of your story from that day, if you're comfortable talking about it."

"With you, I'm comfortable talking. You're a charming man, Langelier. Charming but not warm. Sure, you can fake it when you need to, and bless you for trying, but I like a good, detached man. My second husband was a lot like you, if you remember him."

Langelier nodded. "Harmon Chant. I remember."

"He was detached after a while," she said. She grinned into the last of her teacup. "Then he just up and disappeared. That's when I knew I had to live out the rest of my life alone."

"I find it best to live in solitude, myself," Langelier said. "I should think you did, too. After all, you and Harmon were married, what—five years before he left?"

"About five years and nine months. He told me he was heading to Haverty's and never came back. Never made it to Haverty's either." She shook her head. "Did you know Callfield came around asking about him? Like I'd done something to him. I told him to get off my property and let me alone. That man's always suspicious. As if I'm an axe murderer."

Langelier grinned. "You're not a gentle soul, Mrs. Standish, but you wouldn't be so gauche as to use an axe."

"Not with all this farm equipment, no," Standish said. She started cleaning up the table.

"I always thought it was interesting. Your soil was never any good until Chant left. After that, you could grow just about anything." Langelier looked out the window at the flourishing berry bushes, then over at the compost tiller.

"Sometimes the poison isn't in the land," she said. "Sometimes it's in the people."

Langelier looked back at Standish. There was a look on her face that was full of knowing. She gave him a wink and finished clearing the table.

"That was fifteen years ago," she said. "As detached a man that Solomon was, he loved me. Never laid a hand on me. Took his own life from the pain of The Incident rather than taking it out on me."

"And Harmon Chant—didn't, I take it." Langelier didn't ask. He understood.

"With good bacteria in a compost heap, it takes thirty days to turn flesh to mulch," she said. "So when we had that rat problem, I solved it. Our history—the town's history—is all about the full circle. We come back to the soil. Some a bit earlier than others."

"You're telling me this for a reason. Surely you realize—" Langelier stopped talking when she waved her hand at him.

"You're not going to extort me," she said. "You're a secret keeper. You knew then. I know you knew then. I saw you on your evening constitutional, seeing me."

"I didn't—I hadn't any idea." Langelier's denial in his voice was genuine. "But no, I'm not going to extort you. Your information is far too valuable to turn you over to the simpleton Callfield and his lackey Postman."

He stood up. "Your secrets are safe. Besides, there's no way I could even prove it—and—on top of everything else, those lemon bars are irresistible."

Standish nodded. "I did what I had to do. I always do what I have to do."

"My friend, you don't have to convince me," he said. "I'm rather delighted to add to the town's rich history after you're gone."

"Please do. Before I go, I'll give a deathbed confession. Looking forward to that day, whenever it is." She said.

Langelier stood and made his way to the door. "Until next time, Mrs. Standish."

"Call me 'Esther,'" she said, handing over the box.

"Esther." He smiled. "I look forward to it."

"Have a good evening, Francis."

As he left the house, wooden box under his arm, he ruminated over all the ways a person could die and have it appear to be natural causes.

Perhaps soon he'd be able to explore the subject in depth.

BEFORE THE BEGINNING

"Constance? Connie? Wake up, love. Please. Please wake up."

But she didn't stir. Her husband took a step closer to the bed. "Connie?"

Walker reached out and touched her face—sometimes his wife slept so hard that he had to caress her to wake her—but he recoiled. Icy as the winter morning. Walker cried out and bit into his hand. "This can't—no. Connie. Connie, please wake up!"

The room spun out from his feet and Walker fell backward, putting a hand behind himself to gain ground. No ground to gain. A snap of old kindling rang out as pain shot up his arm, wrist breaking. The man howled.

Outside, scarlet dotted the blanket of fresh snow, leading to a bright red cardinal on the ground, wings fluttering, then stopping. Walker held onto his wrist and looked around, trying to decide where to go. Platt? No help there, not after the incident happened with Ella. What would he say? That the house killed his wife, and that it would kill him, too? The townspeople would think he'd gone mad, as Ella had.

The neighboring house was empty. No one dared live in it after Ella's incident. That left the meeting hall and church, and the Preacher. Walker shook his head at the idea of getting any help from a charlatan and cultist. Walker rejected the myths of Alastor or the Timeworn.

His eyes roved over the broken bird. There was nowhere to go. No one would believe him and the ones who did would say that he was cursed or tainted, and they would kill him.

Walker ran back into the house.

Thoughts raced through his head. Bury Constance in the cellar, if he dared to go there again, and say she wandered into the woods on a walk. He'd have to create tracks in the snow. Her shoes. Yes, he'd use a good pair of shoes, stamp out a trail and then—the ravine was a long drop. If she were to slip—

"I didn't kill her," Walker said to the house. "You killed her. You did and you know it."

The reply was a groan of creaking boards and rats scurrying in the walls. Walker slammed his good fist into it, sending throbbing pain into his knuckles as the wall remain unmoved.

Before he could bury her, he had to set his broken wrist.

The arm throbbed with each step back up the stairs, jarring his body with bolts of lightning. Beads of sweat gathered on his forehead yet the chill gripped him with greater force.

As he opened the door, Walker refused to look at the bed where Constance slept, focused instead on the nurse's kit she carried with her wherever she went. In the small township of Silver Hollow, she was the only person with any medical knowledge.

Walker set the broken wrist on his left hand with a sickening crack. His stomach rolled, and he vomited, nearly missing the chamber pot with his yellow, watery bile. The room began spinning again, and he rolled forward, away from the chamber pot, head between his knees.

Was he hearing chanting?

Chants, in a chorus of whispered, distant voices. Walker closed his eyes and tried to focus on it. No, it couldn't be a chant—just the rats in the walls, or a family of squirrels nesting for the winter.

It isn't otherworldly. It isn't. It isn't.

The paper he'd written on blew off his desk in a strong gust of wind and landed at his feet.

***

One month before, the crisis with Ella met its twenty-year anniversary. Back then, the first whispers of a mustache began to etch out their fuzzy lines on his face. How his Union Army friends teased him (how old are you again?). Now the facial hair was thicker and better trimmed. Today, especially. He dressed in his military uniform and his brass jingled with each step on the freezing ground.

The yellowing grass would give way to the whitewash of winter and the gray sky would continue to be as pale and wan as ever. Just as immovable as the headstones in the cemetery that appeared to grow larger as he walked.

The only things with vibrancy at the moment were the chrysanthemum bouquets he carried in his hand. The red, pink, and gold blooms from his greenhouse gave off peppery scents and clung to his uniform from clutching them so close.

Kneeling, Walker placed them on the graves of Ella's children. She was not buried with them. Forbidden from the cemetery, her body burned in a bonfire after they hanged her.

He hadn't been there. Three-years married to Connie by then, Walker helped put the Western Territory back together after the war had come to an end. When he returned to find that Miss Ella had been possessed by madness and her children suffered for it, he wept for them. Despite frequent tries, he and Connie never bore any offspring by blood, and he cared for children who'd been abandoned by war. The two of them took three home—ages eight to twelve—treating them as his own blood. Raised them to adulthood. When they reached eighteen, they left to seek their fortunes either in the Southern Territory, in Grace City, or by venturing back westward.

Something soft landed on his shoulder. A dainty hand. Walker looked up to see Constance standing behind him, a small smile on her face. "Are you well, husband?"

The man rose to his feet once more. Though he would hardly refer to himself as old, there were runners of gray in his mustache, and his joints made creaking noises when he stood.

Walker picked up her small, gloved hand and kissed it. "Yes I am. This place isn't, but I'm well."

Constance nodded. "They don't want to remember, Walker. Too much pain."

"Bully for them. They should have done something to prevent it." He grimaced.

"What would you do if you'd been there? Stuck your nose in Ella's business? You were a bold young man, Colonel Dubbs, but not so nosy." Her tone remained light and chiding, and her gentle expression softened the cutting truth of her words.

"Yes, yes." Walker waved his free hand at her. "All well and good to say what I would do because of my absence, engaging in hypotheticals. But I'd like to think I'd have tried to help take care of the family."

Connie nodded. "I know you would, but she might not have let you."

"This is so."

She took his arm. "Let's head home and I'll fix you midday meal."

For the past seventeen years, the Dubbs House had seen many changes. They opened it as a hospital for the sick and indigent once his children left. It had remained that way for five years. Once the crisis passed, they turned it back into their home. In the last two years, it was too quiet. Too empty.

The house itself was built over some kind of mass grave that no one ever talked about, and he never knew what it was. Probably a crematorium. Walker always dismissed the mass grave talk as superstitious nonsense that made no more sense than the Timeworn Order or Saint Alastor. Patients told stories to Constance and sometimes to Walker, but they were sick people and dismissed the stories just as easily as the feverish hallucinations of the infirm.

"If there were hauntings," Walker said, "we'd have seen them ourselves by now." Every time someone brought it up, he replied with his pat answer.

"Maybe we refuse to see," Constance winked at him. "And that's why it never bothers with us."

His wife made a barley soup with rabbit for lunch. They ate in the kitchen nook. There were only the two of them in the house. With the dining area a reminder of no more children, a lifetime of quiet meals with clattering utensils against china, it made sense to eat in the smaller space.

On his third bowl, Walker sat back and sighed. "That soup is probably your best yet."

"You say that every time." Constance laughed.

"I mean it every time." He stood and helped her clear the table and wash up after. The cultist men didn't do such things, but Walker Jeremiah Dubbs was not a cultist.

There were times, ever since Walker had the house built, that people would report strange things. One builder went mad, ran into the woods, and killed two children playing by the stream. They strung him up for it, despite his screams that he wasn't responsible—that he was being controlled. There were other times there was nothing out of the ordinary.

"The house slept," Walker said as he helped Connie put the dried dishes back in the cupboards.

"Tell me, how does a house sleep?" Connie grinned at him.

"It doesn't. But I was just remembering something I read by that spiritualist. Can't recall his name, but he wrote that book on hauntings." Walker scratched his head. "Gerald—something or other. Remember?"

Connie nodded. "Gerald Faber."

"Faber, that's the one," Walker snapped his fingers when Connie refreshed his memory. "Well, he went on with nonsense about how haunted houses had periods of time where there was no activity. He said it was due to the energy going to sleep. Then he started on about how the cultists say spirits that sleep in the winter and are active in summer—as if it were true." Walker laughed. "So I thought that since you and I never see these inexplicable effects, the house must be asleep when it's just us."

Connie joined in on the joke. "Must be. Our spirits here must not read, because they're active any time of year, and they go wild in winter sometimes."

They laughed together and Walker went over to her, picked her up in his arms, and kissed her, feeling the soft sleeves of her dress brush against his neck.

When they parted, he looked into her eyes. "How about heading upstairs and trying to wake those spirits from their slumber with some racket?"

Connie nodded, face pink and growing redder as she pressed her lips to his.

***

Constance woke from her afternoon nap to the sounds of Walker's light breathing that was edging on a snore. Lighting the hurricane lamp made it totter and clang against the table, enough noise to make her eyes go wide as she glanced back at her husband. He was still asleep, and she breathed a sigh of relief.

The house was dark—the sun passed from the east side to the west, and Constance checked Walker's pocket watch. Time for supper.

She got dressed favoring a sheer dressing gown. With the two of them alone, Constance preferred a comfortable manner of dress. She admired her figure in the mirror—still slender, but not too slim. The curve of the belly was rounder than it used to be—a little bump under the navel, but she didn't mind. Walker never mentioned it.

The gossamer gown's sleeves were too long to be practical for cooking, so she flattened and folded them against her arms and rolled the sleeves past her elbows. Aunt Beatrice caught fire when her sleeve caught in the woodstove, and Constance would never forget the odor of her charred flesh. Or the sounds of her screams as she fell to the ground. Or the sight of her father, mother, and Uncle Archippus surrounding her with blankets to put her out.

Scarred beyond recognition for the rest of her life, her hair never grew back for all the thick webbing of scars on her head. It scared forty-three-year-old Connie now as much as it scared nine-year-old Connie when it happened. After she saw the surgeons and enlightened ones save Beatrice and fight the infection, her career path as a nurse solidified.

Walker came to the kitchen to help with dinner a few moments later.

"You look a bit peaked," Constance frowned when she turned from the stove and saw him. That had been an understatement. He looked pale and there were dark circles under his eyes.

"Terrible dream. Just terrible. Can't seem to shake it." He stopped cutting carrots and wiped sweat from his brow.

"As though it made you sick." Constance put her hand to his forehead. "No fever. Must have shaken your nerves."

Walker cleared his throat. "It did. Surely did."

"Chase it away," Constance took his arm and made him sit at the table. "Tell me and chase it away."

"It was about the children. Ella's children. Except—" Walker ran a hand through his hair and patted it back into place. "Except I was doing everything through Ella's body, and then it was you. You were on the floor and I was cutting into you and I—"

"You liked it in the same way you like to lie with me." Constance set the rest of the rabbit stew on the stove to warm and added the extra carrots. She sat with him and took both his hands in hers.

"I did." Walker's face flushed with red and he looked at the floor. Connie still held onto him.

"And now you're awake, feeling guilty for your mind's wanderings."

"Yes." Walker's color had come back thanks to the flood of blood to his cheeks. He wasn't sweating any longer.

"Well, don't." Constance gave his hands a squeeze. "Everyone has dreams that test our primal nature, to be sure. Especially men who have seen war and done their killing face-to-face. I saw my share of the destruction out west, and tended to the wounded. I recall what you had to do."

Walker nodded, then sighed. "I won't indulge such dreams."

"I know you won't. Blame the war, or even the spirits if you want—it's of no consequence, Walker. All they are, and all they'll ever be, are dreams." She stood up and went to the stove to stir up the leftover stew. "Are you ready to eat?"

"I am now." Walker stood and helped set the table.

After dinner and cleaning up, Constance joined Walker in the den. He was building a fire when she sat on the settee with her knitting project. The settee made a soft creaking sound as Walker joined her.

"What's your new project?" Constance asked. Hers was obvious now—she was working on an Aran to mail to their youngest.

"Simple scarves for the children. I've ordered watches from Southerlyn's of Grace City for them. Hope they deliver on time." He cleared his throat and held out the beginnings of a burgundy scarf. "Will Jeanie like this? The thickness, I mean—not too wide?"

Connie eyed the craft and shook her head. "No, it's fine. And that's her favorite color. But make sure you make it long. She's a tall girl."

Walker nodded and went back to it. They chatted about the children and he shed the last vestiges of the nightmare he had that afternoon. By the time the fire dwindled to a few embers glowing and fizzling, he was ready to take to the bedroom once more.

Constance went to the bathroom to settle in for a hot bath before bed. As the tub filled with running water, steam billowing off the faucet, she turned to the sink and put oil on her skin. The fragrance of roses, lavender, and jasmine perfumed the air, and Constance sighed, grateful for the indoor plumbing.

Lately, she had not slept well, and when Walker inquired, she blamed it on aging. But the heat inside her, her increased desires, and the reduction of her cycle marked a bigger change for her to come, and soon. The only thing that could lull her into sleep at night was a hot bath and the scents of her oils. Occasionally, she paid for it by waking up drenched in sweat, heart racing, but an open window at night, even in winter, eased things for her.

Recently, Connie compromised by opening the bathroom window while she bathed. It helped her stay relaxed and not get overheated though Walker had scolded her for doing so. "You'll catch a chill and get sick from it."

"I refute the idea that cold air causes illness," Constance said. Walker quieted.

With the window open, the water in the tub cooled off enough not to scald her when she entered. Just in time to put oils on her face to keep the folds of time at bay.

An unfamiliar aroma hit her nose while Constance had her eyes covered. She didn't know it, but it was pleasant. Fruity. She looked around, searching for the scent.

A squeak escaped her lips as she saw a woman in her bath, nude, and staring at her with a mirrored open-mouthed gaze. She reached out to the other woman, trying to speak, but no sound came out.

"What are you doing?" The woman with the scandalized expression asked, voice shrill and sharp.

Constance stepped back to bolt for the door. She started to say something, but then the lady in her tub vanished.

All that was left was a bathtub filled with clean water.

"Walker?" Constance felt a surge of dizziness and sat hard on the floor, putting her head between her knees. Had she called for him loudly enough?

The footfalls in the hallway relieved her. Walker threw open the door. "Connie? What's wrong?" He knelt with her, trying to get a look at her face. She looked up and reached out for him. Walker took her hand and put his other hand on her back, rubbing it.

Connie's tears slid down her cheeks and stained her dressing gown. "I saw something. Insane—I might be going insane."

Walker frowned, brows knitting to form an owl-like 'v.' "Tell me what happened."

Connie explained it and Walker sat on the floor with her, paying no attention to the cold seeping into his robe. He shook his head. "I don't understand it, but I trust you—something happened here."

"But it couldn't be real, Walker. Spirits don't exist."

"No. You're right. Not spirits. Perhaps something scientific we don't yet understand." He stood and went to the tub, putting his hand in the water. "It's still warm. Do you want to take your bath?"

Constance shook her head. "Is it terrible that I don't?"

Walker chuckled. "Not at all. Would it help if I stayed?"

She nodded, and he helped her stand on shaking legs, leading her into the tub. He pulled up the chaise and sat with her, then scrubbed her back. Drips and splashes of water echoed off the porcelain.

"Walker, you don't think I'm going mad, do you?" Connie asked as she leaned back, staring at the white ceiling with the fleur-de-lis etchings.

"No. You're not given to emotionality, nor are you trying to convince me you aren't losing your mind, so that says you're sane, at least to me." Walker reached into the tub and cupped her breast, then leaned down to kiss her.

She snorted a laugh. "At least I haven't scared you away."

"Not yet, madwoman." He grinned at her and leaned back. "It'll take much more than a vision to scare me away."

***

The next two weeks passed without incident. Constance finished her project and mailed it off to her son. The elder son and middle daughter's packages were already en route, and she hoped they would all receive their gifts before Solstice Day. She included similar notes with each gift. Just a few details of their year in Silver Hollow and that they were hopeful they were well, and to write soon.

Walker sent his scarf to Jeanie and sent a similar note though shorter. They made a day of it by stopping at the Jewel Grove Inn for a late lunch and shopping at the large general store for dry goods and winter supplies.

By the time they arrived home, the sun slipped over the horizon and lit the sky in a deep purple display. Walker put the horses in their stalls for the night and gave them their oats and hay and made sure they had unfrozen drinking water. He put out salt licks for them and made sure they were nice and warm with blankets. Once they settled in, he went up to the house and entered through the kitchen.

That's when Constance screamed.

Walker froze as he tried to locate her. Muffled sounds from below.

He grabbed his loaded shotgun from the parlor wall, thinking that perhaps a wild animal entered and attacked Connie—although her screams weren't frightened—they were furious.

When he got to the basement door, he turned the handle and met with resistance. Jammed? No—the door had some give at the bottom, but the knob wouldn't turn. Locked—yet there was no lock put on this door (it was on his list of things to do for the past year). He put his boot to the wood near the knob with all of his weight and it popped open. That's when the malodor hit him.

Rancid, rotted meat and feces overwhelmed his nose and he wretched, but Connie's war cry drove him forward.

A man was on top of her, thrusting, his clothes dirty and covered in reddish brown matter. Connie was screaming underneath him, dress ripped, breasts exposed, and clawing at her attacker.

Walker didn't know what he was seeing—the man wasn't even reacting to Connie's resistance. Her nails sank deep into the man's face.

But not a human face.

Walker aimed his shotgun at the thing and fired. It blew a hole in the creature's midsection and knocked it off of Constance. She scrambled away, blood covering her body and rushing to pull her skirts over her lower half.

"What is it? For the love of Stèphanie de Montaneis, what?" Walker could feel his voice working but not hear it as he went over to the thing and kicked it over. His ears were ringing from the blast and Connie was trying to say something.

He turned back to her and tried to read her lips. *I don't know* was the best he got from it. Walker looked back at the lump of being on the floor.

It had a man's body and a wolf's face. He stared at the creature for a moment, then set down the shotgun and knelt beside it, gripping the sides of its head and pulling. It had to be a mask.

The head didn't budge. Walker inspected the thing. A wolf's head, furry and soft with the skin underneath his fingertips growing cold—how?

Without a word, he dragged the wolf-man up the back steps to the outside, leaving a bloody trail behind him as he moved.

Inside, Constance's ears were still ringing, and she hobbled to her feet to run a bath. All she could think about was washing that *filth* off of her. She reeked of it and it clung to every pore in her body. Connie tossed her clothes—and her boots—into the furnace and trudged up the stairs to the bathroom.

She got to the water closet in time to retch up the faint remnants of her late lunch. The speed at which everything happened made her dizzy. One moment she heard a commotion in the basement and went with her broom to chase out whatever animal was there. The next, she was on the earthen floor of the cellar with that creature on top of her and inside her. The creature wore a man's clothes, and its wolfish head snapped at her.

Connie didn't care. She wanted the bastard off and out of her.

Skin crawling, she ran the water as hot as she could stand and filled the tub with her oils, grabbing a strong lye soap and her roughest washcloth. The water stung at her skin, bringing blood to the surface, but Connie stayed. She scrubbed, layers of scum coming off her, out from her. She shoved the cloth inside and scrubbed herself numb.

"It's dead. Dead. Walker killed the thing. Gone." She cleaned her face and drained the tub, then filled it again, watching the fresh water rise to meet her breasts.

Outside, Walker dragged the body into the woods, off-trail, thumping and thunking as it hit rocks jutting up from the ground. He stopped with a jerk as its mouth caught on a thick tree root. Walker kicked the head to move it. The thing's face made a sloppy crunch noise as something in its face broke.

He tossed the corpse into the ravine, surprised at his own strength, and watched it grow smaller and smaller until it splashed into the water. There was no point in reporting it or talking about it. Walker turned and dashed back to the house. Connie. He had to make sure she was safe.

With water from the pump outside, he washed the bloody trail on the steps. Snow and season would wash away the rest and he could always blame a wild animal. Connie was more important.

The bathroom door was ajar, but Walker knocked anyway. There was no answer, so he peeked inside. Red as a beet, nude, and scrubbing the tub. Walker grabbed her robe and a towel before he approached.

"Connie?"

"I have to clean this. I have to make it all clean." She looked up at him with a tear-stained face. "I can still smell it."

"The scent is gone, Connie."

"It's all over you. You have to get clean."

"I will." Walker put the towel around her and offered her the robe. "Come and lie down on the chaise and I'll clean up. I don't want you out of my sight right now."

In Faber's book, he talked about possession and how people behaved in a different manner, as though something guided them. Walker saw this in Connie—the thing attacked her, and now she displayed these curious symptoms. Or not so curious. He had seen this before and called it shock. There didn't need to be a fancy, otherworld explanation for it.

Despite what they'd seen, Walker told himself it was just a mask that the assailant had glued onto his face. A sickness. Madness. Perhaps he believed he was a werewolf or other nonsense.

Walker threw his clothing in the hamper and climbed into the bath, washing with a new bar of the lye soap. Constance sat in the chaise and stared out the window.

Once he finished, Walker dried off and put on talc, then donned his own robe. He knelt by her side. Constance continued to look away from him.

"How can I help?" His voice sounded small and weak to his own ears because of the ringing.

Connie turned to look at him in the dim light. "We will never speak of this again. That's how."

Walker nodded. He respected her wishes.

She raised her arms to him and he picked her up, carrying her to bed. Her skin was hot from the bath, and he opened the window when she requested it.

Falling into an uneasy sleep, Walker saw Ella dancing nude with the wolf-head man as they ate the entrails of the children—her children. He watched her breasts jiggle as the creature took her, and then it was Constance again. Only this time, her screams weren't anger—they were pleasure.

He woke with a start as the shotgun blasts spattered their innards into each other's, intestines commingling, moving snake-like into each other as though their coupling continued in death.

This was wrong, and he dismissed his visions as he turned to face his wife. She was awake, staring at the ceiling.

She looked over at Walker, unsmiling. "I'll get breakfast started. It'll be ready once you're back from your chores."

Walker nodded and reached out for her hand. She hopped out of bed before he could touch her.

He stayed outside for a long time with the horses, making sure everything in the barn was secure and they were still warm. After that, instead of going inside, Walker checked on the greenhouse. Despite the bitter cold just outside, the glasshouse made a testament to midday in May. So much so that Walker took off his overcoat as he examined his plants. Fresh tomatoes bud on the earthy, spicy scented leaves of their plants. Soon, he'd be able to harvest them and surprise Constance with his success. A fortnight or less. They were small and green, still. He wanted them a luscious red before plucking them from the vine.

He had medicinal plants growing as well. Mint and ginger for indigestion, yarrow for inflammation, and so on—guided by Constance's knowledge of medicine when their supplies ran out during the Great Shortage.

His flowers. His precious mums and lilies. He smiled at the blackberry lilies growing next to them and doing so well. He clipped two and brought them inside for Connie.

She smiled faintly at the lilies and put them in a small vase, setting it on the kitchen table. "Thank you. I know you're trying to make me feel better."

Walker nodded. "I love you."

She swallowed hard, and he saw a glint of tears in her eyes, but she set her jaw and he could see her wrestling with herself to not let them fall. "I love you, too."

The rest of the day was busy with chores as were most days. When they sat down to dinner, things almost seemed normal again. Constance had more color in her face though she didn't smile. Her body was tense, as though she expected the wolf-faced creature to jump out at her any moment. She didn't speak much, and there was no joy in her voice when she did.

Walker filled the spaces of silence by chatting about things he read in the library, and how he thought of purchasing a newspaper subscription and making them deliver from Jewel Grove.

Constance did laugh at that. "They'd deny you service—imagine driving the horses all that way just to deliver one paper."

Walker chuckled. "I suppose they'd charge me more."

"A bit." She clapped her hands and finished her pot roast.

"Excellent dinner, Connie. Your best yet." Walker touched her hand. She let him.

"You always say that." Connie squeezed his hand. Her fingers were dainty threads of ice.

"I always mean it." He didn't say anything else as he helped clear the table.

The darkness fell earlier than the night before, but to Walker, it seemed to get dark hours before instead of minutes. They retired to the den.

Connie began a new knitting project. Knit one, purl two—for three rows. Walker started a fire and for a while, the only sounds were a clack of the knitting needles and the snap of a reply from the kindling in the fireplace. Clack, snap, clack. Clack, snap, clack.

She stood up and jammed her needles into the ball of yarn. The large window seemed to call to her to come sit. She did. She stared out the window.

Walker joined her.

"What are you looking for, Connie?"

Connie put her face in her hands and wept.

***

"Constance ill?" Old Haverty shook his head. "I don't see you out here often."

Walker gave Haverty a smile. "No, she's as well as ever. Just working on a new project in the house and can't tear herself away, so she sent me to pick up some staples."

This was a lie. After her night of weeping, Constance was quiet throughout the next day. She ate nothing and just sat in the den, staring out the window. Walker sat with her and stared at her.

"I don't feel well." Constance ran her hands through her hair, undoing the pins and letting her curls drag around her face.

"I'll help you to bed." Walker stood and offered his hand.

"No. You've done enough." There was an icy note in her voice that he'd never experienced. The chill reached his heart and gripped it.

He watched her leave the den and heard her ascend the stairs. Walker sighed and left as well, but headed in the opposite direction—to inspect the basement.

The room still reeked of feces and blood as Walker descended the stairs. Each footstep caused them to creak and pop, and the spirit of dread—of heavy air and mist around his body, squeezing his breath from him—grew in his descent.

What he found at the bottom landing made that sensation tighten and grow, filling him with shivers. There was—his mind couldn't make sense of it at first. He grew dizzy. A faint chanting came from every direction of the basement. He gagged.

The walls were covered in a scarlet liquid that stank like the inside of a slaughterhouse—an array of symbols and pictographs he didn't recognize.

Walker remembered his mother's advice from when he had to take care of the sick animals that stank up the barn. *Keep breathing and you'll adapt.* But here, the more he tried habituating to the odor of rotting carcass and the sickly copper tang of blood, the worse it got. That's when he realized it was getting stronger.

He wretched, falling to his knees, and emptied his stomach onto the earthen floor. He watched the yellow liquid sink in as he took his handkerchief to his mouth to wipe off the greasy residue. A cough tugged at his throat and he cleared it, trying to swallow the bitter, burning bile.

A groaning sound caught his attention from behind himself. Walker turned and choked out a scream. A hand—feral, oily black—emerged from the shadows and grabbed at him.

"We seek revenge for our brother," the chanting voice said. It clanged from every direction, echoing in his head. "Revenge for our brother. Revenge for our brother…"

Walker pushed off the ground with his legs hard as the hand made another grab for him. Swipe and a miss—he fell against the wall and another hand from behind held him fast. The hands tore at his legs, moving up his thighs, and inside of him. The burn of his insides and blood flowing into the floor below only seemed to make them move faster and harder. If he didn't get out, and soon, he'd die.

He screamed and wrested away from his captor, pulling up his trousers to keep from tripping as he ran up the stairs. A scream came from above his head.

"Connie?" He forgot about his own pain, the burning in his hind end—the sick roll of his lower abdomen—in favor of getting to his wife and making sure she was safe.

When he reached the bedroom door, there were no more screams. Connie was asleep in bed, looking relaxed and peaceful. He kissed her forehead. She was cool to the touch, but the window was open and a northern breeze picked up enough to blow the curtains aside.

"I don't know what to do," Walker's mousy tone irritated him and he banged his fist into the wall. In the distance, laughter.

Connie didn't stir.

She was heavy sleeper some nights, so Walker left her be and washed himself using quick, broad strokes and called it good enough. He dressed for bed and sat at his desk with a pen and paper.

Something is happening in this house. I am a man of reason and logic, but my eyes deceive me, or I am going mad. I refuse to believe what has happened in the past few days. I reject the premise. Houses do not live—they are not animate. That means, logically, there is a yet-to-be discovered force trying to enter here. A malevolent race, I imagine. I am far more convinced of otherworld encounters. During my time in the war, our troops saw many odd things in the sky out in the Western Territory, and many believed them to be visitors. Those were no ordinary meteors or comets.

It is logical that man is not alone. If they have the ability to travel though space just as one travels in the ocean on a ship, then perchance they have other abilities too.

I still sound like a madman. Given my injuries tonight, I have either hallucinated on gone-over food and done this to myself, or there is something even more sinister going on here. But I shall not wake Constance for this nonsense. I will bear it.

I do believe it is logical to leave this house come morning.

***

Pink and red hues streamed through the window when Walker's eyes snapped open. He gasped, as though something had been sitting on his chest. When he looked up, eyes full of morning debris, he thought something disappeared into the walls.

More claptrap. Or they had gone mad.

Walker turned to find Connie. She lay on her back and had a strange smile on her face. If it meant her dreams were pleasant, he was happy. He rose gingerly so as not to disturb her. The poor woman didn't stir a bit.

He went to the bathroom to do his morning routine. Walker planned to go downstairs and make breakfast, bring her to the kitchen, and tell her his ideas. That they needed to leave the house. For whatever reason, it was no longer safe.

The man prepared a simple breakfast of toasted bread, bacon, eggs, and strong coffee. Walker ate as he cooked so that he could focus on Constance and ensure that she resumed eating.

"We'll go to Jewel Grove. Stay at the Inn. Then we can make plans. Investigate. Hire a health expert to inspect the house. Contact the Elburn Institute. Let them investigate." He was talking to himself, but it helped diminish the weight of eyes on him. Of something behind him. The tickle on the nape of his neck. The tick-tock of the grandfather clock in the parlor seeming to be louder than ever.

"Whoever you are, go away."

The creeping sensation dissipated.

Walker took the stairs two at a time, driven by his good idea to have a brief holiday in Jewel Grove while they tried to regroup.

He entered the bedroom in full stride, almost smiling. Something he hadn't done in days—days that stretched out like weeks.

"Time to wake up, Connie." Walker wrapped on the door as he closed it. Usually a noise like that would wake her.

"Constance? Connie? Wake up, love. Please. Please wake up."

But she didn't stir. Her husband took a step closer to the bed. "Connie?"

Walker reached out and touched her face—sometimes his wife slept so hard that he had to caress her to wake her—but he recoiled. Icy as the winter morning. Walker cried out and bit into his hand. "This can't—no. Connie. Connie, please wake up!"

The room spun out from his feet and Walker fell backward, putting a hand behind himself to gain ground. No ground to gain. A snap of old kindling rang out as pain shot up his arm, wrist breaking. The man howled.

Outside, scarlet dotted the blanket of fresh snow, leading to a bright red cardinal on the ground, wings fluttering, then stopping. Walker held onto his wrist and looked around, trying to decide where to go. Platt? No help there, not after the incident happened with Ella. What would he say? That the house killed his wife, and that it would kill him, too? The townspeople would think he'd gone mad, as Ella had.

The neighboring house was empty. No one dared live in it after Ella's incident. That left the meeting hall and church, and the Preacher. Walker shook his head at the idea of getting any help from a charlatan and cultist. Walker rejected the myths of Alastor or the Timeworn.

His eyes roved over the broken bird. There was nowhere to go. No one would believe him and the ones who did would say that he was cursed or tainted, and they would kill him.

Walker ran back into the house.

Thoughts raced through his head. Bury Constance in the cellar, if he dared to go there again, and say she wandered into the woods on a walk. He'd have to create tracks in the snow. Her shoes. Yes, he'd use a good pair of shoes, stamp out a trail and then the ravine was a long drop. If she were to slip—

"I didn't kill her," Walker said to the house. "You killed her. You did and you know it."

The reply was a groan of creaking boards and rats scurrying in the walls. Walker slammed his good fist into it, sending throbbing pain into his knuckles as the wall remain unmoved.

Before he could bury her, he had to set his broken wrist.

The arm throbbed with each step back up the stairs, jarring his body with bolts of lightning. Beads of sweat gathered on his forehead yet the chill gripped him with greater force.

As he opened the door, Walker refused to look at the bed where Constance slept, focused instead on the nurse's kit she carried with her wherever she went. In the small township of Silver Hollow, she was the only person with any medical knowledge.

Walker set the broken wrist on his left hand with a sickening crack. His stomach rolled, and he vomited, nearly missing the chamber pot with his yellow, watery bile. The room began spinning again, and he rolled forward, away from the chamber pot, head between his knees.

Was he hearing chanting?

Chants, in a chorus of whispered, distant voices. Walker closed his eyes and tried to focus on it. No, it couldn't be a chant—just the rats in the walls, or a family of squirrels nesting for the winter.

It isn't otherworldly. It isn't. It isn't.

The paper he'd written on blew off his desk in a strong gust of wind and landed at his feet. He could read it from his position.

In vitae dolor est. In dolor sit amor. In vitae dolor est. In dolor sit amor.

Something cold touched his forehead, and he looked up to see Constance hovering over him. She was smiling, leaning closer. Smiling. Closer. Her eyes a milky blue, face sallow and drawn. The grin wide and unreal. This wasn't *his* Connie. She was still in bed, in her eternal sleep.

"What's happening? Please—what's happening?"

His screams unheard outside the walls, then silenced by the life draining out of him.

DEATH KNELL

The yellow school bus lumbered down the highway. Light streamed in the windows as the trees broke the morning sun with shadows and lines over the man's face. No other cars passed the pale gray stretch of road.

Hale Lemley didn't always rise this early, but today was his special day. Today was Monday. The day all the children got picked up.

Every day, Lemley picked up the children from Silver Hollow and brought them to Central School. Boisterous on the way home from school, quiet in the morning. The bus driver preferred them quiet, and wished, every afternoon, that they would stay that way.

But they never did.

And every day, *every goddamn day*, he thought, he'd wind up going home with a headache. Horrible headaches. This wasn't always from the smell of the diesel, but from the noise. The children made so much noise. These hadn't always happened, no. Maybe six months—or a year—he didn't keep track. Lemley didn't go to a goddamn doctor who'd charge him half his paycheck only to tell him to take aspirin.

Some days, the pain in his head became worse than others. Some days, his skull threatened to split in half. By the time he got home on those days, he would rush to the bathroom, vomit, then crawl into bed and sleep right through to the next day. Fridays were the worst. With the kids worked up for the upcoming weekend, they were loud. Sometimes he'd have to yell, or pull the bus over to get them to be quiet.

But at least with Fridays he had the weekend to sleep it off.

He didn't dislike children, but he didn't like them, either. Lemley never married—found no one who could stand him and he couldn't find anyone he could stand, either. The man never had nor wanted any of his own, either a wife or children. The kids would make too much noise, and sometimes the idea of a wife with her shrill voice and constant nagging made him cringe. Women and children were fine when they were quiet, and that's when he liked them. When they were loud, though, *that's* when he hated them, children more than women.

Overall, mornings were best.

Mornings were the key to happiness.

Children should be seen, and not heard, his mother always said.

Friday evening, Lemley came home to his empty, four-room house (which was more a converted shack than anything else), a terrible headache having descended on him. The worst one he'd ever had.

This was unusual. No nausea yet, but that would come. The throbbing of his head matched the ringing in his ears, and a chill flowed through his body. That's what was so unusual. *The chill.*

Hale, true to his name. As an adult he had plenty of headaches, but that was because of the noisy kids. He had never had so much as a cold in his adulthood and only had the flu twice when he was a boy. Otherwise, it seemed as though he was impervious to illness.

Feeling this foreign chill come over him, he wasn't sure what to do about it. Running a hand through his greasy, dingy salt-and-pepper hair, Lemley figured he'd wait till he threw up, chew aspirin, and sleep. The headache would be gone by morning.

Hale puked in the toilet after watching the clock go around halfway and crawled into bed, chewing five aspirins from the bottle on his nightstand. He closed his eyes and waited for the medicine to work like he always did.

That was the hardest part. The waiting. The pain was incredible, and he wondered through ringing ears, watering eyes, and throbbing down his neck and spine, if he would die from it. Death might be a relief.

The fifty-eight-year-old man who looked older than six decades curled up onto his side and placed his hands over his eyes. That helped, having icy hands over his eyes.

Not this time. His hands were too hot and uncomfortable. With a grunt, he turned over on his back. Now he was sure he had a fever.

Not to worry, he thought. The aspirin would take care of that. Come morning, he'd be fine.

Driving down that long, empty highway to collect the children might be the death of him.

The highway is covered in shade. The path is long—stretching out forever, and Lemley drives on. There are kids everywhere, and he isn't stopping. The bus is full of screaming children. They aren't screaming in delight, but terror, faces pulled into grotesque masks of pain, confusion, and fear.

Hale is smiling, face covered in blood. There is a red hand print on his shirt, no bigger than an eight-year-old's hand.

Black teeth breaking as he smiles, pulling into a wider, toothless grin.

Hitting bump after bump, passing all the stops as the engine roars. The miniature soldiers fall, wet splashes of red flying up to the windshield. The wipers leave streaks.

ten ... nine ... eight ... seven ...

Bump. Screams.

Lemley laughs.

six ... five ... four ... three ... two ...

He is no longer on the highway. The bus is on a field. A field undisturbed by people. The grass is tall, and birds flutter and fly out of his way. Smells of petrichor and iron filling his nose.

The children on the bus are silent now, little bodies collapsed and sprawled out, over and under the seats. A hand juts out from between the cushions, but it has no owner.

A little girl with red hair appears in front of the bus, holding a stop sign in the middle of the field.

Hale obeys. She drops the sign.

The driver in the blue-gray coveralls gets out, helpless in his state. He opens the door and goes to the little red-haired girl with the freckles and green eyes. Does he know her? No. She must be a new girl.

There are tiny flowers on her dress, now filling the surrounding field.

'You know what to do,' she says.

'No.' Hale says. Tears are streaming down his face.

'Pick me up,' her voice rings with the command of a general giving orders.

Hale picks her up.

They move together through the field of flowers and head toward the sound of running water, and get in where the water is warm. Tiny hands wash the blood away. He sets her down. The freckle-face girl swims to the center of the river, where he cannot reach.

'You know what to do,' she says again.

'No, I can't. Not you.' Hale says, no longer crying.

'Yes, you must. It's time to pick them up.' The girl smiles at him, still in her dress, soaked with the clear river water.

'This isn't right,' he says. His voice cracks, and he hates himself for feeling so feeble.

'Nothing is right. But you will make it right.' Nodding, the little sage submerges herself into the water, and is gone.

one ...

Lemley woke up with a start, surprised that it was morning. His head still throbbed as it had the night before. The chill was no longer on him, but he still felt feverish.

He slept through the day that Saturday, and when the sun set, his eyes snapped open and he sat upright.

There, at the end of his moldy, come-stained mattress, was the little girl. Starched white dress with daisy print, clean auburn hair pulled back in a neat ponytail, and smelling of dried roses.

"You know what you need to do," she said. Still that serene smile, green eyes glittering with something sage but cruel behind them.

Lemley blinked and rubbed his eyes, but she was still there.

Then he noticed his headache vanished. He inhaled, smelling the rose-scented air around her.

Wherever the girl was, his pain was not.

"It's time to pick them up?" His voice was raspy, and to him, it sounded far away.

The little gem nodded. "Yes. All of them."

"No more pain?"

"None. For any of us. Save them, Hale. You know how."

She crawled up onto the bed as Lemley's limbs went weak, life oozing out of him. As she got closer, he drew back, lying flat. There was no fear pumping through him—just a sense of having to surrender.

Hale closed his eyes as her hand came near to his face, cool over his feverish forehead.

"Sleep now," she said. The dainty hand connected, soothing.

He closed his eyes.

Sunday, he woke up as the sun filled his bedroom with light, hitting his eyes and making them sear with a different pain. His headache was still present, but it was mild. The chill left him, and the fever had passed. There was still a ringing in his ears, not familiar to him.

Slight throbbing in his head didn't matter—he could cope with that. He chewed another three aspirin and got up to make himself breakfast.

The headache, it stayed.

That was a first. Those aches always evaporated by Saturday. Sunset, at the latest.

He wandered into the kitchen and grabbed a can of lard out of the refrigerator, and several eggs. After he found a pound of bacon that was still before the expiration date, he set about making breakfast and coffee.

As the four eggs in the lard and bacon grease popped and sizzles from cooking the pound of bacon, he thought he heard a noise in the living/dining area. Letting the eggs set a minute, Hale turned away and looked. There was nothing there. He shrugged and went back to his eggs.

They albumen turned white (one of those know-it-all kids taught him that word), yolks kept runny for his bacon and toast. Once they were ready, he dug them out with a spatula and put the eggs on top of one slice of hot, buttered toast. Then he took them to his kitchen/dining table, along with a large mug of coffee.

Sometimes, the coffee helped make the ache go away, but he wasn't sure if it would work this time.

The little girl sat at the table, and what headache remained disappeared again.

He ate as the little girl watched him, large green eyes never leaving his face.

"You hungry?" Hale shifted in his seat, awkward about eating in front of the little moppet.

"I'm always hungry, but not for food." The girl smirked.

He snorted. "What for, then?"

"Silence."

What did that mean? Lemley wasn't sure if she meant she was hungry for silence, or if she wanted him to be quiet. Either way, he didn't respond.

He found he preferred things to be silent, too. After work, he'd come home and rest in front of his television, not bothering to turn it on. Instead, he'd sit and think. The noise on the TV annoyed him. When he wanted entertainment, he'd read a newspaper or a book. The past few weeks, though, he found he couldn't concentrate enough to read anything but the comics section. It wasn't always like that. Lemley had loved collecting articles about the Ladies Legion of Silver Hollow and Jewel Grove. They used to do all kinds of functions and quilting bees. Pretty ladies—he liked to look. Never got up the nerve to socialize with any of them, but he sure watched them. He'd clip their pictures and paste them up in his scrapbook with their eyes scratched out.

The little girl sat with him through breakfast and followed him into the kitchen while he cleaned up. Once he finished the dishes he turned to her. "Why doesn't it hurt when you're here?"

The girl smiled at him and giggled. "Because you'll do what you have to do when I'm here. Pick them all up."

She faded. As she did, the pain returned.

"Don't go," he said.

"I'll be back soon," she said. "When it's time, I'll come back."

She disappeared.

Lemley's face got wet with tears. The pain returned, worse than ever.

He went to his medicine cabinet and took out a bottle old painkillers he still had when he knocked out his back two years ago. They'd work.

Hale chewed on two of them, then crawled back into bed and begged for the pain to go away.

When she appeared in his dreams, the pain faded again. She stood watch like a sentry as he drove the bus to the far ends of Silver Hollow, picking up the children.

They boarded the bus. Then the noise began. The screams, the excited laughter, the fights—*are not! Am too! Nuh-uh! Uh-huh!* It was just too much.

Lemley slammed on the brakes and watched in his rearview mirror as the children lurched forward. A few of them hit their heads with a meaty *thwack*! That made Lemley smile.

But the little ginger girl, now wearing a blue dress with a starched, white pinafore, stood still, her face wearing a placid smile.

"Do it."

He parked the bus in a field.

He grabbed a machete.

Slice. Chop. Hack.

Hale came. There was no more pain.

He picked up the children and put them in the field.

Everything was quiet.

The little girl stood behind him, giggling.

"Pick me up," she said.

"I can't."

"You have to, and you have to take me with you."

Hale awoke with a start, his sheets a mess which hadn't happened to him since he was a teenage boy.

The pain had returned, and there was no little girl in the room.

He wept.

This was something Lemley didn't want to do. But how else could he make the pain go away?

You'll do what you have to do, echoed the little girl in his head. The pain disappeared when she spoke.

He closed his eyes as the high throb returned to his head. Sunday night dread settled into his stomach. Hale took a deep breath. The agony had to stop.

Tomorrow, he would make the pain go away.

No! I couldn't do that! This was wrong. So wrong. He sobbed. Why did he have to do this? They were just children.

"Noisy, little bastard children." The little girl said as she appeared at the foot of his bed. Now her dress was bright yellow with a large lily print on it. "You made a mess." She said, face twisted in disgust.

"I didn't mean to," he said, face getting hot from his cheeks to his ears. But at least there wasn't any pain.

"No, you didn't." Her eyes were cold, but her voice was sympathetic. "You can't help yourself, can you?"

"No." Tears stung his eyes.

"Your mother would be ashamed again." This time, her voice was casual as though she were discussing a sudden weather change.

"Yes," Lemley said. *Mother was always ashamed of my mistakes*, he thought, an image of her standing in front of him with a thin hickory switch in hand floated by, and he shivered, pulse rising.

He wondered how the little girl knew about his mother.

That's when the little girl giggled. "I see everything about you, Hale Lemley."

She said his name like a winter breeze, and the chills came back to him. "How do you?" He asked. "I don't even know your name."

"It's Daisy," she said. "I'm your long-lost friend."

Daisy? He didn't know any little girl or woman by that name.

"You're not my friend," he said.

"I make the pain stop. You need me."

The tears flowed down the wrinkles in his weathered face. "I need you."

"It's time for work," Daisy said. "Get up, get up, get up—"

Lemley sat bolt upright in his bed. It was Monday. It was four o'clock in the morning, and his alarm had melded with Daisy's voice—the ring-ring, ring-ring, ring-ring—was threatening to split his head in two. He slammed his fist into the alarm off button, and the clock rattled a death knell.

Time to get ready for work.

His head hurt again. There was no little Daisy in the room with him.

Hale shrugged. Maybe it was just a weird fever dream. But the headache worsened. Still. He wished he could see that girl again.

Daisy. That was her name. Didn't her little floral print dresses have daisies on them sometimes?

He got up, showered, got dressed, and ate breakfast with a large mug of coffee. The headache was still pressing on the back of his head and moving its ugly way toward his eyes.

"No noise today," he said out loud, and considered calling out for the first time in his entire career. But that wasn't an option, he thought again. Calling in sick was for liberals and pussies, his father had told him, and just days before the man blew the back of his own skull out with a shotgun.

Since he was neither liberal nor pussy, he would not let himself down by calling out for a headache.

He'd just have to tell the kids to be extra quiet today.

Pick them all up today.

"Shut up," he said to no one.

As he went to the door, he found a rusted machete leaned up against the door knob. He stopped.

He didn't remember putting it there, and he didn't remember even removing it from the shed. His father had used it to work the cane fields in the Southern Territory, back when migrant farming was the only way for the Lemley family to make a living. He inherited it when the bastard blew out his brains. The edge glimmered as though it had been recently sharpened, even though the majority of the blade was still rusty.

How did he manage to do that and still be sick all weekend?

Daisy did it.

No. That was ridiculous thinking. But she seemed so real.

"Enough of this!" He said out loud again. This time, he heard a little girl giggle. He spun around, away from the door.

She wasn't there.

"Take it," Daisy said. Although he couldn't see her, the pain in his head dulled a little when she spoke.

Lemley took it and went out the door.

There was not a soul in the maintenance bay that morning, which wasn't unusual. Lemley always got there a half-hour even before the boss did. He punched his card, went to his bus, and did his maintenance checks. The machete stayed out of view, behind and underneath the driver's seat.

Once finished with his routine checks, Lemley left to pick up the kids. His route started in Jewel Grove, but today, he'd do his coworkers a favor and pick up all the kids starting with Silver Hollow, too.

He picked them up, one by one, in Silver Hollow.

A group at the little meeting hall that used to be a church was waiting for him. He picked them up, too.

The bus rumbled its way to the general store, leaving a trail of acrid, black smoke from the exhaust as it squealed to a stop. There was a special surprise there, sitting on the steps of Haverty's, in the form of the little red-haired girl in a white dress that seemed to glow in the sunshine, and a daisy in her hair. Little feet in white patent leather shoes climbed the metal steps of the vehicle. She smiled at him and looked up at his name plate.

"Good morning, Mister Lemley," she said. Her voice was airy and pleasant, like wind chimes.

The pain in his head vanished.

"Thank you for picking us up today."

Lemley's vision blurred as his eyes watered. "You're welcome," he said, a crack in his voice.

The other children boarded the bus around her. The little girl took the first seat on the passenger's side, where he could see her in his rear-view mirror. None of the other children would sit with her.

Hale drove on, picking up all the children in Silver Hollow. The bus was full of the buzz of children talking. He kept driving.

He made his way through the small town, picking up forty-four children in total.

Hale drove away from the town, in the opposite direction of the school.

The little girl in the starched white dress watched him, a small smile playing on her lips.

The noise was getting to be too much. He drove faster.

He found the field that the little girl had told him about before—led there in a dream.

"It's time." Daisy's voice was soft, and she hummed an unfamiliar tune.

The bus driver pulled over and the children quieted. *Whack. Hack.* Blow by blow, inch by inch, they fell one by one. Their cries and screams drove each blow harder, deeper—then blissful silence—and oh, what bliss. His pants grew tighter, wetter, and relaxed again.

Hale grabbed the machete and took the remains to the field. There were still little bits left to clear up.

When he finished, he turned to Daisy. Her white dress was still immaculate, despite the gore that soaked through Lemley's coveralls.

"Pick me up," she said.

Lemley picked her up, her little white dress getting smudged with red.

"Take me in and tell them what you've done. Hand me over to them. I will make all this pain go away." Soft lips kissed his cheek.

Turning to the bus still on the edge of the highway, he walked. Machete in hand, he held Daisy in his free arm. Over his shoulder, he carried the extra burden of a large, olive green, canvas duffel bag. Lemley filled it with enough pieces of candy to sustain the hungry girl. They boarded the bus.

He set her in the aisle, and she took a seat in the spot she'd been before. She was looking at him with a soft smile, eyes heavy-lidded.

"You're doing fine, Mister Lemley. Now, start the bus and let's go."

He turned the bus away from the field and headed back down the highway toward the town of Silver Hollow. While the town wasn't big enough for even a police station, it had a constable's office. That's where Daisy wanted him to go, so he could tell them.

Then all the pain would go away. It made perfect sense. She made his pain go away, so why wouldn't he do what she told him?

The constable's office consisted of one small building. Its innards contained a receiving desk, manned by a deputy, and a holding cell off to the left of the reception area. This was where Lemley knew he had to go. He was under orders.

The place smelled of a musty, old basement. The hardwood floors, dry and untreated, creaked and complained under his feet. Daisy was right behind him. He was glad not to be alone—the place was empty except for the deputy and the constable. The jail cell door hung open like a hungry mouth.

The constable and deputy looked up to see him, mouths rounded and eyes wide.

Lemley dumped the contents of his duffel bag onto the floor. To his surprise, the decapitated heads of twelve children came rolling out. Where had those come from? The sack had been full of candy—sugar skulls, toffees, chocolate-covered cherries.

But he knew. He knew it had been Daisy the whole time. He was just the instrument.

Standing before him, their eyes fixed in horror on the sight at their feet. The deputy turned away and retched as constable paled, but remained on his feet.

"What—wh-what in the fuck have you done?" He said to Lemley, his voice pinched, near hysterics.

Lemley turned, and Daisy was gone, along with the pain. Problem was, the world was fading away from him, turning black.

He fell to the floor, convulsing, feeling a gush of hot blood oozing from his nose, and then wetness near his ears. Warm. He let go and gave up. His crotch flooded with hot liquid, and the stench of blood and urine filled his nose.

The constable knelt over him, screaming.

"WHAT HAVE YOU DONE? ANSWER ME, YOU SONUVABITCH!"

Lemley could do nothing but croak and bubble out one last sentence as the darkness smothered him.

"It was time to pick them up."

END

Printed in Great Britain
by Amazon